LEGENDS of
AZUREIGN:
DRAGON and ORACLE

Joy Oestreicher

Omega Cat Press — California

Joy Oestreicher

Omega Cat Press, independent publishing since 1990

This is a work of fiction. All characters and events in this work are fictitious. Any resemblance to real persons, living or dead, is purely coincidental and not intended by the authors.

ISBN: 0-9631755-7-2

ISBN-13: 978-0-9631755-7-1

1 2 3 4 5 6 7 8 9

For the dragonriders among us

Table of Contents

Joy Oestreicher

Some Things You Might Want to Know

This is the story of a girl and her dragon. He's a great hulking beast that may, in fact, be too big to fly. She's an orphan, who has been chosen to ride him mostly because she's small.

Now, you might think that a story with a girl and a flying dragon (well, he's supposed to fly) would be a fairy tale set in some far away long-ago place. There'd be magic and weird creatures and probably a princess and a quest involved.

This is not that story. There is a bit of a quest—besides the quest to get Nizael to fly, I mean—did I mention the dragon's name is Nizael? And you might consider a great hulking dragon a fairly weird creature. But there are no princesses in this story at all. There are several Queens, though not the kind you might expect.

So, quest, yes. Weird creatures, yes. Princess, no. And *no magic.*

It does take place in a far distant time and place, on a frontier colony world called Azureign, a few thousand years in the future, which is a sort of magic. There's no ray guns or space ships. In fact, Shala's job—I think I forgot to tell you the girl's name is Shala—her job would have been much easier if there *were* space ships, or even jets or an ancient-fashioned airplane. Then she wouldn't have cared if Nizael ever flew, and this would be a very different story. But that's not how it is.

So, quest, future times and far away places, yes. Spaceships and princesses, no. Ray guns and magic, definitely not.

Dragons, though. Very nice, large dragons...

WESTERN MAP of AZUREIGN

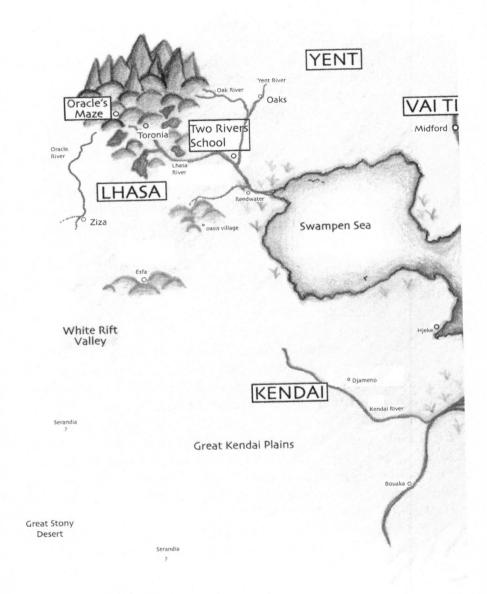

EASTERN MAP of AZUREIGN

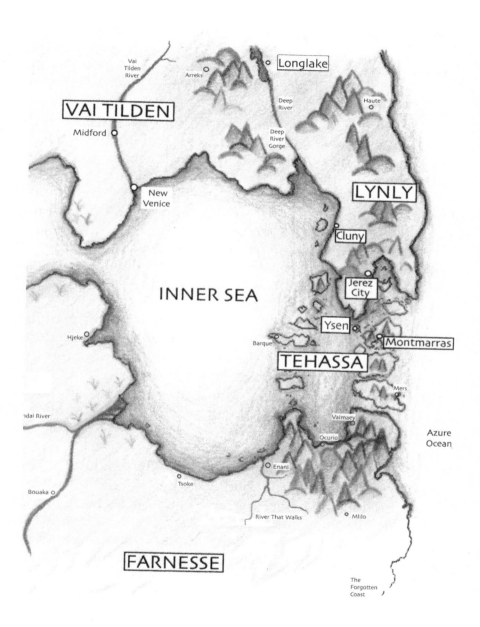

PROLOGUE — A Legacy

The noonday sky sparkled when Shala drove into camp. She guided the colorful wagon between the tents of the traders, goat herders and miners. She touched her father's shoulder. "Papa! Wake up! We have arrived."

He startled and looked around. "You are so good with the horses. Has anyone camped in our space?" He finger-combed his hair, put on his best green vest, and waved to the other caravanner families.

"New shears," he called. "Sharper and longer lasting! Cooking pots, lighter and faster cooking. Embroideries! Sweets for the children."

The adults waved back, and crowds of children followed the wagon. Her father sat down, but kept waving. He turned to Shala. "Isn't this wonderful? They are so happy to see us."

Shala had no reply. She concentrated on avoiding tent lines and children. Her small hands deftly controlled the reins as she maneuvered the wagon into the narrow canyon where her family traditionally set up their itinerant store. The slim break in the rocky ravine offered a natural corral and enough shelter from the desert sun to grow lush browse for the horses.

She checked the sky. No clouds. Three days of high winds had driven the bad weather to the Swampen Sea and beyond. Her mother read the signs a tenday ago. Shala and her father had tied the caravan shutters closed to protect the family from flying debris. They'd sat together inside in the dark while the wind roared.

Now the shutters were wide open, baring the windows for light and sight. She knew her mother looked up from her embroidery every few minutes to see where they were: to greet a familiar tree, or see how the brush and sand had been changed by the wind.

When the wagon stopped, her father stood and addressed the crowd of children. "You may purchase one item each, then we are closing for the day. We've had a long journey, and are tired." They quickly sold the chosen treat to each of the dozen children, then flipped the sign closed. "Please return tomorrow when we will be open all day."

Disappointed faces slowly dispersed into the sandy spaces between the drab, woolen tents and the other, colorful wagons.

"I never tire of the enthusiastic reception we receive." Papa smiled at her. "Thank you for driving, Shala." He paused a moment, his hands still on the harness he was examining. "You are becoming old enough to think about your future."

Shala had been avoiding this discussion for days. With her parents getting older, and her brother planning to apprentice as an ironsmith, the future—oh how she detested that word—was on everyone's mind. She bit her lip.

"We are at the biggest gathering of the summer, now, and I hope you will make some effort to meet the boys your age who are here," Mama said, coming around from the back of the wagon, water jugs in her smooth-skinned hands.

"I know all these boys," Shala said, scowling. "I have always known them. Pulling my hair, kicking dirt in my food."

"They have changed. So have you. You are all growing up. We need to think about finding you your own wagon, your own family," Mama said. "The best matchmaker is here. She will help us make a good bargain."

Feeling like a piece of leather being traded on the open market, Shala shook her head.

Rather than reply, she walked to the horses and led them to graze in the triangular pasture behind the wagon. But the horses refused the protected green space and bolted between the wagon and the rock wall. They slowed at the entrance to the triangular site, and she caught up with them. She gripped their halters and led them back. This time she tied them to stakes she drove into the ground with Papa's sledgehammer. She stroked their withers to calm them. "What's wrong? Eat some nice grass and I'll get you a bucket of water."

Her father ignored the horses' strange behavior. "Shala, this is a good life, moving from camp to camp, respected and appreciated. Soon a wagon like this one will be yours."

She had dreaded this moment since she'd been old enough to calculate money and bargain with the customers. She did not want her own wagon. She did not want to continue on this same old route, year after year. She wanted to leave the White Rift Valley, to see the big cities of Azureign, the waterfalls at the edge of the world, and maybe even travel off planet to see the rings up close.

"I should go fetch water," was her best reply.

She climbed to the roof of the wagon where they stowed her carrying poles among skeins of yarn and sacks of ore her father had received in trade. She tossed the wooden poles down. They landed with a dull thud.

"Be careful!" her mother shouted. Shala peered over the edge and saw the poles had barely missed Mama.

Shala jumped down and hugged her. "Sorry! I was distracted."

"I know you don't like talking about the future. I used to hate that word, too, when I was your age. I remember hating the idea that I must follow in my parents' footsteps. I wanted to travel and learn, not be stuck in the same old pattern. But my family bequeathed this wagon to me, when my sister refused it. And so I was trapped."

"Oh, mother. I never knew that."

"Yes, it is true. My sister Andrya is settled now, a landowner. So we know it can be done. You will not be stuck here, if you do not wish it. I have been saving. When the time is right, the false bottom of my jewelry box holds enough gold coins for you to go wherever you like, and follow your heart's desire. Perhaps after some travels, you will return and take up the reins of this wagon."

Eyes wide, Shala tightened her hug just slightly, realizing how thin and weak her mother had become. "I don't want to leave you."

"My time is not much longer, and my wish for this life has always been a better opportunity for you."

Shala felt tears rolling down her cheeks and turned to hide them. "I should go fetch water."

"Wait! Wait!" Her mother reached into a deep pocket in her multi-colored skirt and removed a thin chain with a globular pendant.

Shala looked at the tiny crystal ball with an even tinier metallic-looking flower floating within. "What is this?"

"This is the charm of our Nizael family, passed from mother to daughter. It was my mother's and her mother's before."

Shala's tears flowed anew, and she placed the delicate circle around her neck. Mama fastened the hook through the loop. The crystal felt warm between her budding breasts. She hugged her mother. "I want to stay with you."

Within the comfort of a gentle embrace, Shala heard, "You have so much to accomplish. You are good with animals, and the pendant will help."

Shala meant to ask what that meant, but her brother arrived, frowning, and snatched up the carry poles.

"No, I will get the water," Shala said.

"The horses are thirsty," he growled. "*I'm* thirsty."

"Yes. I'm going." She took the carry pole, adjusting it to better balance the empty pails on either end. They'd be easier to carry when they were full and not bouncing around.

She took a few steps, then kicked off her sandals so she could wash her feet at the well. Barefoot, her sandals slung by the straps over her arm, she approached the well. A group of women took turns filling their buckets.

She felt a tremor, a trembling in the earth beneath her feet. She climbed onto the well wall and peered deep to the bottom. She turned to the other women. "Look. Do you see that? The water is roiling a like tea kettle."

Before anyone replied, the shaking increased. "Earthquake!" Shala jumped off the wall like it was aflame.

Several water buckets fell off the edge and splashed into the water below, their ropes following them like slithering snakes. Amid shouts of "Quake!" and "To the ground!" everyone dropped what they were doing, and waited out the earthquake away from walls and things that might fall. For what seemed like forever, the ground shook. The shaking went on so long and hard that the wall around the well collapsed. Rocks tumbled onto the damp sand outside or splashed deep into the water.

Frightened for her family, Shala looked back to the hills.

Worse than she feared, the earthquake had triggered a rock fall. Dust and boulders filled her family's special alcove. She could not see the wagon, nor anything but dust and tumbling rock.

Appalled at what she *could* see, she started moving in that direction, but someone caught her shoulder, another man blocked her way. They held her back.

When the boulders stopped rumbling and the dust had settled somewhat, she could see that the canyon had collapsed, burying everything that had been at its base. She could see nothing of her family or their wagon or horses. Hoping to see Papa or *someone, anyone* appear through the dust, she strained against the men holding her back. More dust roiled out, escaping the vee-shaped canyon. Could anyone have survived?

The rumbling quieted, the dust settled. No one came out of her family's camp. Not even the horses, who had tried to escape earlier. No one had lived through that.

The earthquake, the boulders, the rock fall: they had taken her family. Everyone, everything was gone, and there was not one thing she could do about it. They had all been crushed into nothing.

As was traditional among desert people, the survivors held the funeral within a tenday. Shala knew little of funerals. She cried for days while rescuers with horses and donkeys and even a pair of big oxen tried and failed to move the boulders that buried her family's last campground.

She would have tried harder.

She would have kept trying to move the rocks away. But no one wanted to listen to a grieving orphan girl. Before the tenday was over, the camp held a funeral with no grave goods and no bodies to bury.

"They have their wagon," the preacher-woman said. "They have their trade goods. They are buried safe now in the good earth."

"May they travel well," all said.

May they travel well, ran through Shala's mind over and over. She bowed her head as people dispersed after the simple ceremony. The blessing was her people's version of the "amen" many settled villagers used. It was one of many differences between them, traveller versus villager.

She could not leave the landslide or stop crying.

She climbed among the rocks without eating or sleeping until she found a smooth face on one of the largest boulders, one of those that guarded her family's grave for all time. She carved the names of her father, mother, and brother.

She wrote, "They travel with gods and dragons." It was a line from one of the stories her mother had told. Shala could not let herself think beyond her sadness and loss, but the epitaph seemed right, and she felt she had at least done something to mark her family's last camp.

She kept thinking she would wake up from this horrible nightmare, and her mother would be there, shaking her awake. Her brother would grump at her for taking so long with the water. Papa would flash his quick grin.

She kept making deals with invisible, improbable gods. If they would bring back her family, she would enter religious service. She would create magnificent artworks to honor them. She would spread the story of the miracle far and wide.

But she knew, in her deepest heart, that was not going to happen.

They were not coming back.

She gathered greens and accepted goat milk from the herders. She borrowed a pot and cooked and ate the first meals of her new life alone. She slept on the ground in silence, without the family snores and grumbles and snorts she'd heard every night for all her short life.

Two mornings after the funeral, wearing some mismatched, donated clean clothes, she climbed up into a northbound wagon and set off to her mother's sister, the aunt who led what would be her new foster family.

Her aunt who lived in a village, and who had turned her back on travelling and trading, and who was unlikely to welcome an impoverished orphan of the traveller clan. Would she honor the ancient tradition among travellers, to care for orphaned children, or would she turn Shala away, as villagers often did?

Shala did not know, but there was nowhere else for her to go. She had nothing to offer a prospective husband: no wagon, no horses, no trade goods. Even if she had been willing to take up a new life as a very young bride, the matchmaker just tsk'ed and shook her head.

The distant cousins who owned the wagon going north of course expected her to help as they travelled. She took care of the animals, feeding and grooming the horses, making sure the tiny herd of goats had ample forage and water.

"Bring some water for the soup, please, girl," the woman said.

"Give some of this grain to the horses tonight," the man said.

She worked for her passage toward an aunt who might refuse her. Then what would she do? Shala scowled, driving the wagon, imagining herself finding a few goats that had gone feral, starting her own herd. Getting a horse would be harder, but she had heard tales about a wild herd of "mustangs" that ran among the foothills at the south edge of the Kendai plains. She imagined herself walking there with her three feral goats. She could do it.

She could do it, but she was not certain she wanted to.

As they pulled out of Asfa village, now heading northeast into the wasteland at the edge of the desert, Shala felt her heart grow chill. It was dangerous to care for people, when they could just be snatched off for no reason, with no warning. It was better to keep her distance, to not care so much.

She went now to her strange aunt, with her stranger cousins, having no vote in the matter. When this journey was over, she vowed, she would never again place her choices, her life and her future, into someone else's hands.

A week later, they left behind the last oasis, the last water before they would come to the tiny village and its deep well where her aunt had settled.

Shala moved into her future, empty of everyone and everything she had known.

CHAPTER 1 — Dragons

The sun edged up above the sand hills surrounding the oasis, tinting the sky pink with dawn light. Shala grabbed the hem of her tan linen skirt, pulled it above her knees and stepped up onto the stone paving around the well. This well never ran dry. It was the only reason for the existence of her aunt's tiny village.

She worked the pump handle several times to bring water up into the cistern, then moved her water jug to the cool stone rim.

Her gaze wandered off to the far southwestern horizon. Azureign's pale morning sky met the sand in a hazed blue line. There was nothing of note in that direction for many tendays' worth of travel, as she well remembered. North of the oasis were hills, mostly old sandy dunes, that she'd explored a only a little.

"One is like the next," her aunt Andrya said.

But still, Shala wondered and yearned to see. Or the south or the east, for that matter. Anywhere had to be more interesting than this village, which was so tiny and unimportant it did not even have a name.

Shala looked back down at the well. She opened the cellu-plass spigot at the base of the reservoir and let enough water out to fill her jug.

A very pregnant calico cat ambled up and looked at her expectantly, rubbing herself against Shala's bare calf.

"That's the trouble with being first out to the well," she told the cat. "I have to fill your bowl, too!" She poured several ladles of water into the large stone bowl the villagers always left on the ground beside the well. "You'd better hurry up before the dogs get here!"

"Talking to the cat, again, Shala?" Embry's voice was sweet-humored, and her eyebrows danced above innocent but very old brown eyes. The ancient herb woman moved stiffly, joining Shala at the well.

Shala smiled. "The cat has the good sense to say little and mean much," she said.

Embry laughed. "Philosophy at the well! You could write a book!" Embry set down her basket-covered jar beside the spigot and rubbed her hips.

"All achy again," she muttered. "I wonder if someday we could all go to the Oracle and find cures for our various ailments."

"We don't all have ailments," Shala said. "I suspect until we do, there won't be much interest. Why would I go, for instance?"

"To drive the goat-cart for me, of course!" Embry said, a wry grin on her wrinkled face. "And for the mystery, the learning."

Shala snorted and picked up her jug. She gathered her skirt again in one hand and stepped onto the dirt, her bare feet making dust puff up from the ground. "Not likely. There's too much to do here." She glanced at Embry, but the old woman wasn't smiling. She was staring at the ground.

Thinking, *snake,* or *scorpion in the dirt,* Shala scanned the ground also. There was something moving, but it was only a shadow. A big winged shadow. A pair of them, in fact. She looked up.

Oh, dragons!

"They're so big!" Her surprise must have been clear from her tone.

"Heh," Embry said. "They aren't even halfway down yet. They'll get bigger before they land."

"Land?" Shala watched the pair circling lower. One of them had a rider; the other did not. "Why would they land *here*?"

Embry gestured to the well. "Water, I would guess."

"Oh, my." The dragons' wings were wide and leathery, something like the dead bat that Jono had found in the garden once. Their bodies were slender, rather like a sand-lizard's. Shala watched in admiration as they circled down. They were magnificent! Then she startled herself into motion. "I've got to get out to the herd. There will be lots of frightened goats!"

Embry nodded absently, still looking at the big flying reptiles.

Shala hurried to her foster home. Her aunt glanced up from the stove as Shala pushed past the door curtain. "There are dragons landing by the well," she said, thrusting the water jug at Jono, her littlest foster brother. "They'll need help with the goats."

"Yes, they will," Andrya said. The woman smiled at Shala and called out as the girl was leaving again, "I'll send Jono out with breakfast!"

Shala trotted through the dusty side yard. It was already much warmer out in the sun than inside the adobe house. She grabbed a still-damp rag from the wash line as she passed, twisted it expertly, and wrapped it around and around her hair, taming the dark cloudy mass atop her head into a neat package that she tied off with a saucy bowknot above her ear. Besides keeping her hair out of her face, it helped keep her head cooler and cleaner.

Dragons! She imagined traveling upon one of the great winged beasts. She could probably fly all the way to the western sea, on a dragon. That would be the way to see the world! There were still places people had never been on Azureign. Imagine discovering those new places, on dragon-back!

She grimaced and shook her head. She was not going exploring, especially on a wondrous dragon. Not when her aunt needed her here.

But did she?

Shala trotted out past the familiar small gardens, the lentil field, and past the band of poplar trees the first settlers had planted to keep the sand dunes from rolling over the village. Now the trees shaded the ground, and brown grasses grew between them, a grazing area for goats, sheep, and the two village mules.

The goats were indeed restless, heads up, ears back, nostrils flaring.

She came up to the herd and her brothers. "Hello, Jhude, Logyn," she called, letting her two older foster brothers know she was there among the herd. She stood and stared a moment. How on Azureign could anyone justify needing three herders for sixty goats? They just didn't, that was all. Shala bit her lip.

The lead billy rolled his eyes and shifted past a pair of kids. She walked to him and spoke gently. "They aren't here for you, you cranky old thing," she said, standing between him and any view he might have had of the big flying predators. "You wouldn't even taste good." Unimpressed with her logic, the billy lifted his head and flared his nostrils again. His ears twisted back and forth as he tried to identify the danger he could sense nearby. She fondled those ears, scratched his forehead, and then walked among the other goats, leaving a path of serenity behind her.

Jhude and Logyn worked the dogs to keep the herd confined in a tight bunch while easing them out to the north and east, further away from the village. After a few more moments of coaxing, they got the herd out of sight among the tall dunes that encircled the oasis. Shala continued to pass among them, soothing them with her voice and gentle caresses, but she knew her brothers could have managed without her. Even if Logyn went off to the monastery like he wanted to, there was no reason Jhude couldn't care for the animals alone. He had the dogs. He had Jono, if there was an emergency.

16

This was just a job they pretended they needed Shala for. She looked toward the village. She couldn't see any dragons in the sky, now. They must have landed long since.

A few outlying palm trees and their shadows were the only things moving in the gentle breeze. High haze dulled the sunlight, and she could make out the rings that circled the planet, a brightness far above and curving down to the horizon.

Azureign didn't have a moon, but the planet did have a spectacular set of rings: ice and rock that circled the equator like a necklace of fine jewels. The rings were what made Azureign unique; usually only gas giant planets had them—that's what the teacher at the Traveling School had said.

Shala stroked the incredibly soft ears of a brown and tan nanny goat, lost in musing. She had learned a lot at the school.

She had been allowed to go to classes three different times, now. Andrya thought it important that even goat herders knew how to read, and something about what made their planet work, and how the weather was affected by the Great Stony Desert and the Inner and Swampen Seas. And it was helpful to know what grew on the plains of Kendai to the south, and so forth.

Shala had also learned why they were saving money for a solar collector—the entire village could use it to cook, taking advantage of their free sunshine and saving their scant wood. Instead of burning the animal dung, they could spread it as fertilizer, and thus earn the approval of the Priestess at Ysen for their environmental care, which might mean a license to raise more than goats, eventually.

Jhude, when he had attended classes, had learned some things at the school that helped make his cheeses better. Jono was looking forward to his turn.

But Logyn, her middle brother, had detested the classroom. He gave up his second set of classes so that she could go again. "You like to learn such facts much more than I do," he told her, and Shala accepted the royal gift with glee.

As soon as it was Jono's turn for school, Shala planned to question him each day, both to set the knowledge into her littlest brother's head, and to help herself do the same, remembering.

The nanny lowered her head and took a step forward to eat an artemisia plant the same way Jono ate noodles, starting at one end and sucking up the whole thing with a slurp. Shala patted the goat's head. "Not that you slurp, though." The nanny eyed her with calm brown eyes, chewing. "More like a crunch." The goat blinked, then bent her head and sniffed the ground for scraps she might have dropped.

Jono jogged out to them, having followed the trail of goat tracks and fresh droppings. He handed Jhude and Logyn their breakfasts, and turned to Shala. "You're to come back with me, if everything's okay, which it is," he said, eyeing the herd which was sniffing out tufts of dry artemisia or pawing the sand to find thorn tree leaves or miniature palo verde to munch.

"Oh," Shala said. "Okay, then."

Jhude pulled the cloth off his breakfast, and took a bite of cheese and egg pie. He nodded. "We're fine," he said in his raspy voice, eggs sticking to his lip. "Go ahead."

Of course they were fine. They'd never really needed her in the first place. She nodded to him, waved to Logyn, and turned to walk back with Jono. He handed her a third cloth-wrapped bundle. "You might as well eat on the way," he said.

"What does Andrya want me for, do you know?" She bit into the pie shell filled with cheesy eggs.

Abruptly transformed into a little bratty brother, Jono smirked and said, "Ha! You'll find out."

Even before they could see the well, they could hear the squeals of the village's three littlest children. When they passed the corner of the Dylun's corral wall, they could finally see what the commotion was about.

The two dragons were on the ground sucking water from Andrya's big washing vat. Children were clambering on the back and legs of one of them, a large dark brown dragon, using the straps of what looked like a carrying harness that might be used for a goat or donkey, except much bigger. Shala supposed it was for the rider and his belongings.

The other dragon, a smaller green and tan one, also with a set of straps around its neck and shoulders, seemed more aloof. No one was climbing on him. Or her, Shala thought, unable to tell the difference.

Dragons. Definitely not lizards, but not dinosaurs either. Shala felt a thrill inside just to be standing so close. On the ground, the dragons were something like plump, two-legged lizards with bat wings. Very large magnificent lizards. Calling them lizards did not do them justice, though.

Shala found herself enthralled; they were so much bigger than she had imagined, but not nearly so fierce. She shook her head at Clery, the youngest Dylun family child, who was on the beast's neck, leaning forward to peer into the brown dragon's eyes. The boy backed down the neck, then used the dragon's elbow as a step to reach the ground.

Dragon: Two large legs with long, slender but sturdy feet, and two wings rather than front paws. They folded their wings tightly against their flanks. She noticed the smaller dragon used a joint of his folded wings to lean on as he reached his long neck down to the water, bending forward from his haunches.

Smaller being a relative term, she thought as she approached. Her head was near the top of the dragon's shoulder, where the wing material descended into a neat folded package along the dragon's side. If the dragon stood up to its full height, she judged, that shoulder would be well over two meters off the ground. She walked around it, staring.

Their heads were long and narrow, with long nostrils as though a horse's nose had been stretched lengthwise a bit. The eyes were large and dark golden brown, with a slitted vertical pupil like a cat's.

The dark brown dragon stood up and Shala felt dwarfed. Clery now clung to the slender tail like a bug on a log. The dragon blinked as Clery slid down the tail to the ground like a little monkey.

Shala stepped forward and ran her hand down the dark dragon's scales. They were warmer than she had imagined, silky smooth beneath her fingers. She started to pet the long fluffy feather-like hairs that sprouted between the scales around the dragon's neck and shoulders, but as she reached up, the dragon turned its head and looked her in the eye.

Suddenly it seemed undignified to be petting the noble creature as though it were a dog.

"Do you mind if I look at your feathers?" she asked it.

The dragon whuffed softly, blowing a puff of air out through its nose. She took this as permission, and lightly touched the feathery hairs. They were stiff enough to be springy at the base and along the stem rather like cat whiskers, but the thin, feathery edges were quite soft, like goose down.

As she looked more closely, Shala realized the brown dragon was old; she could see the lumpy joints that marked arthritis, like grand'ers' hands often were. Irrepressible Renel, Clery's older brother, clutched a small pot of ointment and was smearing it on these lumps at the bigger dragon's shoulder.

"Bodo thanks you, young sir," a man's voice called. "He's getting a little too old to fly. His joints are stiff, and they hurt. The salve helps a lot."

The man who spoke was younger than Andrya, but older than Jhude. He wore soft leather leggings and a loose and dusty linen shirt. He stood only as tall as the brown dragon's shoulder, a small man compared with the dragon, of course, but a small man compared with her foster brothers, as well, she saw as she came closer to him.

This must be the tan and green dragon's rider. She turned to the green dragon and looked it in the eye. It tossed its head, like she had seen horses do, and moved a step back from her. "Are you Mister Snooty, then?" she asked the dragon.

The man laughed. "His name is Simba, and he's very conscious of his dignity. It wouldn't do to have children climb on him," he said. "And my name is Sylvan, and you must be Shala, as your aunt told me."

She nodded to him, still looking at Simba. Then she wondered why her aunt and this Sylvan would have been talking about her.

She held her hand out to the green and tan dragon and let him sniff her fingers, then she reached up to stroke his nose. He flared his nostrils and lowered his head so that her fingers reached the bony eyebrows.

"He likes to be rubbed just above the brow ridge there, in that dent," Sylvan suggested.

Shala did that, and grinned as a small groan escaped Simba's throat. "Yes, I can see that he does."

Andrya came out of her house, then, crossing the dusty road while she wiped her hands on a cloth, her

21

fingertips stained blue from the dye she was working today.

"This is my Shala. As you can see, she is quite small."

Shala looked at her foster mother, wondering why being small should matter. And why they had been talking about her.

"She is the only teenager in the village?" Sylvan asked.

"No, there are my boys, but they are all three big louts, likely to get bigger. Renel, there, is twelve, but he is not mine to speak for," Andrya said. "His parents are the Dyluns," she pointed to their house.

"He is too young. They grow a lot from twelve to fifteen."

Shala couldn't stand being talked around any longer. "Why does growing a lot matter so much? What are Jhude and Logyn too big for?"

Andrya faced her foster daughter and smiled. Did Shala see a tinge of sadness in that smile? "Master Sylvan is looking for dragon riders. They have to be small people. I told him you might serve."

I might serve what? Shala stood with her mouth hanging open, looking just as stupid, she was suddenly aware, as Logyn did when he stood like that, trying to figure a puzzle out. She snapped her mouth shut and narrowed her eyes at Sylvan. "Dragon rider?"

"A worthy duty. Dragon riders serve towns and villages by carrying news, making delivery of mail and packages, and sometimes people."

Shala could feel her heart pound, as if she had been running. She did not like the idea of Andrya and Sylvan planning her future. But—to ride a dragon! To fly!

To fly away, she thought. Away from tiny oases in the desert and out into the world.

Her arms prickled. Her soul ached with yearning. Was it possible she could do this?

Renel with the pot of ointment and his little brother in tow, approached Simba. The younger dragon backed off from them and opened his wings with a whump. Then the dragon took three running steps and lofted himself into the air.

"Ah, too many people," Sylvan said, watching his dragon rise into the sky. Then he looked at Shala again. "It is good you are not afraid of them, even the 'snooty' ones," he said with a grin. He looked back up at his dragon in the sky.

"You would become a guild member," he said, head tilted back. "This would be your profession, the care and riding of dragons. You would be paid a small sum for your work, as well as receiving room and board from the community you and your dragon serve," Sylvan said.

He looked at her, seeming to gauge her reaction. "We have a clutch of dragons that hatched almost six months ago, who are now big enough to be trained. You would choose or be assigned a dragon to care for, to train, and ride." Sylvan then looked at Andrya. "If her brothers are big, she could yet grow also."

Andrya shook her head. "She is my foster child. The boys are not her blood brothers. My husband was a tall man. Shala's family were caravanners. My sister and her husband were short and very small-boned, rather like you."

"The rest of the family?" Sylvan asked.

Tired of being talked around again, Shala answered before Andrya could. "My brother was a little taller than my mother. He died when he was fourteen, when my parents were killed. There was no one else."

Master Sylvan looked her in the eyes. "How old are you, do you know?"

"I was eleven when I came here. I've been here five years."

"So, about sixteen." Sylvan nodded. "You have started your female courses, then?"

Embarrassed to be asked this by a male stranger, Shala flushed and nodded.

"How long ago?"

"Two years."

"Well, then, I think you will not be growing much more. That is good. If you are too heavy, too big, your dragon cannot carry you. But if you are too small, then you are not strong enough to ride, to control your dragon. You are just right," Sylvan smiled. "You could be a dragon rider, if you would like to, and if your foster mother wants you to do this thing."

Shala frowned. It wasn't really Andrya's choice, was it? It was *Shala's* life they were talking about.

Andrya tucked a strand of her graying hair behind her ear, and gave Shala a tight smile. "We have talked about your future. You have no home or flock of your own." She glanced at Sylvan. "We thought she could work with the cloth. She is good at beating the flax and cleaning it, is not as good with the goat hair. It is my skill, I have been teaching her."

"Or trying to," Shala said. "But truthfully, Jono is far better at it than I am." Somehow, her fingers were never as nimble as Jono's or as strong as Andrya's.

"Yes, he is," Andrya's laugh was gentle, and then she sighed. "We have wondered what might be Shala's gift. She is very good with goats and other animals. She has brought home and rehabilitated a variety of injured beasts." She smiled. "This is why it seemed like this was a good idea for you—it could be a fine way for you to make a living. But I will not send you away, if you do not wish to go." She looked from Shala to Sylvan and back again.

Sylvan stared at her as Andrya spoke, but he did not say anything.

"She is my only daughter, for all that she is not my own child, and we would find work for her here."

Sylvan nodded. "I understand. This has to be something Shala wants to do." He looked up into the air where his dragon was gliding about in a circle, rather like a large—*very* large—hawk.

He's so beautiful, Shala thought of the young, rather arrogant green dragon. And the old dragon was very sweet.

Dragon rider. Out of the blue, literally, a way for her to leave, to not be a villager or a caravanner, but still to travel, and to work with more than goats. And she need not be embarrassed and feel inadequate because of her clumsy fingers.

She looked at Sylvan. "You said I would be paid?"

"A small sum, in addition to your room and board." He quirked his lips in a wry smile. "I cannot tell you an amount, because it will vary depending upon the kind of posting you get; if you are part of a pack, you would be sent to a larger city. A city can afford to pay for all of you—but because there are many of you the individual share might not be as much as you think.

"On the other hand, if you are a solo, or part of a small pack, you could be messenger for several small villages, who can afford to pay less, but there would be fewer dragons and riders to support, so you might end up receiving more. And it may not be coin, but trade items the village makes." He nodded at Andrya, "Such as your foster mother's fine linen and wool cloth."

Renel and Clary started wrestling near the old dragon's feet. "Please move away," Sylvan called to them. "You don't want to get stepped on."

The boys separated, then complied rather reluctantly, stomping to the other side of the well with small steps as if to move off as slowly as possible.

She felt a bit like that.

Moving off with small steps.

"Whatever you earn would be yours, Shala," Andrya said, anticipating Shala's concern. "We are self-sufficient, here, and there is enough for the three boys."

She could still send some coins, as she got them. But no need to argue about that now. "Well, it is good if Jono can weave instead of taking a share of the goats."

"Yes," Andrya said. "So, it is about whether you wish to stay here, or go to some new place. And whether you like dragons better than goats," she said, with a tight-lipped smile.

Shala looked around at the tiny village, the well, the four houses and fala-bird coop. This had been home for some years, now: the workshop where Luann made pots, and Embry kept her herbs and medicines; the goat yard, and the Dylun's chickens and fala birds ever-squawking in their yard. She had known long ago there was no one here she could marry; she would have to leave the village eventually to start her own life. And her heart always rose at the start of a journey, however short or familiar the trip. She loved traveling. She loved the journey to the annual trade fairs Andrya sometimes let her attend in Reedwater. It was where Jhude had met his future wife, so Shala hoped perhaps one day her life would change in a similar way.

She could not have imagined anything like this—a realm of possibility literally falling from the sky on dragon wings. And some traitorous part of her mind said: *If you leave first, they can't leave you behind.* As her parents had left her. Which was not at all fair, she knew, since they hadn't chosen to leave. But it had happened, nevertheless.

"When would I leave?" she asked Sylvan.

"You can ride back on Bodo today, or come on foot to the school at a later time if that is better. It would be one, maybe one and a half tenday's walk from here, which means many of the babies in this year's clutch would already be chosen; you would have less of a choice in dragons."

Her heart sank. Today was much too soon. But the delay to arrange a trip, followed by a couple tenday's walk wasn't appealing either, and it sounded like she might miss the fun of choosing her animal. "I would like time to say goodbye," she said, realizing she had made her decision. She would go to the dragon riders' school. "Today seems too fast. But several tendays seems too slow."

"It may be that you could ride along with some other trainees, assuming I find any beyond here. You could possibly ride together in a wagon, or in a small mounted group," the dragonrider said.

"Where is the school?" Shala asked.

"At Two Rivers," Sylvan said.

"That's north of Reedwater?" Andrya asked.

"Yes."

Andrya seemed to come to a decision. "If you wish to go, Shala, I could send you soon with Jhude. He has been pestering me for a trip to visit Netke—he hopes to bring her home before the end of winter," she added for Sylvan's benefit, glancing his way, then back to Shala. "You could help him harvest some flax there by Reedwater, then go on to the school. Jhude can then bring back the flax and his new wife. It would serve three purposes at once. He plans to leave in a few days."

Shala took a deep breath. It was a good plan, and a generous one.

Seeing the tears well up in her foster mother's eyes, she felt her own eyes fill. She turned abruptly toward the big brown dragon and pressed her hand against the old animal's warm brown neck. Did she really want to leave?

"She always has wanted to see over the next hill," Andrya said. "We have teased that it's her traveller blood, the caravan wanderlust." Shala felt her foster mother's hand on her shoulder. "If this is what you would like, then I will make the arrangements, little one."

Shala nodded, afraid if she spoke she would cry, and she didn't want to cry in front of Sylvan. Who wanted a weepy dragon rider?

"Good," he said behind her. "We will look for you at Two Rivers before mid-winter, then."

Shala blinked, then turned to smile. She was reluctant to cry, but she wanted them to know she wasn't reluctant to go at all. Andrya nodded, gathered her long tightly-woven wool skirt in one hand and walked back to their house, stepping carefully past the pile of dragon poop Bodo had just dropped.

Sylvan put his fingers to his mouth and let out a long piercing whistle. Simba immediately tipped at an angle, slanting into a downward spiral. He landed and neatly folded his wings.

Shala admired how elegantly done the landing was.

Could she fly a creature like that? Truly?

Still not certain she believed it, Shala stepped back from Bodo. Excitement lifted her heart as she considered the majesty of the dragons, and the magic of flight to distant places.

It seemed like a dream, not something that could happen to her. Sylvan reached out to rub Simba's brow ridge just as the tan and green dragon let loose an enormous, noisy fart.

"Augh!" Renel cried, fanning the air away from his nose. Clery gasped and pretended to be choking to death; they staggered and collapsed to the ground.

A bit of cinnamon earthy scent wafted to her nose. It wasn't that bad, really, Shala thought.

"They do that," Sylvan said, a tiny grin on his face.

"Well, that pretty much spins your dignity off to the rings, doesn't it?" Shala said to the tan and green dragon.

Simba pretended nothing whatever had happened. Sylvan snickered and scratched his dragon's chin.

Renel climbed back to his feet. "Does that help them fly faster?"

"You might think so," Sylvan chuckled, "but no. It's their digestion." He grinned at Shala. "Your dragon will do it, too."

He mounted the dragon by placing one small, soft-shod foot into the big dent between the base of Simba's left wing and the dragon's deep chest, then swinging himself aboard, like straddling a large, lean horse. He fitted his legs behind the belly straps. It was a little like a horse's saddle, but less constructed, softer. There was no halter or bridle, no reins. How did the rider guide the flyer? Clearly, they didn't just go wherever the dragon wanted. *I guess that's what I will learn at the school.*

Shala gave Bodo one last pat. She would not ride the big brown dragon to her new home today. "I will see you another time," she told him, and Bodo nodded his head, as though he understood her, though of course he didn't.

She would have her own dragon to ride, soon enough.

She stepped away, made shooing motions with her hands at Renel and his brother, warning them to make room.

Simba, with Sylvan aboard, ran a few steps fanning his wings, and then lifted off the ground. Bodo had a harder time of it, running most of the way through the village before his feet left the ground.

Sylvan looked quite secure, holding straps and Simba's neck. Shala stood in the dusty street and watched them fly away, until they were the merest specks in the eastern sky.

She was going to Two Rivers, to become a dragon rider.

Think of the things she would learn, the places she would see!

Suddenly she shuddered, a weird little shiver running from her head to her feet. She clasped her arms around herself and rubbed her arms as if she could wipe away the little prickly bumps that galloped up and down her skin. Her hand found her great-grandmother's pendant and clasped it.

Shala the dragon rider. Who could have guessed?

CHAPTER 2 — Choices

She and Jhude spent two days in Reedwater. While Jhude visited Netke and her family, Shala explored the town, and took several pieces of Andrya's linen to the shop her foster mother had made arrangements with. They were happy to have Andrya's fine cloth, and asked for more.

They came to know Netke's family a little better, and Jhude asked for and received permission to return to pick Netke up and take her home with him after he took Shala to Two Rivers. They would be married in the tiny oasis village before Year Turn. Her family would join them there for the celebration.

Plans made, Shala and Jhude left Reedwater, traveling a half-day south to the swampy lands of the Yent River delta and the shore of the Swampen Sea. They spent the rest of that day harvesting flax and putting it to ret—soaking it so it would be workable. Then they headed north. She was excited and nervous and a little bit sad all at the same time.

In gradual stages, they left behind the swamp and its grasses, then the desert palms and tamarisk, mesquite and saltbush. Two days later, they entered a scrubby forest of piñon pine that transformed little by little into stubby oak and madrone and plane trees. Then taller ones, a real forest.

"And that's one of the platecone trees that Logyn talked about wanting to see," Jhude pointed to one.

It had no branches for a long way up its trunk. Then a flat ring of branches all around the trunk, which was then bare again up to the next flat level of branches a meter or so above the first. Three large flat waffle-like cones hung down from the second disk of branches.

"This one should have been called the plane tree," Shala said.

"Some people call plane trees sycamore. But these are different, however planar they look. Have a look at one of these platecones on the ground. You can see how it got its name. The nuts are good eating. I'll be sure to take some home for Logyn."

"Take a whole cone to show him, too. I think he'd like that." Shala picked up several of the cones and tossed them onto the fire that night. The cones shriveled away from the seeds, leaving a sort of platter with nuts sitting on it: a plate, from the cone, hence the tree's name. She made a pig of herself eating the nuts, but they had so many she also made sure to pack some in a spare linen sack to bring with her to the school.

This time with Jhude was like a long goodbye. She found herself wishing they had Logyn along, too. She missed him already.

So, it was her path to leave, to go to new things, to try this riding of dragons, and find new family and friends. That was what she wanted, after all. It was just a difficulty that going to new things meant leaving the old ones behind.

She envisioned herself on the back of a dragon. Her own dragon, in the sky above the tiny village, and herself on the dragon's back, guiding it down to the stone-walled well. She would see her family and friends, and even the stupid billy goat. She wiped tears from her cheeks and stared at the steam rising from their little pot of soup.

She was leaving. But she would come back to visit. It did not make the ache go away, but it did make it hurt less. She decided to keep her focus on what she was moving toward.

Two days later, Jhude and Shala crossed the Yent River on the sole bridge between Two Rivers and Reedwater. They trotted the mules into Two Rivers—which was not a town, or even a village. It seemed to be just the Dragonrider's school and farm, which stood on a promontory above the lake. A sheer cliff dropped down to the green-blue water below.

The lake was surrounded by trees. Redwood trees, with ferny green branches and deep red bark were mixed with oak and madrone and a few white-barked trees which had lost their leaves for winter. The redwoods impressed Shala with their majestic height.

She and Jhude kept the cliff on their right as they rode up to the buildings, taking special care to keep back from the edge. They passed a row of wind turbines that helped generate electricity for the school.

"I can see why the wind turbines would be here. But you would think they would lose people over this cliff," he muttered. "Why put a school here?"

"Sylvan said it's easier for the dragons to learn to fly if they can launch off a height and glide down. Later they learn to take off from the ground." She dismounted and walked, leading her mule, which was puffing as hard as she was. Jhude stayed on his, looking all around at the layout.

"It seems strange that they have to learn to fly."

"Yes, just like birds. That's what Sylvan said, anyway. They don't grow up as fast as birds, though."

"Huh." Head swiveling, Jhude examined the cliff, the trees, the paddocks and fields, and the buildings.

As if he won't let me stay here, if it's not nice? she wondered. Perhaps that's exactly it: Andrya has asked him to make sure his sister was going to be safe and cared for. It would be like her to put that burden on Jhude, for he was the one coming here with her, after all.

Her foster mother had helped Shala pack as though she were some kind of princess, off to marry her prince. Sylvan told Shala she would need trousers for riding. "It's difficult to climb on and off the dragons in a skirt, and the wind catches them when flying." So Andrya had devoted hours to making clothing. She cut some of the nice green linen she had just dyed and made up two new pairs of loose pants. Then a pale blue set and an entire outfit of fine peachy-gold linen, along with several shirts of good cotton she had traded for. She made some warmer pairs of pants and a jacket of fine goats' wool, and even had made headscarves to match the new outfits—then packed it all into one of Logyn's beautifully tanned goat hide satchels that would serve as a saddlepack for some time to come.

Shala added her sewing kit, her old brown linen pants, a soft old cotton djellabah and a couple of her old skirts, and Andrya at last had pronounced her well dressed and ready for anything.

Now Jhude checked out the school itself. Shala would have been amused if she hadn't been so relieved. She wasn't going to be abandoned to her fate here, if things didn't look right.

They approached the closest building, a sizable two-story wood and adobe structure. Solar panels covered the sloped roof. As they neared, Sylvan came out a low arched doorway, followed by a young man and woman, who wore matching denim jeans and plaid flannel shirts.

"Hello, Shala," Sylvan called.

"Hello." What did she call him? The, "Sir," she settled on seemed too formal.

Jhude dismounted and stepped forward. "I'm Jhude, Shala's brother," he said, and he looked tall and strong and a little threatening. He was a good deal taller than any of the dragon riders. He stuck out his

34

hand, and he and Sylvan clasped wrists. Sylvan then made introductions.

"This is Aimee, who will be Shala's advisor, and Dene who is the boys' advisor this year."

Shala and Jhude greeted the others, and Shala examined Aimee just as Jhude was doing with Dene and Sylvan. Aimee would be the teacher she worked with the most. Sylvan was the stablemaster for Two Rivers School. He also served as veterinarian and recruiter. It was the resident Queen dragon and Queen's Mate riders, Dene and Aimee, who would teach the new students.

"Dene's Kharmin is brooding," Sylvan said.

Shala tilted her head. "Brooding? I thought the new dragons were six months old!"

Dene and Aimee smiled, and Sylvan laughed aloud. "Yes, they are. This confuses everyone. Kharmin will hatch a new clutch that will be ready to ride *next* year," Sylvan explained.

Dene was nodding. "We are here with her at the school until she hatches her eggs. The Queen—the mother—of the clutch your group will be riding has already returned home. Her children are big enough to be left on their own, now, ready for training. That is why we needed riders to come soon."

Jhude spoke up, "The Queen does not teach her own children to fly?"

"Left in the wild she might stay and do that," Aimee said. Her voice was smooth and soft; Shala liked the sound of it. "We don't know, because these are an engineered species—natural behaviors mostly don't exist yet. We use the original creatures' behaviors as a sort of 'expectation map,' but what the dragons would do naturally is as much a puzzle to us as it seems to be to them."

"And in this case," Sylvan put in, "Kharmin's arrival made Jana—your group's Queen—decide it was

35

very much time to go. Two brooding Queens in one place does not work at all!"

"Would you like to meet the dragons?" Dene said. He spoke as if she was only ten years old, but she decided not to take offense. Some people were better at teaching than others.

"Of course," she replied, and beside her, tall Jhude nodded also.

"You can put the mules in the stable back here." Sylvan led the way down a dirt pathway between a fenced area and the buildings.

The stable was almost empty. A single white horse and a mule were visible as they went past. Their mules—borrowed from Benar—were turned loose in a box with sweet fresh hay on the floor. While they unloaded the animals, Sylvan forked a couple flakes of alfalfa into the manger and the mules were crunching it up with relish as they left.

They went out a different gate than they had entered by and walked down a path to a large, noisy barn. Squawks and chitters and croaks greeted them as they entered.

The building had adobe walls with a high log roof covered with what looked to Shala like thatching made of palm leaves. It was open to the sky at either end, above the adobe wall. She noticed how much light there was, and good ventilation.

Around the edge of the big open space were smaller rooms like storage sheds, and stalls rather like those for horses, but much bigger. An assortment of odd equipment hung from the walls and posts by each stall. A couple of young people were using two of the stalls, but she couldn't see much past the wooden gates.

Sylvan moved out of the way, and what then caught her attention and would not let go were the young dragons. They squeaked and grunted, clambering around on the pile of hay on the floor. The dragonlings were not as clumsy as she expected. They might be babies, but they were already the size of a pony. One charcoal gray fellow waddled up to her and stuck his nose in her face.

Beside her, she heard Jhude's indrawn breath.

"He's looking for food," Sylvan said. "That's Tomaso's dragon, Tanzi. They are always hungry, no matter how big or little they are."

Heart pounding with excitement, Shala patted the baby dragon's nose. "I don't have anything to give you little one," she told it, and beside her she saw Jhude shake his head.

"She's always talked to animals," Jhude told the others. "We've decided it's because they don't talk back!"

She laughed and gave her brother a quick hug.

Then she stepped back and watched dragons again. She caught a whiff of dragon poop on the air; it was heavier than mule droppings, but much less rank than a cat or dog's. Unlike goat clumps or horse droppings, the dragons made large cone-shaped pies. Dene grabbed a shovel and scraped up the two fresh cones from the barn floor. He carried them to the barn door opposite the one they had entered by and tossed them onto a manure pile just outside.

"Later it gets mixed with compost and spread on the fields," Dene said when he saw her watching him. He leaned the shovel against the wall.

Then another little dragon came up to see if she had anything to eat, and Shala forgot about dragon poop. She was entranced; she was also surprised by how many colors the dragonlings came in. This one was pearl white.

Sylvan stepped forward and handed her some apricot-sized hard green and brown lumps. "Dragon chow," he explained. "Step into the center of the area,

Shala. As the dragonets come up, give each one a kibble."

Oh, they call the babies "dragonets," not dragonlings. "Okay," she said, taking the kibbles. She fed one to the white dragon, which had followed her the few steps to the middle of the barn. It opened its mouth, and she dropped the kibble onto the dark pink tongue.

"Now, half of them have been matched to their riders already," Aimee said. "Let's see if I can point out the ones that are available."

Two dragonets were in the stalls with their riders. Of the seven baby dragons on the floor, four had not been chosen yet.

The pretty pearl white dragon Shala had her eye on was already claimed. She looked over the four riderless dragons.

A big olivey green guy, a tan and reddish-brown female, a good sized leafy green male with a few brown speckles, and a very small, pale lime green female, who seemed too shy to approach.

"I don't know if you were told about the tradition, but each clutch of dragons is named as a group. These dragonets must have the letter 'Z' somewhere in their names," Aimee said. "It's to help distinguish each pack, so for example, you'll be known as 'Z' year. Kharmin's brood will be the 'A' clutch or maybe 'B' if the Queen that's brooding at Toronia hatches her eggs first."

The olive green dragon, bigger than the others, came up to Shala again. "This is the second time for you. Are you just a starveling, then?" When it sat up, the dragonet's head was higher than Shala's by half a meter. He looked like he was begging, the way Benar's little dog would. But instead of front paws, the dragon had neatly folded wings.

"I think he likes her," she heard Sylvan say.

"I think he likes food," Shala said as the dragonet poked his nose under her arm. "Do you think I keep kibbles in my armpit, silly?" He sniffed down her arm until he found her hand, and the concentrated kibble smell. He opened his mouth. She laughed and dropped the kibble onto the dragon's tongue. He crunched it twice and swallowed, blinking. His mouth opened again, and this time even Jhude laughed.

"He's pretty large already," Dene said. "He is a good candidate to be Queen's Mate." He glanced at Shala, and met her eyes. "That means he would be a pack leader."

Aimee added, "The dragons choose. They pick the strongest, bossiest female as Queen, or she just takes over and they let her. Then the biggest male, or the one she likes best, or to whom the rest of the pack defers, becomes the Queen's Mate, and fathers the offspring." Aimee glanced at her, to see if she was listening. Shala nodded her understanding.

"And it doesn't matter if you're a girl or a boy rider, or what sex your dragon is, as long as you like him or her—and the dragon likes you."

The olive green dragon butted Shala with his head. She lost her balance and took a step away from him. He honked, sounding like a large, irritated goose, and hopped on both feet to make up the step she had taken. He sniffed her hand.

"Well, mister, I can't have you pushing me around like that," she told him. "Do you really think I should give you a reward after you almost knocked me over?"

Not at all embarrassed, the green dragon whuffed, and opened his mouth again.

"You seem to think so, whatever I think." She raised her eyes and looked over the other three unclaimed dragonets again.

The other large green male was nice, and the tan and red one seemed pleasant, too. She did not think she cared for the timid pale green one. Olive green was still sitting with his mouth open.

"So tell me, why should you be my dragon?" she asked the hungry one.

He tilted his head and blinked. It looked like he was batting his eyes at her, like a flirt trying to get a dancing partner might. Since his mouth was still open, he just ended up looking goofy, and Shala had to laugh. She popped a kibble in his mouth. "I think you have a sense of humor, fellow."

He hopped closer yet, and nuzzled her hands and arms. She knew he was looking for more food, but he was gentle and sweet about it this time, no more head butts. She gave him her last kibble. After crunching and swallowing it, he snuffled around on her palms, then licked the crumbs off. His tongue was dark peachy pink. It tickled her fingers.

"Okay. I think you are my dragon."

As if he agreed with her, the dragon crouched down and leaned his neck against her thigh. Like he was giving her a hug.

She glanced back over her shoulder at Jhude. "What do you think?"

He spread his hands. "It's your choice! He seems to like you, though."

The dragonet did appear to have chosen her. So be it. "I will name him Nizael," she told her foster brother. He raised his eyebrow and nodded once at her.

"That's the name of my birth family's caravan," she told the olive green dragon. "Since it already has a Z in it, and my grandmother's work robes were almost the same color as you, it does seem like it was meant to be."

The dragon farted, a rather long and noisy process. Shala grinned. Even if that was his opinion of her name for him, she couldn't help laughing, because his eyes were wide open and rolling a little as though he had surprised himself.

"They do that," Sylvan said.

"A lot," Aimee agreed. "Especially when they're little."

Jhude said, laughter in his voice, "I wonder if that's his reaction to his name, or his new rider?"

Shala turned and made a face at him. But it was good Jhude was making a joke. It meant he had decided this dragon-riding thing was going to be okay for his little foster-sister.

"So, Nizael. Let's see how friendly you are when I don't have food for you." She reached one hand to his eye ridge and scratched him where Sylvan's Simba liked to be scratched. Nizael pushed his head forward and closed his eyes. It looked as though there was a blissful smile on his green dragon face.

"That's a good sign," Aimee said. "I think you have your dragon, Shala."

"Nizael for Shala," Dene said. "I'll write it in the log book."

A dragon, for Shala! She kept waiting for someone to say she had to give him back, that they'd just been joking. How could this be true?

CHAPTER 3 — Training

The only thing more amazing than how fast the dragons grew was how much they ate. Shala could feel the muscles in her arms building up from toting sacks of dragon kibbles. Of course, a little muscle also came from rubbing an aloe-based salve into Nizael's pebbled hide twice a day, too.

"It helps the skin smooth out and encourages scale growth on their necks and backs—which they need to keep up with their growth rate," Sylvan had told them in the lecture that morning. They were learning a lot about dragon physiology, feed requirements, and basic dragon medicine from Sylvan, along with *people* first aid from Dene and Aimee.

Shala understood now why Jhude had been careful to pack his first aid kit when they traveled. He had helped her create hers, and now she learned more things that should go in it. She selected some things from the school's supply to put in her carry sack that would always go traveling with her. A few of the more expensive items like the antibiotic ointment, she would have to buy when she could with her earnings-to-come.

Aimee and Dene had also talked about dragon kibble, which was manufactured in Midford. Mostly of fish, and bodhaata, a kind of antelope which were raised on the plains near Midford. But since dragons were omnivorous, the chow also included bits of dried fruit, such as bandova and raisins, greens for minerals and roughage, and some carbohydrates for energy: potatoes and yams.

Cooked and baked into dragon-sized kibble shapes, the chow was delivered quarterly by a long oxen-pulled wagon train from Midford. In civilized areas, the dragons were not allowed to pillage herds and farms. To protect the balance of nature, they were prevented from constantly preying on wild game. Other, wilder locales often had nothing for the dragons to hunt, and food had to be brought along for them.

One sunny afternoon in late fall, Shala squinted against the bright sun as she worked with Nizael in the dragon paddock area. There were few trees, and she'd been a little late finishing her noontime chores, so she'd gotten stuck with one of the full-sun areas of the paddock. Nizael didn't seem to mind, and of course Shala was used to the sun from her days at the desert oasis.

"I do think I'm going to get some sunglasses or a hat," she murmured, using one hand as a screen so she could examine Nizael's wing structure. She was supposed to be able to determine whether she was exercising him enough by how well-developed the lateral muscle group was, and how thick the tendons connecting the wing segments together at the joints were.

She was about to signal her dragon to close his wings when he decided to play. He curved his neck around and butted her with his nose. He was tall enough now that he had to duck his head down to thump her in the shoulder blades like that. It tipped her over and she fell forward, throwing out her hands to catch herself on his rump. She heard air "oof" out of him as she lost her footing and fell against his side.

"Hey, mister! That's enough!" She pushed his head back with her hand, laughing. "We'll play ball in a minute, okay?"

He seemed to understand the words "play ball" well enough. Shala was impressed at how quickly the dragons learned the hand signals, and some of them like Nizael picked up the meanings of a lot of the

43

people-words too. That made them at least as smart as goats and dogs, and Shala thought perhaps they were much smarter than that.

Sylvan finished with Ben and Lizard and walked over to look at Nizael. "What is your measurement on him, Shala?"

She held up the leather gauge strap they'd each been given that morning. "He's about a three at the major joints and under two at the minor ones."

Sylvan nodded. "Yes, I thought so. He's developing a little more slowly than some of the others. He's putting a lot of calories into growing, so you'll see more development when this growth spurt slows down."

"You said it takes about a year for them to be full grown," Shala said, "but could it be longer for a big dragon?"

Sylvan nodded. "I've seen a few take a year and a half before growth stopped completely. And the bigger they are, the harder the rider must work to build wing muscles and develop the dragon's bellows, because it will take extra strength and breath to get that extra size up into the air."

Shala ran her fingers through Nizael's feathery ruff hairs. The tips were almost as soft as a nanny goat's ear. Nizael poked his head in front of her, begging for a brow rub.

Sylvan snorted. "He's not shy about asking for what he wants, is he?" He signaled Nizael to open his wings, which the dragon did. The sun shone through the wing leather, making a kind of olive green tent or sunshade over them. "Yes, he—and you—have a way to go to get those measurements up. That will determine when he flies, too."

Shala heard shouts of laughter, and glanced across the paddock. Some of the students were having a water fight with their buckets of dragon bath water, sloshing it over their dragons, themselves, and each other. Nizael turned to look too, and leaned himself in that direction, as clear a sign as any that he wanted to join the fun.

"Hmm," Sylvan said. "Looks like I'm done out here!" He beat a hasty retreat from the paddock, and soon Shala and Nizael were as soggy as everyone else. Even Sparkellz and Erisse were laughing and soaked to the dripping point.

Wyant turned around just in time to catch a part-bucketful in the face as Tomaso threw the last of the sudsy water in his container on his friend. Wyant grabbed Shala's bucket away from her and made sure to toss water on her and Nizael when he got his revenge on Tomaso.

Nizael then discovered stomping in puddles was fun, and everyone nearby was sprayed with mud just about the same time Erisse and one of the guys came up with the hose turned on full. They were drenched, but all the mud was washed off, and the dragons whuffed, curled their tail tips and began moving into the sunniest spots for naps.

Shala polished Nizael dry with a smile on her face.

Later, Aimee called out that she had just posted the list of First Dance partners. Breathless from laughing and running, three of the four young dragonrider girls arrived in the dining hall just about the same time that the boys got there from wherever they had been. The dance was a traditional part of the Year Turn Day celebration pretty much everywhere on Azureign. Usually, parents or grand'ers of a village assigned the dance partners, but that method wouldn't work, here.

Shala skidded on the wood floor. Her leather sandals slid on the waxed surface, and she bumped into the wall before she came to a complete stop. Laughing and windmilling their arms in a wild thrash,

Erisse and Tarva also skidded, crashing into Shala and the wall as they stopped. Meanwhile, little Alu walked with calm steps up to the board and became the first of them to read the list, though she'd not raced with them to get there.

"Aha!" Alu said, "I dance with Tomaso," she told them with a great big smile. "And the gift assignments are also listed." She opened her notebook to write down something.

Shala waited while Tarva and Erisse ran their fingers down the list, getting their information. The boys hung back, watching. Once the other two girls stepped away, she looked at the list. She'd be dancing first with Kiny. She and Wyant were to give a gift to Alu; also, she and Kiny were to create a gift for Tomaso.

This was the way Aimee and Dene had decided to arrange the Year Turn party and gift-giving. At home, Shala had given each of her brothers and Andrya a small gift she had made, and they had done so in return. But she knew Tomaso and others had not given gifts at all. Instead they did their family members or their community some service, such as repairing the stables roof at the inn, or clearing weeds from someone's garden.

The teachers had also been thinking up ways for the riders to get better acquainted. They'd added their own Year Turn activity: each young rider would introduce one of the others to the group. Shala would introduce Wyant. She would get to know him by asking him questions, and then present what she learned to the rest of the group in some way.

Each of the other eight riders would do likewise with their assigned rider. Aside from the oddness of introductions at Year Turn, they would celebrate the Day in as normal a fashion as the school could devise under the circumstances.

46

CHAPTER 4 — Campout

A few nights later, they were assigned to groups to camp out in the yard, using the materials they had packed for themselves. The sleepout included a food search, and how to build a fire, the best way to pitch their tent, and how to make an emergency lean-to.

Shala had been cold ever since she arrived at Two Rivers, so she made sure to pack an extra layer of clothing, three blankets for her bedroll, and she took her goat wool jacket, wishing she had a sweater to put under it. She was going to shiver all night.

Kiny came up behind her as she crouched down and laid out the firemaking tools she had brought. "Hadn't that ought to be the guys' work?" he asked.

She glanced over her shoulder at him. "Guys' work? Why would it be?"

"Well...I just thought I might have more experience at camping than you would, I suppose."

Shala straightened up and turned to face him. "Maybe you do. But I've built loads of fires for dye vats," she told him, "and I'm pretty good at it."

Erisse's giddy laughter preceded her. "Oh, Shala, let Kiny do the manly thing and build the fire," she said. "We can go set up the house and make up the beds!" She smiled at Kiny in a way Shala thought odd, then took Shala's hand and led her to the area they had chosen for their tent. Shala noticed the other two groups already had their tents up and their gear inside. Why were she and Kiny and Erisse so slow?

"Okay," Erisse said. "First the tarp, right?"

They stretched the cellu-plass tarp out flat, and took turns pegging down the corners with the mallet and stakes. Shala had selected the tools from the work kits Dene and Aimee provided. The plass was made of wood-pulp which had been treated with a biological agent that turned it into thin strong sheets of waterproof fabric. It tended to curl if it wasn't weighted down, so they drove a stake into the ground at each corner through the mounting rings fastened there with heavy stitching. Shala fingered the heavy hemp threads. She hated sewing with the stuff, it was coarse and hard to work with, but it did the job.

Next, they squared up the bottom of their tent, and Shala drove more stakes into the ground while Erisse pulled the tent corners taut with the cords at each corner. They tied the cords onto the stakes, then ran the stiff plass rods through the mounting pockets and raised the tent dome.

Erisse wandered over to where Kiny wasn't getting the fire started, and Shala struggled to post the last rod end into the tent pocket where it belonged. It was difficult to hold the tension in the rod, so it curved enough to get the rod into place. She managed to jam it in at last, and the tent was up. She glanced at Erisse, who was kneeling beside Kiny.

Shala turned and picked her bedroll and pack up and put them in the tent against the right-hand wall. Erisse was going to want to be in the middle, she guessed. When she finished, Shala went back outside and watched Kiny's struggle with the fire. She hoped her expression didn't show her dismay. How did he expect those three leaves and two pinecones to be enough kindling to start the fire?

"Erisse, do you want to go look for dinner?"

Erisse's blue eyes flashed as she stood up. "Sure. Dinner. Are you really going to live off the land?" She pointed to her backpack. "I brought some eggs I swiped from the henhouse; we could have those."

"Oh," Shala didn't say anything more, but she felt a headache begin between her eyes. Weren't they supposed to fend for themselves? Maybe stealing eggs was part of "fending," but she didn't think so. "I guess

I'd like something a little more than that," she told Erisse. "There's some platecone trees just down the slope; the nuts are quite tasty. And I'd like to collect some greens for a salad."

"Well, there's the veggie garden for raiding," Kiny pointed out.

"Um. I don't think we're supposed to steal our dinner," Shala said, feeling like the odd one out. "It's just as easy to gather it from the hillside here as climb all the way back up to the garden, anyway."

"Point," Kiny said, writing an invisible tick mark in the air. "Go ahead. By the time you get back, I'll have the means to cook it, whatever it is." He glanced up at the sky, where clouds were tumbling in from the south, hiding both the rings and the sunset. "And it's going to get dark soon, so you'd better be quick."

Despite her initial grumbling, Erisse was actually helpful at finding and harvesting some salad greens. They came back about a half-hour later, arms full of goodies. Erisse tossed the wild onions onto the ground, and showed Kiny the prize of their collection: a shelf of ruddy splaid fungus. It would be delicious baked among the coals of their fire, which Shala noticed, Kiny had gotten going quite well. Perhaps there were other ways to start a fire; she shouldn't have been so quick to judge his efforts.

Erisse didn't seem inclined to help cook, so Shala took over that chore. She wasn't a very good cook, but Andrya had taught her a few simple dishes she could make with the supplies she had. She peeled the onions and put them in a pot of water with some of the watercress and a handful of broken platecone nuts. She set the grate over the fire, spreading its folded legs and seating it so it was steady, and put the pot on it. Then she went down to the small creek where it splashed over a low waterfall before joining the muddy Yent a half-dozen meters below their camp. She filled a bucket with water. After she washed the salad greens, she set the bucket beside the fire. She knew from experience it would be nice to have warm water to wash up with after they ate.

Erisse and Kiny had spread a blanket by the fire and sat side by side with another blanket around their shoulders. Shala noticed they still hadn't put their things inside the tent. Should she mention it? The dark clouds in the twilit sky looked like rain.

Well, it wasn't her business, was it? She hated bossy people, and assumed they did too, so she said nothing.

She went into the tent to get her jacket, and discovered it was two of *her* blankets Erisse and Kiny had taken out to sit by the fire with. She felt anger begin to simmer. She buttoned her jacket and wrapped her arms about herself.

What was she supposed to use to sleep with? And why had they gone to all the trouble to go inside and take her things when their own were lying outside right beside them? Shala flipped the tent flap back and leaned through the opening.

"Guys, did you take the blankets from my bedroll?"

"*Your* blankets?" Erisse asked. "Oh, my gosh. There were three, so I thought you packed one for each of us, and these two were ours!"

"You didn't pack blankets?"

Kiny looked over his shoulder at Shala. "No. We have sleeping bags. You don't?" He unwrapped the blanket from himself and lifted the other end off Erisse's shoulders. "I'm sorry, Shala. I just assumed you did, too, and these were extra." He handed her the one, but the other lay in the dirt.

Kiny saw the direction of her gaze. "Hey, we'll shake it out before bed, okay? I'm sorry!"

Erisse made a face. "No sleeping bag! You'd think they would provide such things, wouldn't you?" She looked at Shala, her expression bland.

Beginning to feel very bad for making a fuss, Shala shrugged. "I'm sorry, too. It's just I've been so cold ever since I got here," she reached a hand out and took the blanket Kiny handed her.

He snorted. "This! This isn't cold! I mean, it's winter, but this is warm compared to home."

Erisse laughed her giddy laugh. "He's from Queensland. He's used to an igloo!" she said.

"Igloo?"

Kiny shook his head. "No. It snows a lot, but we live in a real house, just like you do. Don't let her fool you!" He saw how she was wrapped in her jacket. "I guess it doesn't get this cold in the desert, huh?"

"It does at night quite often. But it's dryer, somehow." She shook her head. "I don't know why but this cold seems to get in my bones. And once I'm cold, I can't seem to warm up."

"Well, that's a problem, isn't it?" Erisse said with a bright smile. "Too bad you aren't in Wyant's group. Then you could snuggle!"

Shala couldn't imagine for a moment why being in the other group would be a way to warm up, then she remembered how Kiny and Erisse had been sitting wrapped together. Did Erisse think she and Wyant were a couple? Shala was surprised at how pleased she felt at that idea—though it wasn't true. "Well, snuggling would be warm, all right!"

Erisse laughed.

Shala sat down by the fire, and yearned for the soup to be ready. That would warm her, and much better than Wyant would, no matter what Erisse was thinking. She stared at the flames of the fire as Kiny and Erisse put their things in the tent and got their coats out.

No matter how hard she tried, she didn't seem to be fitting in with the others. The students and school were not what she expected, and it felt as though she was not what they expected, either. It made her miss her family. All at once she wanted the warmth and comfort of Andrya and the three boys and a cat and dog or two sitting around the fiercely-burning dung brick fire.

She should write them a letter. One of the grown-up dragonriders who came by delivering mail could take it onward. It would get there long before she would.

Maybe one of them, Logyn no doubt, would write back.

Then she remembered the book he had given her, and vowed to read one of the meditations in the morning when she could see the words. It would be like being with him, a little.

Year Turn Day arrived, and Shala was busy putting the finishing touches onto the hems of Tomaso's pants when a giggling Erisse came into the girls' dorm and plopped down onto the bench beside her. Erisse reached across Shala's back and set her fingers on the outside edge of Shala's shoulder.

"Gosh, you are small, aren't you?" she said, and then just as abruptly as she came, she went, leaving Shala with a raised eyebrow. *What was that about?*

Alu turned around on her bunk and leaned over the edge. She brushed her blonde curls, watching as Shala knotted the thread, reknotted it, and snipped it off with the small stork-shaped scissors from her sewing kit.

"I wish I could sew," Alu said. "I've never even threaded a needle."

"I could show you, sometime, maybe," Shala said, glancing over at her. "I don't have enough time right now, and then it takes some practice. Though I should warn you, my foster mother had nasty things to say about my stitching quality."

"That would be great!" Alu grinned, her dimples making her face look merry. "Even bad stitches would be better than nothing. Could I see your scissors? I think my grand'er had a pair like that."

Shala handed the scissors up. "Those were *my* grandmother's. My foster mother said they came all the way from Earth. That was the style back then, to make them in fanciful shapes." Alu handed them back and she put them away. "They aren't very sharp any more, but it's kind of a tradition."

"They were your real grand'er's?"

Shala nodded. "She wore them around her neck on a ribbon. That's all I have of her. Those, and an old piece of her dress."

"What happened to your parents?"

"They were killed in an earthquake, along with my brother."

"Oh, how awful! You must miss them, a lot."

Shala sighed, folding Tomaso's pants into a neat rectangle. "Yes."

"That's sad, Shala. It must be hard to grow up without a family." Alu tossed her brush into her clothes chest, and flopped over onto her back. Head hanging upside down over the edge of her bunk, she said, "I'd be unhappy without my family, I know."

"Well, I lived with my foster family after. My mother's sister. They *are* my family, now."

"Oh, I see." Alu sat up. "Do you have brothers and sisters?"

"Three brothers, whom I miss very much."

"Gosh. No sister. Are you the youngest?"

53

"No, Jono is younger. Logyn and I are almost twins, and Jhude's older."

Alu grinned. "I have two sisters and two brothers, and I'm in the exact middle. "I miss my oldest brother and younger sister the most, and my dad." Alu jumped down off her bunk. "I wonder if I can sneak into the kitchen yet." She picked up a piece of paper and waved it. "We're making rabbit stew for Kiny; Ben snuck the recipe from Kiny's cookbook, and Sylvan provided the rabbit. It's the last gift I need to make," she said.

"I'm about done, too. I just need to finish the drawing I did for introducing Wyant."

"Oh, that's right, you have Wyant. I'm introducing Tomaso." She rolled her eyes. "Can you imagine what that was like? I felt like I was prying words out of him with a blacksmith's lever!"

Shala smiled. "He's pretty quiet. I'll be glad to hear about him," she said. She got up and pulled out the tissue paper Wyant had found and smoothed it out on the bench. Taking care with each fold, she wrapped Tomaso's pants in the paper. That gift was finished. She couldn't work on Alu's gift, because it was supposed to be a surprise: a chart showing what desert plants would make what color dye. When Alu went off to the kitchen, she could finish it.

Wyant had discovered that the little blonde girl's family grew cotton on their large ranch on the Kendai plains. Alu was good at making paper from the scraps that did not go to the weavers; she used dyes to tint the cotton slurry into pretty colors. Shala thought she would be interested in desert plants and what she might be able to do with them.

She dug into her clothes chest and found the wrapped drawing she had done of Wyant for her introduction. She took her courage in hand. If she couldn't even show it to Alu, how could she present it to the whole group? She untied the ribbon and unrolled it, and held it up.

Alu gasped. "Oh, Shala, that's gorgeous!" She leaned forward and studied the drawing. "Wow, you are good!"

"Really?" She felt a little embarrassed. "I never know how anything I do compares with anyone else, because we had so few people to compare anything with. My brother draws, and he taught me a little. His work was always much better than mine. But he gave it up to make cheese. I've never thought I was very good."

Alu shook her head, curls bouncing. "No, you could sell this," she said. "You could earn a little extra money that way, if you wanted, I'm sure. It's just lovely." Alu handed the drawing back, and Shala rolled it back up and retied the ribbon, smiling. Alu should like the chart too, then, for she had worked hard drawing it to make the plants look just right and match the tinting chart to the colors she remembered producing for Andrya's cloth. Of course, the paper would take the color in a different way, but it would be a guide.

"I'm going to go take a bath and wash my hair," she said, and Alu nodded.

"Erisse and Tarva were going in as I left. I hope there's some hot water left!"

As this was a joke, Shala laughed. Hot springs under the school was their water heater. They never ran out. She picked up the shampoo and soap Embry had made. She loved the herby smell—it reminded her of home.

"See you later!" Alu called.

Tarva and Erisse were just leaving the bath house. Tarva took the opportunity to ask another question to use in her introduction of Shala.

Shala's drawings were a bigger hit than her presentation, she thought. She even received a commission to draw Tarva's dragon, so the stocky brunette could send it home for her family to see.

Tarva's introduction of Shala had been a poem about an orphan girl from the desert. It was charming, and Shala felt the others might have gotten a good idea what she was like from it. Wyant teased her later about herding goats, so he, at least, had been listening.

The two gifts Shala received were a shawl from Erisse and Ben, and a bookcube from Wyant and Tomaso. Or Wyant, really, since she knew it had come from his home in New Venice: his family owned what seemed an entire library of books.

Some of the gifts were pretty silly, like Kiny's rabbit stew, which he proceeded to eat, making slurping noises punctuated by, "Mmm!" and everyone's laughter. Ben mended a strap on Granger's pack, which would have been practical, if he hadn't decorated it all over with the fat striped bumblebees Granger had once mentioned liking.

"Oh well, at least I'll know which pack is mine!" Granger had said with a grin.

Kiny and Tarva braided Erisse's hair for her, in a style that lay close to her head, and with a promise to braid again any time she needed her hair out of her face to ride.

Shala felt a warm glow when Tomaso unwrapped his package and saw that his T'ai Chi pants had been shortened. His sweet smile was thanks enough.

Alu gave a packet of her pretty paper to Erisse, who grinned and nodded thanks. A couple of people asked Alu if there was something they could trade for the paper, so they could have some, too, which seemed to please the little blonde.

Before they knew it, all the gifts had been exchanged, and it was time to dance. Hoping she wouldn't disgrace herself, Shala smiled and made a little curtsy as Kiny came up to her.

He bowed and grinned. "Off we go," he said.

Their first dance was something Shala could pretend she knew how to do, with a promenade, and lots of passing back and forth. They danced in back, so she could see what the other couples did before it was her turn. They held hands to make a bridge for the others, then took their turn ducking under the bridge. This was a dance often done at weddings. In fact, Jhude and Netke probably had danced it at their wedding, just a few days ago.

Kiny told her, "We spin, next, you know," and with a wicked grin he grasped her waist, lifting her up off the floor a bit as he swept her into a series of fast turns.

Breathless by the end of the dance, she could only laugh and beg to sit down. "Thank you, Kiny, for a wonderful First Dance."

"My pleasure," he said.

As she rested, Dene and Aimee announced the partner system for the next dance. Grateful for the dances she had learned at the fair the times she had been able to go, Shala felt perhaps not confident, but at least not the worst dancer there.

She laughed and made the fringe on her new shawl twirl. Erisse and Ben had gotten a lightweight wool, in an aqua so deep it was almost turquoise. It was constructed of an open, loose knit, but was warm despite all the openwork. And, she had learned, Erisse was "measuring" her, when she'd come in that morning and given her that strange, brief hug.

Now Granger came up and suggested they dance. She smiled and got to her feet. She did not think he looked as good with his hair so short—the haircut was his gift from someone—but it pleased him, and Erisse had been seen running her fingers through it.

As they danced, Shala thought about Wyant's face as she had held up the drawing she had done of him. He seemed happy as she explained each part—the books in his home, what his home was like and where it was, his mother the Professor in the New Venice college, his father the biological scientist. She'd mentioned his siblings, and the horse he had raised and trained—all of which were in the drawing, arranged around his face in a sort of frame. She also spoke of what she hadn't drawn: his political ambitions, which his father had tried to discourage, and how much his family like to talk, discussing all manner of topics.

Wyant's expression had been serious when she finished, but—she thought—appreciative. And he and Alu and the others complimented her on her drawings.

Alu had been so excited about the desert plant dye chart that she had actually jumped up and down, making everyone laugh.

Shala smiled as they spun past Wyant and Tarva, Ben and Alu, Erisse and Tomaso. Aimee and Sylvan swept by, grinning, while Kiny sat out with Dene, who watched everyone with a huge smile on his face.

It wasn't home, but it was a real Year Turn Day celebration.

Some Things You May Want to Know About Dragons (And How the Heck Can They Fly, Anyway?)

Think of a pterosaur. Or a big—very big—bat, with lizardy scales, a long slender neck and tail and hollow, waffle-structured bones, and enormous leathery wings. The tail is thin and ropy, with long wisps of hair at the end. The chest is deep and beneath the wings are gill-like bellows which supercharge the dragon's bloodstream with oxygen, giving them additional power for flight.

Dragons are not natural creatures. They were genetically engineered from a pterosaur-like native flyer once found on Earth, and a similar beast from the planet Oni. Modifications were made so they could become a true Helper Species for human colonists; thus, they fly well in the atmosphere of terrestrial planets, and can carry light loads, which the original species could not do well.

Average wingspan varies between seven to nine and a half meters. Average speed is about 50 kilometers per hour, and up to 65 or 70 kilometers per hour when diving or gliding under ideal atmospherics. Average flight endurance, four to five hours. With significant gliding time, or a break to rest on the ground, two to three additional hours flight time per day may be added. Thus, depending upon atmospheric conditions, a dragon may cover between 250 to 400 kilometers per day.

The head is smaller and the snout shorter than a pterosaur's, as though a horse's face had been elongated. Heavy brow ridges protect the eyes. Those eyes are double-lidded, with an inner protective lining, like a cat's. Nostrils are oversized, the jaw large and powerful, eyes like those of raptors: good at long distance, not as good close up. Dragons probably have a limited ability to see colors. Small pointed ears are set at the top of the head above and behind the brow ridges. Hearing is good but not spectacular. They tend to use scent as their primary sensory input.

The body skin is pebbly and tough; imagine a rhinocerous crossed with a monitor lizard. Dragons also have flat scale-like divisions in the skin on their backs, shoulders, and upper legs, which overlap the pebbled skin. These are similar to the scales on a snake, which serve as a protective and temperature regulating system and probably make them more aerodynamic.

The skin of the wings is leathery, and tough. The wings are on a joint permitting them to be cambered (tilted, or angled) like a bat's, so they are agile in the air. The wing camber system can also be used as drag, to assist in landing (think of the flaps on an ancient airplane, if you have ever seen one).

Long fluffy fur grows out between the scales on the dragon's shoulders and neck. The long manelike ruff across the back of the head and neck may be a temperature-control mechanism, or a genetic engineering artifact.

Colors vary; geneticists believe their scale and fur colors will consolidate over time, but natural selection has only had about 1200 years to exert pressure, and Queen selection and mating has little to do with dragon color and much to do with size and strength.

Packdrones, which are thought to be "throwbacks" to the original species, are slower and smaller, and tend to be short-tempered; they generally cannot and will not take on a rider. They are never accepted into a dragon pack. They tend to be treated (by "real" dragons) rather like a cow that has an embarrassing tendency to look somewhat like a real dragon. Mostly packdrones are ignored by their dragon cousins.

Everything on a dragon is about flight: A cross section of dragon bone reveals the waffling that makes the wings strong but keeps the dragons light. Wing joints and leg strenth help with takeoffs and landings. The valved bellows system helps make burdened flight possible. This is a sort of super-lung, which functions like a four-stroke piston engine:

1. dragon raises wing; valve opens, inhale
2. dragon lowers wing, valve closes, pressurized oxygen is forced into bloodstream
3. dragon raises wing, valve stays closed, lungs suck carbon dioxide from bloodstream
4. dragon lowers wing, valve opens, exhale

This supercharger system gives the dragon more power for flight than most large flying creatures such as an eagle.

This Helper Species is utilized as couriers and aerial guardians on the colony worlds Bootai, Azureign, and Little Shanghai, and casakin holdings at Linlary Catap*y, where gravitic and atmospheric conditions make burdened flight possible.

(Author's note: In the case of Azureign, additional neon in the atmosphere means thermals (currents of rising air) go up faster and higher in the atmosphere. This more energetic thermal system assists the dragons in faster flight. It also results in more aggressive weather systems on Azureign, including extraordinarily strong tornados, waterspouts and dust storms, and extensive and frequent forest and grassland fires.)

The Oracle's Encyclopedia for Young People
Terra, 1875 Galactic Era

CHAPTER 5 — Whistling

Shala stuck her fingers in her mouth and whistled again. The shrill sound seemed to have potential, but across the grassy field, Tomaso shook his head—again, no.

It was his turn to try. She saw him take a deep breath, insert his fingers, and let loose. It was loud, but it wasn't shrill, and would not carry up to a dragon's level in the sky. She shook her head.

She tried again, with even less effective results. Tomaso shook his head.

"This is stupid," she muttered to herself. "How can I learn everything else, but not be able to whistle? How am I ever going to call him down?" She sighed. "Assuming he ever flies, of course." She glanced over to the dragon paddock. All nine dragons, plus Simba, were in the yard, sunning themselves in little wallows they'd made among the clumps of long spring grass. The sky above was blue witness to her failure, but the dragons, at least, were oblivious.

They each tried the whistle again, failed again.

In the paddock, one of the dragons trumpeted. It was Arzid, challenging Lizard for a spot near Sparkellz, who stood with her neck arched in the meadow. Sparkellz preened the feathery fur that fluffed out between the scales on her shoulders. The splendid gold female was exactly what a dragon should be: lithe, elegant, swift, and strong in the air. She was even pretty on the ground. And she was a natural leader. Most telling of all, the other dragons in the pack bowed to Sparkellz, honoring her. She would undoubtedly be the pack's new Queen.

The pack was made up of the eight dragons that flew. All of them except Nizael. Simba flew, of course, but the Z-year pack mostly ignored him. He wasn't one of them. Nizael almost was.

Shala shook herself, and tried the whistle again, changing the angle of her fingers, and this time, making no noise at all. Tomaso wasn't even sure she'd blown. She waved for him to try, which he did. It was kind of a limp little whistle, all wheezy and thin.

"Oh, that's wracked!" Wyant said, coming up from behind Shala. She jumped, then turned to see what he wanted. "Tarva just got it," he said. "You two are the last ones without your whistle," he said. "But—" he made a dramatic flourish, "Sylvan sent me out with some help." He handed her a silvery tube. "You blow here, as hard as you can," he explained.

Shala took it and did as he'd said. This time, the whistle was shrill and carrying. Tomaso waved both arms and grinned. He trotted over to them. He arrived out of breath, already reaching a hand out for the other whistle Wyant carried. He blew that one, and all the dragons in the yard turned their heads.

It was eery, with ten dragons all facing the same way, toward them.

"Weird," Tomaso said.

"Cool," Wyant said.

Tomaso held up the whistle. "I knew there was a better way."

"Well, you still have to learn how to do it yourself," Wyant said. "Because you may not have the whistle when you need one."

Shala put her fingers in her mouth and blew again.

"Close," Wyant said. "Try it without the fingers; just shape your lips as though the fingers were there," he suggested.

Shala did that. She startled herself and both boys with the volume and depth of the whistle that came out. "Wow! I can't believe I did that!"

Tomaso tried it that way, too. His first effort was no good, but he tried several times in a row, and each was an improvement on the last. Finally, red-faced and gasping, he emitted a respectable whistle then collapsed on the ground, half-laughing, half-wheezing in relief.

Wyant threw his arms out wide. "At last!"

"Now we have to get our dragons to understand what the whistle means," Shala said, rolling her eyes.

"That's not so hard," Wyant said. "They're curious about things, so if they're aloft, they'll come down to see why you're making such a racket!" He tilted his chin in a proud pose. "I got Denez to land twice this morning." He grinned that great lopsided smile Shala liked so much. "Of course, you have to reward them with food when they come, so they think a whistle is a wonderful thing!"

"Alu got Ozala to come, too," Tomaso said. He rolled up into a sitting position, resting his forearms on his knees.

Ozala and Denez both flew and flew well. That made it easier, Shala thought. Now that she had her whistle, how could she train Nizael to land at the sound, if he wasn't up in the sky in the first place?

Wyant jerked a thumb toward the barns. "I'll go tell Sylvan how well the whistles worked!"

"Hey, wait," Tomaso said, getting to his feet. He lifted his whistle to Shala in a jaunty salute, and ran to catch up with Wyant.

Shala patted her thighs, realized this pair of pants was the one with no pocket, and tried to figure out where to put her whistle. She ended up sticking it in her mouth as she walked over to the dragons.

"Hi, Niz. Ready to work?" she said, slurring her words around the whistle. Nizael heaved a deep sigh, but instead of standing up, ready to go, he stretched out his neck and flattened himself so he was lying on his stomach, haunches reared up with his feet splayed out behind him, and his tail flat on the ground.

"You look extremely silly," Shala told him, but he didn't seem to care at all. "I guess that means we aren't working now," she said. She scratched his brow ridge and tried to figure out how she was supposed to train him to come to the whistle, when he wouldn't even get off the ground. She rubbed his head and neck, and he curled his toes up in pleasure, making a hump in his foot. She was still standing there among the dragons when Erisse came out from the dining hall and walked across the yard.

Shala watched her come, admiring the way the other girl always managed to look so put-together. Erisse was wearing a pretty blue sweater that made her eyes look even more blue. She had on black pants with blue embroidery down the side of the leg.

I could do that, Shala thought. I could embroider something on my pants.

Then Erisse was there, smiling a hard, bright smile at her. "I heard you have your whistle," she said.

Shala nodded.

"Well, the fact that Nizael isn't flying yet is a concern to everyone." When Erisse turned her head, Shala could see there was a blue ribbon in amongst the black curls. The same blue as her sweater and eyes, of course.

Shala sighed.

"Listen," Erisse said, leaning close. She spoke so softly that Shala leaned forward and pulled her hair back, trying to hear better. "I have an idea you may want to try."

Flattered that the popular girl would take the time to talk to her, Shala listened to each word. She knew Erisse could be friends with anyone she wanted. But Shala had to work hard to make friends among the other riders. After all, she had no experience with flocks of girls, and no real family history. She had no famous father, no status to claim. Not like Erisse. Erisse had friends, and an important family, and money, and everyone liked her.

Erisse was everything Shala thought she wanted to be, herself. She listened carefully, indeed.

"I mean, dragons are supposed to fly, aren't they?" Erisse said. Her black curls sparkled in the sun. Her blue-violet eyes sparkled, too, like diamond chips that lit up her creamy cheeks.

Shala felt very brown, in comparison. Even her clothes were brown today. She pinched her nose, feeling a sudden headache strike between her eyes.

"Especially a strong dragon like yours," Erisse was saying. They both looked at Nizael.

The big dragon still sprawled haunches up in the sun, an ungainly olive green hill. He wasn't very dignified. He couldn't fly. But Niz was big. She tried to be proud of that. His wingspread was almost four meters now, and he was still growing. He stretched and spread the toes apart on his big feet, content.

Shala looked back at Erisse. She still didn't understand. What was the point of this conversation? Was it some kind of game? Shala became stiff and nervous. She wasn't very good at games. Especially girl games. She'd had plenty of boys to grow up with, but the only girls had been left behind with the caravanners, years ago.

Erisse laughed her soft laugh. "He needs your help, Shala. And my Sparkellz is one of the best fliers, so I know what I am talking about." She grinned and gave an admiring look at her own dragon. The gold Queen-candidate was sunbathing now, her iridescent leathery wings spread open to the light, so she glowed in the sun.

Shala groaned. Nizael looked like an enormous pile of cow droppings, by comparison. Ungainly on the ground, and who knows what in the air? One had to assume he *could* fly...because they certainly hadn't seen any real attempt.

"All his size and strength are just being wasted. You can train him to get better."

At that, she felt herself become annoyed. "That's what I've *been* doing, the training and strengthening exercises for his wings and his breathing." She could feel the heat of anger and embarrassment in her face. "I've worked his legs so they're strong enough for the loft-up." She shook her head and met Erisse's eyes. "He just won't get off the ground."

The dragon should fly. No one could really explain why he didn't. But Shala didn't think it was because she wasn't training him enough. If training exercises were all that mattered, Nizael was ready. But apparently something more was needed to make her dragon fly.

She was ready, too. She had passed ground school—all the classwork and map studies—with the highest score of the pack's riders. She knew every detail of the dragon-civilian protocols, the health care of dragons, and the flight paths in the lands that circled the Inner Sea and crossed the Rift and Drystone Deserts. But in the dragon department, they were in last place.

Shala loved her dragon. But honesty forced her to admit that in contrast with the others, and especially Sparkellz, Nizael was one big clumsy goof. Great wingspan and strength. But so far as anyone could tell, a ground-hugger of major proportions.

What good was a dragon who wouldn't fly?

What if he *never* flew? It was enough to make Shala wonder if she had chosen the wrong dragon.

Was it possible she could choose again, maybe from Kharmin's brood? Or would they blame her, say she was a bad dragon rider and send her back home, dragonless?

"Okay, so you should try this," Erisse said. "I think it will work: Just get him to the lofting cliff and *push* him off the edge. His wings are strong enough to hold him up. Even if he is afraid to fly, he can just glide down to the lake."

"Oh, he's not afraid to fly," she said in stout defense of her dragon. "It's more like his wings or his bellows aren't developed enough yet. Or something." She hoped. But how could she tell?

Niz now lay on his right side in the dust wallow, left wing extended high into the sky. The bellows on his left side was thus exposed, and Shala could see it stretch open. Even from this far away, she could hear the air Nizael sucked in through the gill-like structure, into his lofting chamber.

During flight, the bellows supercharged a dragon's blood with oxygen, and helped the lofting chambers fill with air, making them more buoyant. That was why they could fly well and carry loads.

Or at least most of them could.

He should be able to fly. Shala knew that, and so did everyone else.

Erisse snorted, a rather unlovely sound coming from her. "It looks like he's trying to grow his wings bigger in the sunlight," she said. "Does he think he's solar-powered?" She laughed at her own joke.

Niz was looking back at them. He blinked. Did the dragon know Erisse was making fun of him? He folded his wing, rolled onto his other side, and raised the right wing. His whole right side was covered with dust from the wallow. He could hardly make a worse contrast with Sparkellz or the other dragons sunning in the meadow.

Why was she defending him?

Okay, she thought. Erisse cares about this, too. She's showing you some attention—just go with it. She turned and met Erisse's big blue eyes.

"I think you may be right," she said. "Maybe he would fly if I pushed him off the launching cliff. But...I can't imagine how I would get him there, or push him over the edge if I did."

Erisse's bright smile faded. "Oh, Shala. Surely a clever girl like yourself could think of a way."

Her heart clutched. It was wonderful that this lovely girl would set herself to solve Nizael's problem. But now she was disappointed in Shala. Would she lose her new friend on the same day she had found her?

"Maybe if I dragged the chow wagon out there, he would follow," she blurted out the first idea that came into her head.

"Yes," Erisse said. "That would probably work." Erisse turned to her and smiled again. "And if you do it at night, no one will miss the wagon."

Shala nodded, sudden doubt entering her thoughts. She thought about stolen dinner eggs, and other choices Erisse had made that were less than stellar.

But Erisse's smile quirked. "And...if you used the tractor to pull it—why, I'll bet you could nudge him over the edge with the tractor, while he was distracted by the wagonload of food!"

It was Shala's turn to stop smiling. "Well, maybe," she said, trying to imagine doing that.

Erisse touched her shoulder. "Come on," she said, walking toward the barns. "I'll show you where the keys to the tractor are." Blue eyes flashed. "But you mustn't tell anyone I told you, or Wyant will get into trouble!"

"Oh," Shala managed. "I wouldn't want Wyant to suffer because of me," she said faintly. Wyant was one of the few who talked to her as if she was a real person. But now Erisse was helping her. Perhaps she was making friends after all.

"They'll forgive anything you do, if it gets Nizael into the sky. We all think he's going to be the pack leader, because he's so big," Erisse said. "And they need a strong leader." She stopped walking. Shala stopped too, to avoid running into her. Erisse looked at her, lips pursed, and forehead crinkled in a tiny scowl. "Granger's Arzid could lead the pack, he's big enough and strong enough and a good flyer. He would be a good Queen's Mate for Sparkellz. But Nizael is so much bigger—they want the biggest one in charge, that's the way dragons like it. So, you see, Nizael has to fly, so the pack leaders can be chosen." They started walking again.

Shala looked at the ground, at her feet, thinking. She thought about all that her new friend had said. It was true everyone thought Nizael would be the pack leader.

Each pack had its hierarchy figured out before the end of their year's training. They picked their Queen and Queen's Mate before they flew their final training run, at summer's end. Like wolves, they liked, *needed* someone big and strong to boss the group.

Shala knew Erisse's boyfriend Granger had worked hard to get his brown dragon, Arzid, ready. Erisse and Granger were very serious about the pack, and how strong it was. And where they were going to be posted when they graduated.

Erisse was right about that too: Arzid could easily be the pack leader if Niz wouldn't get off the ground. Even if the people were willing to wait, the dragons wouldn't. They would make their best choice at the end of summer.

Nizael had less than four tendays to fly, establish dominance, and become a leader.

"If he doesn't fly, he can't be Queen's Mate. And he's so big, if he isn't pack leader, you know what the other dragons will do." Erisse patted her shoulder. "We wouldn't want to see that happen."

Shala's breath caught. Nizael could be a threat to the pack and the new Queen and her Mate. They might drive him off. He would not be permitted into the pack. The other dragons would make him outcast.

They might even kill him. Shala felt her skin prickle all over.

"I'll see if I can figure out how to drive the tractor," she said.

"Good," Erisse said, a bright tone to her voice. "I think this plan will work."

Shala looked around the school grounds. The redwoods that fringed the paddock were a dark green and rusty red. The spring grass was still green, and the ground was damp from the rains and fog that appeared almost nightly. The sky above was just beginning to haze over with the arriving fog, but the rings were a bright white arc across the deep blue sky above. She took a deep breath and turned to go into the dining hall.

She could face the other riders now with a satisfied smile on her face. The afternoon's training session had gone very well. Nizael had been cooperative, and seemed strong and willing. He had fanned his wings hard enough to lift most of his body up, though his feet had not left the ground. Perhaps she would not need to resort to drastic measures to get him into the sky.

Her sandals slapped on the wood floor as she entered. She sniffed the air. It had been Kiny's turn to cook. What had he made? It smelled like greens and rice. Again. She picked up a bowl, spoon, and glass at the service counter, and walked toward the two long polished ash wood tables. She found a spot near the window where a cool draft blew in, and sat down. The bread basket was full, so she took a couple of chunks of the warm multi-grain loaf and glanced up in time to catch the server's eye. It was Alu on duty tonight.

The cheerful blonde pushed the serving cart over to Shala's table. This tiny girl from a wealthy family seemed to make everything fun. She had a great time training her dragon, reading the training holocubes— even examining dragon droppings for signs of disease—all with an adventuresome and eager grin. Alu also took her turn at service without complaint. Her arms looked so delicate they might break if she picked up anything heavy, and Shala hoped someone—maybe Kiny or Tomaso—had helped get the big tureen full of soup onto the serving cart.

Alu ladled stew into Shala's bowl, gave a pleasant nod at Shala's murmured, "Thanks," and pushed the serving cart on to the far end of the table to serve Aimee and Dene.

Shala dipped her spoon and tasted the sauce. It was green and garlicky, and she dug in. No weird spices tonight, thank heavens. Sometimes their fellow student cooks got too playful for the others' taste, and everyone went a little bit hungry. Everyone except the dragons, who appreciated a little "people food" now and then. Scraps and leftovers of the daily meal went into the chow wagon, along with their regular crunchy dragon kibbles. That's what she would use to lure Nizael with, when she— Well, *if* she followed the plan she and Erisse had made.

As she chewed, she thought about it again.

It wasn't really her plan, at all. She ought to call it Erisse's plan. She was still pretty nervous about trying it. And maybe it wouldn't be necessary.

Her thoughts were interrupted by Wyant and Tomaso, who sat down on either side of her.

"Hi!" Wyant said cheerily, thumping down his bowl.

Tomaso, as usual, didn't say anything at all. He was even quieter than Shala. She wondered if that meant he was shy, too, or if he just didn't like to talk.

She held out her bowl for seconds when Alu came around to serve the guys.

"Wow," Wyant said. "I can't believe we get to go on our first real training flight."

Alu set the ladle back in the pot when she finished filling bowls and clasped her hands. "Oh, it's going to be so much fun!" she said. "I washed Ozala and shined her up this afternoon. She's so excited!" Alu demonstrated her own excitement with a little bounce. Shala had to grin. Alu's happiness was like a virus, you caught it just being next to her.

"Yeah, they seem to know something's up," Wyant said, meaning the dragons. "But Ozala is always pretty, like her rider!" he added with a wink and a long sidewise look at Tomaso.

Tomaso flushed deep tomato red and stared at his bowl, not looking at Alu.

Oh! Shala realized. Tomaso likes her!

Well, what was not to like? Alu was very sweet and friendly. Secretly glad that it was Tomaso and not Wyant who seemed interested in the little blonde girl, Shala winked at Wyant, who gave her a conspirational smile. Matchmakers united, Shala thought, admiring Wyant's curly brown hair and golden-brown eyes.

Tomaso nodded his agreement with Wyant, after such a long delay that Shala was startled into thinking he'd read her thoughts and agreed with her matchmaking.

"Ozala is the prettiest dragon in the pack," Tomaso said. He raised his head and smiled his sweet smile at Alu. "You, too," he said.

"Why thank you," Alu said with a grin at the boy's gallant compliments. She said nothing about being compared with a pretty dragon, Shala noticed, imagining what Erisse would have said. Alu just took the compliment in the manner it was meant.

And Alu's dragon *was* as lovely as her rider. Ozala was the gorgeous pearly white Shala had looked at the day she chose Nizael. In the sunlight, Ozala gleamed with rainbowy swirls in her scales, and multicolor sparkles in her ruff fur. The pearl dragon was prettier than Sparkellz, many thought, though she was probably too small and sweet natured to be a likely candidate for Queen.

Rather like Alu was much nicer than Erisse. Shala stared down at her bowl. Why would she think unkind thoughts about her new friend? No, Shala decided, it's just that Alu is so kind. She isn't better than Erisse, she's different.

Now Alu nodded toward her serving pot. "You probably want to eat plenty tonight, because we'll have trail rations tomorrow."

Even Tomaso groaned at that.

"Great," Wyant said. "The dragons are stuffed, but we get to run on an empty stomach."

"Light and fast," Shala said, wishing she and Nizael were going.

Of course, the dragons would fly on the training flight. But their trainers could not ride them yet. By the end of summer, the young dragons would be strong and well-developed enough to bear riders. Until then, the students would follow on the ground—so their packs needed to be as light as they could make them. That meant trail bars for the people, because they each had to carry their dragon's high-energy chow, along with their own food and gear.

"Are they going to let them forage?" Wyant wondered.

"It sounds like we have to," Alu said. "We're gone overnight. Can't carry enough food for them without a truck coming along. And the dragons are going to be competing, for speed and strength," she wrinkled her nose, "and that includes finding food."

"So, they can decide—" Wyant began, but then Shala felt Tomaso's swift kick under the table that shut Wyant up. They'd realized whom they were sitting with. The girl whose dragon wouldn't fly. The Queen's Mate candidate who wasn't going to be a candidate for anything in the pack if he didn't fly soon.

Shala kept her eyes on her food. She wasn't going tomorrow. Alu and Wyant and Tomaso and the others were going, but she was not. The only thing slower than people walking on the ground was a dragon walking on the ground.

After that, Wyant said nothing further about the trip. Alu moved on to the kitchen door across the room, and Tomaso's heartsick gaze followed her.

Shala thought about what a great foursome they would make. Tomaso and Alu, herself and Wyant. She wished she could join them on the trip. It wasn't just the dragons that were setting their hierarchy, and bonding with others in the pack.

What were she and Nizael going to miss by staying here at the training grounds? Maybe just friendships.

Maybe Nizael's place in the pack.

Maybe everything.

She felt as if both her and her dragon's futures were teetering on the brink. If they were outcast, it would obviously change the rest of their lives. If they could make friends and fit in with the group, then they would go with the pack when it was posted.

Of course, if Nizael would just fly, they would be going on this trip. She scowled at her bowl, deep in thought. It wasn't too late. Maybe she should try Erisse's plan tonight.

If she could demonstrate her dragon's flight ability in the morning, the instructors would surely add them to the training journey.

CHAPTER 6 — Plan

The hitch of the food wagon was just a little lower than the pin assembly on the little tractor. Shala grunted, straining to lift the hitch over the pin. Her arms shook with the effort. Then it slipped into place. She snapped the lock on, and checked everything again. She didn't want anything unpredictable happening. This was going to be tricky enough.

She glanced at the paddock where Nizael was watching her. Did he know what she was doing? It almost looked as if he did. She stared at his big shadowy shape in the dark. He was so still she could hear him breathing. In the distance, she heard the baa of sheep in the fields just beyond the dragon paddock, and a few lazy crickets. Everyone else was asleep.

The spring day had been hot, but now it was cool; a soft breeze blew moist air in from the Swampen Sea, two days flight to the south. It would get foggy soon. A few drifts eased up the slope toward the school buildings like tentative, reaching fingers. She'd waited until everything was quiet. She'd waited until the last golden glow of a lantern was put out, and the darkness became more intense. But she shouldn't wait any longer, now. Get on with it, Shala.

She took a deep breath. She unlatched the paddock gate, sat down in the tractor seat, turned the key and started the tractor again, wincing. Even a solar battery-powered electric motor made *some* noise. She was certain someone would hear the ruckus she was making and come out to investigate.

She turned the tractor toward the path to the lofting ridge. There was a clunk as the food wagon lurched into motion behind her, then she was trundling along the path.

She glanced back at the paddock to see what Nizael was doing. He was still sitting there, eyes glued to Shala. Or the food wagon. She hadn't fed him much at dinnertime; he had to be hungry.

Sure enough, the next time she glanced over her shoulder, he had pushed past the gateway and taken a couple of steps out of the paddock. Yes!

He followed her all the way to the lofting ridge, where the cliff dropped away down to the lake, and warm updrafts created perfect dragon-launching conditions. All the dragons would be able to do ground takeoffs once they became expert fliers, but they enjoyed gliding, and it was the best way to begin their flight training.

That is, all the other dragons enjoyed gliding. Nizael had never gone off the cliff.

Shala had taken him there numerous times, in the company of other dragons and also alone, in case the others were making him nervous. He would open and fan his wings, he would lift himself up, stretching to the top of his height, standing on his toes. But he would not push himself off for a launch.

Well, now she would give him a little help. He would go over the edge, spread his big strong wings, and...she swallowed a sudden lump in her throat. What if he didn't?

Surely, he wouldn't just plummet to the ground below. No, he would open his wings, the updraft would catch him, and he would glide down and out to the lake. Shala swallowed again. She just needed to place the tractor at the right angle, set the shovel blade so it would go under Nizael's rump, and...scoot him off.

She scowled. Of course, that required Niz to be seated, which he was *not* going to be doing next to the food wagon. He was going to be standing there stuffing his face. Well, she would solve that problem when she came to it.

She drove down to the far, lower end of the ridge. A few scrawny madrone trees screened her from the buildings of the school. She could see the barn, but the only thing in the barn that could see her were some dragons who were housed indoors at night. They weren't going to be telling on her.

She swung the tractor around, placing the food wagon near the edge. Leaving the engine idling, she set the brake, hopped down and disengaged the wagon, got back aboard, and placed the tractor and its blade in line with her target. Which would be her dragon, when he got there, which he wasn't yet. He was very slow on the ground, but Nizael was coming. His reptilian, dinosaur-like form was silhouetted against starlight and the faint glow of the rings.

She was uneasy with being sneaky. It was the scariest part of her plan. Well, it was Erisse's plan, really. But Shala was pretty sure she didn't want anyone else knowing about it. She carefully did not think about why.

Nizael rubbed his head against Shala's shoulder. She picked up a handful of dragon chow and put it under his nose.

"Yeah, you can't figure out why you're out here in the dark for dinner, can you?"

Niz snuffled at the food, opened his mouth, and she dumped the smelly mixture into it and jerked her hands back. His teeth were omnivore teeth—dragons could eat anything—but she still didn't want those big jaws to close on her hand. He chewed, and blew a breath out through his nostrils, almost like a snort.

"Okay, guy. Are you ready?" She waited till he finished swallowing, then gave him the signal to open his wings, a firm rap on his shoulder with her fist.

He flared them open, just missing the food wagon on the right side. Fortunately for her plan, he remained sitting rather than standing up to spread

79

them. Shala showed him the flat of her hand, the "stay" signal. She turned away, walked to the tractor and slid onto the cold metal seat. When she started the motor, Nizael glanced back at her over his shoulder. She gave him the stay signal again.

He kept looking at her as she drove the tractor closer to him. He jumped up into a standing position, looking alarmed. Shala opened her mouth to shout at him for disobeying her order, but he swept his tail out of her way then sat his rump back down again.

Well, that was fair; he didn't want his tail run over. And it was good, because now it was wrapped around him and she could get the shovel blade under his back end without the risk of hurting him.

She crept up, moving the tractor by centimeters until the blade was fitted against Nizael's rump.

He made an odd whistling noise, "*Whree*," and a snort. Still looking over his shoulder, his eyes moved from the tractor blade to Shala and back to the tractor.

"It's okay, Niz," she said, hoping it was okay. "You're going to fly now." She signaled him to flap his wings, and to stay—keep flapping. He flapped. Then she nudged the tractor forward again.

When Nizael felt the pressure against his rump, he *whree'd* again, then looked away from her and the tractor and out to the open space in front of him.

The tractor did not seem to be moving the dragon at all, at first. Then Shala thought she detected a slant to Nizael's posture, as though he was leaning backwards. Or his rump was moving forward, faster than the rest of him. Then he did slide forward a little, still leaning back.

With no warning, he rose to his feet, tipped forward, and disappeared off the edge. Shala scrambled to keep the tractor from going over, too: suddenly freed of resistance, it lurched forward. She jammed the brakes, reversed it from the edge, and stood up to see what Nizael was doing.

Heart thumping, she searched, and for a long moment could not see him at all. Then off to her right she caught sight of him. His wings were not spread. He held them in, half-tucked. He was not gliding so much as dropping with a partial brake now and then. He never extended his wings full out.

"Flap!" Shala screamed. But he did not.

He banked, spreading one wing a bit more and tilting, so he was aimed more at the lake. Then he pulled both wings in tight against his sides and dropped like a stone.

He hit the water with a dreadful smack and disappeared beneath the enormous splash that rose up all around where he had been, as if the lake had swallowed him in one gulp.

"Oh, dear heavens," Shala mumbled, already running down the path. "Oh, please don't let him be dead!"

She could not see him in the lake.

He ought to float up; dragons were very buoyant. She ought to be able to see his silhouette against the shimmering black water, but she could not. She chanted a prayer of protection, even as she thought, *It's too late to pray!*

She spun around the hairpin turn, lost sight of the lake as the path slope steepened down to the next switchback.

At the next turn she ran out onto the cable slide platform that had been built onto the outside of that hairpin turn. She grabbed the bar-loop, flipped the brake pulley off, and pushed off the platform. She dangled from the slide as it swooped down, skimming along its cable. She still couldn't see Nizael, just glimpses of the lake between the trees. In moments she let go at the lower slide platform set in the top of a platecone tree. She ran across the platform and grabbed the second slide handlebar, pushing off hard so she would go faster.

She let go at the bottom, dropping into the sawdust pile there, sprang to her feet and hurtled to the lakeshore.

The black sand was as empty as the water was.

Gasping, Shala spun around on the sand, searching in all directions. "Nizael! Oh, please, Niz, I'm so sorry! Please be all right!"

She heard a splash, and spun to her left. She saw, or imagined she saw, movement along the shore beside some scrubby bushes. She remembered that there was a rocky promontory that stuck out into the lake in that direction. Several years back a dragon in training had made a bad landing there, hitting the rocks instead of the lake. He had broken both his feet, both bones in his left leg, and one in his right. He had healed after three months of hanging in a sling, legs and feet encased in shrink-wrapps.

Shala gasped for air, thinking of what Nizael could have done. The dragon that had crashed did recover, after seasons of therapy. He never walked well, and he had great difficulty launching himself into the air. Though his wings worked, he was not a good flyer because of the launch problem.

But at least he was alive, Shala remembered, running. At least that. She ran out onto the promontory, then had to slow down to pick her way through the rocks.

She stood panting on the end of the promontory and searched. Whatever she had seen moving, it must not have been Nizael. She scanned the lake. She searched the shoreline to either side of the promontory. She turned and faced inland—perhaps her dragon had crawled out of the lake and into the trees. But she saw nothing.

"Nizael," she yelled. "Oh, please," she whispered, and began her search all over again, examining the lake, the beach, the trees along the shoreline.

Then her gaze was caught by a shadow climbing the lofting ridge trail. A big hulking shadow.

"Nizael!" She ran in that direction, slipped off the rocks of the promontory, into the lake. She gasped at the sudden chill, then swam a few strokes until she could get her feet under her on the gritty edge of the beach. She ran as soon as she reached solid sand. "Nizael!" She ran up the beach toward the trail.

Now under the trees, she could no longer see the trail, or her dragon. She could not see where she was going very well either, and smacked her head into a branch. Still rubbing her forehead, she snagged her dripping shirt on a bush, tripped over a root, and fell headlong. But she got up and ran again. At last she reached the bottom of the switch-backed trail. Nizael was lumbering along, about half way up. Was he moving okay? She could not see him well enough to tell; she could only hope.

"Nizael!" she called again. She was certain he could hear her, but he did not look back.

When she clambered over the top of the ramp onto the ridge, she was frightened to see the tractor and food wagon were gone. She spent a moment catching her breath, and looked all around. No, they were nowhere in sight. She looked over the edge, wondering if Nizael had shoved them off in anger, but of course she would have seen and heard them coming down the cliff edge onto the trail. They were just gone, which meant someone had driven them away.

Well, that was not good news, but it also wasn't important now. What was important was checking her dragon.

She trotted toward the meadow area of the paddock, where the sleeping hollows for the dragons were clustered together beneath the shelter of a grove of wide-branching plane trees. She tiptoed among the dragons, making her way through the maze of packed mud paths to Nizael's usual spot.

He was there, curled into a shadowy lump. He raised his head as she approached, but his gaze was off into the darkness under the trees.

"Nizael," Shala murmured.

He did not turn his head her way. He tucked it back down by his wing and ignored her.

"I'm so sorry," she said. She took a step closer and ran her hand along Nizael's neck, using her fingers to straighten the fur there. He liked that, and on other days he would stretch his neck, or curl his toes in pleasure. But not tonight. Shala's heart ached even more. "I'm so sorry. I will never push you again. You are a fine dragon, and you will fly when you're ready." She continued stroking him, having no idea if her words were getting through to him, but hoping at least her tone and gestures would. "I'm sorry," she said again.

A voice behind her made her jump in sudden terror.

"They don't respond well to verbal apologies," the voice said.

Shala gulped and turned around. "Sylvan," she said. The stablemaster. It must have been him who had found the tractor and driven it back.

He knew what she had done.

"I checked him over," Sylvan said in calm tones. "It appears there's no permanent damage." He stared at the darker lump that was Nizael. "His feelings were hurt, no question of that."

"How—" her voice cracked, and she cleared her throat and tried again, "How can I apologize, then?"

Sylvan squatted down next to Nizael, rubbing what he could reach of the dragon's bony feet. "A little foot massage will help. Extra treats. He'll know you're doing it to get back into his good graces, and he will be angry for awhile, but keep at it. After a time, he will forgive you."

"Oh, how could I be so stupid?" Shala moaned. Would Nizael ever trust her again?

"I think I can understand," Sylvan said. "The first training flight is important."

Important to me. I wanted to impress my friends, Shala did not say. I almost killed my dragon because I want the most popular girl in the pack to like me. How could I put my own wants before the needs, the very safety of my dragon?

"It's important but not that important, right?" she said aloud. "It's not important enough to risk a dragon."

"No, that was not a good thing," Sylvan said.

What a terrible dragon rider she was!

"I'm so sorry," she said again. Now, too late, Shala thought of the consequences. She was irresponsible. She had not trained her dragon right—he could not fly. And then she had compounded her failure by trying to force him, for her own purposes.

Never fly for personal reasons. That was like rule number 2. *Never put your dragon in danger unless it is to save a human life.* That was rule number 1. And Shala had done both. She trembled, realizing the extent of her stupidity.

"You had better get some dry clothes on," Sylvan said, "and then go down and pull the cable slides back up. They may be needed tomorrow morning."

"Yes," Shala mumbled. "Of course," said the very stupidest dragon rider. She mustn't interfere with the properly trained dragons that would be flying tomorrow. Bad enough that the biggest and best would not be flying with them, because of her.

How could they trust her with a dragon, after this?

They would take Nizael away from her, give him to someone sensible, who would treat him with respect.

Tears running her cheeks in streams, Shala swept her sodden hair back from her eyes and trudged back the way she had just come.

She climbed the platecone tree, got hold of the bottom cable slide, and set the rope pulley. She went to the bottom and did the same with the base cable slide. She trudged back up, climbed the platecone again, and towed the base cable slide back up and reset it on the tree. She walked back up the slope to the top and pulled the top slide back into position.

By the time she had finished resetting the top slide she was too tired to blame herself any more. She was just going to have to live with the consequences of her bad decision. Shivering, she pulled on her nightshirt and left her wet clothes in a dripping pile on the back stoop of the sleeping quarters. She climbed into her bed and tried not to think.

CHAPTER 7 — Problems

Shala was one big ache. She woke feeling muzzy, aware someone was shaking her shoulder. She scowled. She had planned to stay asleep until after everyone left on the training flight. But the shaking continued.

"Come on, Shala. Get up. You have to attend the meeting too, even if you're not going," Aimee's voice said. The girls' advisor was a tough but fair young woman. If she said Shala had to get up, Shala had to get up.

She did so, levering herself up to sit on the edge of her bed, stiff as a tree. Meeting? Why was there a meeting?

Then everything that she had done the night before crashed down on her.

Oh, no. They were going to tell everyone about Shala's disaster. They were going to announce that she would be sent home in disgrace—her adopted family would be shamed before everyone else in their village—and—

And Nizael would go to someone else.

Shala became aware of the excited chatter around her as the other girls got up and dressed.

Like a damaged automaton, she washed her face. She combed her hair, pulling a dried leaf out of her still-damp fluff. She dressed, trying to build a shell of not-caring around her heart. If she wept when Aimee or Sylvan told what she had done, the other riders would laugh at her, and she did not know if she could stand that.

She was already outcast—the very thing she had been trying to prevent.

She clenched her jaw. Well, so be it. At least she knew what she was.

She walked alone to the dining hall. She took a cup of tea but skipped the inviting muffins and eggs and fruit put out for the students whose dragons would be flying today. She walked to a chair at the very edge of the room, where she would be a little hidden by the other tables and riders.

Aimee was at the front of the room with Dene. They were setting up an easel with a flip chart on the elevated platform that served as a stage. They were going to diagram flight formations. The ones without Nizael.

She studied her tea as the other students seated themselves. From the corner of her eye, she saw Sylvan walk in and join the advisors on the stage. He would probably be her accuser. Aimee and Dene might not even know yet.

Shala tried so hard to make her feelings numb she wasn't breathing. She realized she was holding her breath, gasped, then took several deep calming breaths. She tried to breathe in a normal way and—sip her tea. Wait for the announcement.

She thought about what she would pack to take with her back home. Overnight bag for the journey. The rest of her clothes and books in her satchel/saddlebag.

No, she wouldn't need her books. She had to leave those for Nizael's next rider.

She had nothing to bring home that she had not brought with her, then, no evidence of her time here at all. Just some wear and tear on her clothes. She was going to have to sleep out in the goat shed at home. Jhude and his new wife would have filled her old room in Andrya's house, with Jono and Logyn in the third tiny sleeping room.

She sipped her tea, feeling like the hot fluid was falling far down into a deep dark well inside her. Like Nizael had fallen down to the lake.

Tears threatened to fill her eyes. She gripped her teacup and breathed again.

All eight of the other riders from the pack were seated and chattering, when Dene thumped a pointer stick endwise on the stage so it boomed through the room. There was immediate silence.

Shala noticed her teacup was shaking. She set it down on the table and folded her hands in her lap.

Another adult walked into the room. Every head turned to watch as the headmistress from Lhasa's Central School at Toronia walked up the aisle. If anyone could be said to be Head Dragonrider, the headmistress would be the one. She was in charge of the largest school, at the Guild's headquarters. She'd come once at the beginning of their training, to welcome them and explain the Guild's rules.

Shala trembled inside and out, now. What was the headmistress doing here? Was her own transgression so enormous that they'd send the head of the Guild to throw her out? Were they making an example of her?

Dene rapped the staff against the floor again. "Mistress Arapunta, I present to you the Year Z pack at Two Rivers School.

"Hello again," Arapunta said. She smiled slightly. "Eight of you flying today, so one is not?" She looked at the pack's riders, and not at their advisors, for her answer.

Erisse stood up and made a cute curtsy. Everyone laughed as she grinned and told the headmistress, "Nizael has not flown yet," she said.

Here it comes, Shala thought. Maybe she should stand up and admit everything. Certainly, Erisse shouldn't be speaking for her.

But Mistress Arapunta just nodded and said, "He will, in time. But he is not your dragon, is he? Yours is...?"

"Sparkellz, Mistress," Erisse said, bouncing another curtsy. It was not as cute the second time. No one laughed.

"Of course," Arapunta said. She looked up, including all of them in her gaze. "It is for a special reason I am here today. You should know, as you embark on your journey this morning, that your pack is to be divided in two."

Murmurs interrupted her, and she raised her hands. Silence fell again. "There are many towns without our service, who are begging for a pack, or even a solo. Also, we have found other packs of three or four to be very successful. They serve smaller towns who cannot support a pack of eight or nine dragons and their riders, like the big cities can." She nodded. "So, you will be divided into at least two groups, plus any solos that develop. That means there will be two Queens from your group, and two Queen's Mates."

Shala felt a small kernel of hope in her heart.

Mistress Arapunta went on, raising her voice above the rising murmurs. "You will begin pairing up dragons to see what the natural groupings may be. You will encourage your dragons to seek flight companions. Riders should form friendships in small groups to see who will work well together. Include your grounded dragon and his rider in all activities as much as possible." She glanced at Dene. "He is the biggest of the pack, yes?"

Dene nodded. "Yes."

Nizael! She means Nizael, Shala thought. This didn't sound like she was being thrown out. But nothing much had been said about Nizael's rider, yet. She listened.

"It is often so," the Guild Mistress said, "that the biggest ones fly last. He will make a strong mate for one of the Queens—who must be chosen and separated soon." She nodded and stepped back.

"Questions?" Aimee said, looking as calm as always.

"Where will the two packs be posted, Mistress? Do you know?" Alu asked.

"One has been promised to Midford, in Rei Tildon," Arapunta said. "The other is due to go to a smaller town, perhaps in Kendai, or one of the oasis towns of the White Desert, who have very little contact with the rest of Lhasa or Kendai now."

Shala felt her heart pound. One of those "oasis towns of the White Desert" was her birthplace. She had never imagined she could go there again, to see where her family was from, where many of the caravans began and ended. Another such desert town was the oasis village where Andrya had taken her in. That would be a great assignment!

But then, she couldn't be assigned yet. She might not even have a dragon any longer. It did not sound as if the Mistress had heard of her outing the night before, but that did not mean she wouldn't.

Dene stepped forward. "If there are no further questions, we should get on our way," he said. "Will you join us partway, Mistress?"

"No, I cannot," she said. "I am here for another reason, today."

Oh, no, Shala thought. Now it comes.

She dipped her head forward in kind of a dismissal, then turned to Sylvan.

Chairs were dragged back, and packs picked up as the eight riders and their advisors left the dining hall for the paddock.

"Shala, would you join us?" Sylvan asked her, indicating she should come with him and Mistress Arapunta. Shala swallowed, and bussed her teacup, joining them as they walked back toward Sylvan's office. At least it wasn't going to be in front of the other riders.

They did not sit down in Sylvan's office. He scooped up a tray of tiny bottles and displayed them to the Headmistress. "Will this be enough, do you think?"

She nodded. "Syringes, too. They aren't going to have an adequate supply. We sent a flyer to the Oracle to get more."

Sylvan turned to Shala. "Do you know where they keep the syringe packets?"

"Yes, in the—"

"Get four packets and meet me in the barn," Sylvan said.

"Er," Shala said as he and the mistress headed out the narrow door. "What size?"

"Dragon size," Mistress Arapunta said. "We have an epidemic."

Shala gulped and scurried down the hall to the infirmary. They kept the dragon supplies with the people and other animal supplies, so it was easy for her to spot the packets of syringes big enough for dragons. They were the largest size. Not even horse shots needed to be as long or as tough as the needles they would need to penetrate dragon scales and skin. She gathered four of the packets and ran out to the barn.

What kind of epidemic?

"Are our dragons in danger?" she asked with gasping breaths.

Mistress Arapunta turned to face her. The woman shook her head. "What is your name, child?"

"Shala, Mistress. Nizael is my dragon. Um. The big one who won't fly."

Mistress nodded, tying a headscarf over her hair. "Well, Shala, your dragons here should be quite safe. This was a problem with the water supply. The Avor peninsula has had too much rain; the wells in Avordan Town are contaminated, and all their dragons are ill. The people have boiled their own drinking water, but they thought the animals would be okay." She shook her head. "Obviously, they aren't." She took the packets from Shala. "Now, you are going to be in charge here until the rest of the pack returns from their training flight."

Shala stood blinking. Had she missed something? It was so much the opposite of what she had been expecting to hear from the Guild Mistress that she did not know what to think.

Sylvan finished loading his saddlebag and backpack and turned to her. "You're going to have to feed all the animals, this morning and tonight, and again tomorrow morning. Including the sheep and goats. But you can manage that, I think," he said. "She has experience with goats," he told Mistress Arapunta. He turned back to Shala. "Keep working your dragon as much as you can, and if possible get Bodo out and rub him down and see if he'll fly."

"Okay," she said. "Feed everyone twice a day. Exercise Niz and Bodo. The packdrones?"

"We'll be using Chester. You'll need to feed Lila and Kinko. You might check Kinko's bandages. Oh, and Kharmin, of course. Feed her outside the brooding barn; she won't want you near her eggs. Dene and Aimee will be back tomorrow evening, so you should be okay," he said and patted her shoulder. "I will return as soon as possible."

She "should be okay," Sylvan had said. Her face and hands felt numb, and her heart heavy. She walked toward the barns. It seemed like nothing was going to be done about her just now. Would she have to live in dread until the final moment?

"Shala."

She spun and looked at the paddock rail where Simba was readying to loft up, Sylvan aboard.

"Rub Nizael's feet," Sylvan said, and he waved goodbye.

Simba and Mistress Arapunta's dragon beat their wings, pumping the bellows, filling their lungs. They stood on their toes, wings pumping, then lifted off. Their combined wings made a strange sound on the air, almost like Andrya's spinning wheel when she had disengaged it for cleaning. It would spin freely round on its hub with a whirr. Shala tilted her head.

Yes, the sound was like that, but much, much louder. The sound of dragons flying.

Shala liked being out in the paddocks alone during that peaceful morning. The air was fresh, but she still was taken aback by the dampness. Wet air would never seem natural to her, after a life in the desert.

She gave some dried grass to the sheep, and little by little managed to move their rolling pen to a different, uncropped area of their field, lambs galloping and silly among the ewes. She left them munching on spring green grass.

The vegetable scraps from the kitchen went to the goat herd. The baby goats were lively, playing king of the mountain atop some scruffy hay bales, and even leaping up and off their mothers who were variously standing or lying in the path of the play group. Despite everything, she found herself smiling at the antics of the kids. Baby goats just looked *happy*. Rather like Alu, they infected everyone around them with friskiness.

Then there were two mules, a fat little pony, and Alu's horse Teek. She levered a section of alfalfa hay from the bale with the pitchfork, picked up the flakes and distributed them among the equines. Later she would stake them out to graze in the commons. They kept the grass down and fertilized it too. She shoved her hips and shoulders against the roan mule's flank to get him to move and dropped his share of the alfalfa into his feed trough.

She fed Teek last. The big white horse had not yet been picked up by Alu's brothers, who were supposed to come and ride him back to their home. Alu didn't need a horse anymore. She would be able to ride Ozala anywhere she needed to go.

Shala realized that trying not to envy Alu was a much harder chore than feeding the animals. Alu and Erisse had everything. But Alu was nice. And Erisse— Shala was not so sure about Erisse. Why had she listened to the girl in spite of the fact she had suspected something was wrong with their plan to force Niz to fly?

She made a decision that whatever Erisse and Alu did needed to be separate from what she herself did. She made an effort to recall the words of a recent reading she had done in Logyn's book. The section about pride and arrogance seemed most relevant to her this morning. She chanted the mantra regarding humility while she crossed from the stables to the dragon barn and her work there.

Once she finished feeding everyone, she made her way out to the meadow to find Nizael. She carried a bucket of warm water and a piece of rag and had a pot of Sylvan's salve in her pocket. She would wash his feet and rub them with salve.

He had landed hard in the lake. Perhaps his belly needed attention too. When she entered the paddock gate, she couldn't see her dragon anywhere.

Well, this was ridiculous—with all the other dragons gone, he ought to be as visible as the rings in the sky. Then she spotted his dark green nostrils poking out from beneath a mound of hay and dead grasses, and made her way over to him. Shala picked away the strands of grass that covered the dragon's feet. Nizael's nostrils spread and he whuffed when she put the warm, wet rag on the bottoms of the big lizardy feet, and Niz's toes curled as she washed between them. Otherwise, he ignored her.

She rubbed salve on the backs of the four big toes and top of the long foot. Careful of the heel spur, she spread salve on the back of the heels and then the pads of the feet. Nizael emitted one tiny groan of pleasure, but did not open his eyes. She was still in his bad graces—not that she had expected a simple foot rub would make up for her actions. She was putting his hay blanket back over his feet when the sound of dragon wings made her look up.

Who was coming back already?

It didn't take long to see that this was both no dragon she knew and that it was in trouble.

Instead of a smooth downward spiral, the pale brown dragon dropped down by jerks and weird angles. As it banked, wing down toward her, she could see that it had a rider, but there was something wrong: that person was slumped on the dragon's neck. The dragon plunged to the ground, striking its wing with a sickening crack.

Shala realized she had already been running toward the spot even before it crashed; she was there in moments. She could see that one long, beautiful wing would not fold closed. A bone was broken somewhere. The dragon had landed badly, wings out, for all the world looking like it was trying to hold its rider on its back regardless of what it did to itself. It folded its good wing and turned mournful eyes toward her.

The rider was still slumped over its neck. Shala stepped around to the folded-wing side, so she could approach the person. She could see now that it was a young man about Sylvan's age. His eyes were rolled up in his head. He had wrapped his fingers through and around the dragon's feathery hair and neck strap, and still clutched them in tight fists. She had to pry his fingers loose to get him down.

In the process, he came partway conscious and stared at her with bleary eyes. "Antibiotics," he murmured. "Saddleb—" and then he was gone again.

"What?" Shala asked. "I should put them in your saddlebags? They are in your saddlebags?"

There was no response. She knew that sometimes people in shock stressed about the wrong things. First take care of the man. "Are you injured or are you sick?" she wondered aloud. She managed to get her arms under his and, resting his shoulders on her chest, dragged him sideways and off the dragon. They fell backwards, onto the open soil of the paddock. She glanced up and met the dragon's eyes. It whuffed and seemed to point its nose toward the saddlebags tied to the leather band that encircled its chest and lower neck.

"Saddlebags," Shala said, nodding. "I know." She had pulled the rider far enough away, she judged, and went back to loosen the strings of the bags.

Inside it were kits not unlike those she had seen Sylvan and Mistress Arapunta take with them to Avordan, small bottles resting in holes in a tray, all covered by cellu-plass.

But this was confusing. Shala looked at the dragon, and then at the rider. This did not seem to be a case of dragon epidemic. It was the man who was ill.

She walked up to the dragon's head, examined its eyes and nostrils. She gripped its jaws with both hands, putting pressure just behind the hinge of the jaw on either side. The dragon opened its—his, Shala could now see—mouth. The male throat sacs were charcoal gray and looked healthy; the tongue was moist, and the dragon's breath did not smell odd. She let him close his mouth. His eyes were clear. "Okay. I don't think you're sick, not that I know all that much.

97

But," she turned toward the now-moaning rider, "you are."

He had felt warm and sweaty, and he was not coherent. "So, there's a fever." Shala walked back to the rider, set down the tray of what must be the "antibiotics," the man had mumbled about. She knelt by his head and pulled up one eyelid. The whites of his eyes were yellowish and very bloodshot. Even unconscious, he was gasping for breath, and his exhalations smelled foul. "So, is the antibiotic for you?" But she hadn't a clue how much to give him, or even whether it was for humans or not. He might have been taking them somewhere for some other purpose altogether and fallen ill on the way with...whatever he had.

Shala ran to the kitchen, got the serving cart and rolled it out to the paddock. With a great deal of effort, she managed to get the limp and heavy man propped aboard it and rolled him in to the infirmary.

She cranked the infirmary bed down to the same level as the cart, set the cart's brakes, and solved the problem of rolling him off by leaning against the adjacent bed and pushing the man with her feet, rolling him from the cart to the bed. Once she had him on the bed and propped up with pillows, she tried to give him water to drink, but he was unresponsive. Glad she had helped with sick and birthing goats, so she wasn't squeamish, she took another careful look in his eyes, nose and mouth, and noted how everything looked.

She ran back and got the antibiotics. The label had said they should be kept cool, so she stuck them in the solar cellar box. She went into Sylvan's office and pulled down the emergency radio. Hoping the school had enough credits to pay for its use, she followed the printed instructions and called the Guild headquarters in Toronia.

She explained her situation. They got a doctor to their radio there, and she guided Shala through the process of hooking the rider up to an IV fluid drip. That would help with the dehydration from the fever.

Shala tried to remember to breathe as she raced through a description of the antibiotic trays. The physician at Toronia had her repeat her descriptions of the white-tipped pustules inside the man's mouth. That and his reddened palms but white, cold fingers, and the bloodshot eyes all seemed significant. The physician instructed her to inject the rider with a regimen of drugs from one of the tiny bottles. She followed the instructions, giving him his first shot.

"He must have been on his way from the Oracle to someplace that needed that medicine," the doctor had said. "Try to find out where and take the whole tray and some syringes to them as soon as you can! All right Miss Shala?" Her voice was kind but firm. "It's urgent."

"Yes," Shala said. But how could she find out where, when the rider was unconscious? She put the radio back in Sylvan's office, and left a note explaining how long she had used it and what for. Then, after a brief pause to check her still-unconscious patient, she grabbed a packet of shrink-wrapps and a splint bundle and ran outside to the injured dragon.

It was easy to see which slender bone had snapped in the wing. The pale brown dragon still had his wing spread wide open, and a little bit of the afternoon sunlight glowed through the leathery skin, so the bones were dark shadows. Shala stepped forward to get a good look at the break, and the dragon took a step away from her.

"I'm just looking, okay?" she told him. "We'll fix it in a few minutes," she said, hoping she could fix it.

But it was a clean, simple break in the second "finger" bone down from the leading edge. That big edge bone would have been much harder for Shala to set, but this one was slender. And the rest of the wing was perfect. "Now I'm going to look closer at this break, okay?" She glanced at his face.

He was looking at her as though he understood— or was that her imagination? No one claimed to know how smart the dragons were. Shala felt they often listened to what people were saying. They understood at least some human words. She made her tone calm. "It hurts, I know, but I need to be sure you don't have grit in there."

The waffle-like structure of dragon bone cross sections was strong though lightweight. All she should have to do was line up the grids of the waffling, then set the bone. But if there were any tiny pieces of bone broken off, they could irritate the re-join and prevent it from healing. Shala gently but firmly pressed her thumbs against both ends of the break. She could feel the edges of the broken section through the skin of the wing, and she did not feel any grit crumbles sliding around in the wound, as she had in the sample Sylvan had made them all study.

Since the skin was not broken, she would not make an incision and risk infection. She felt all along the break, pressing down the swollen tissue beneath the skin so she could judge how to line up the two pieces of bone.

"All right, fella," she said. "I know what to do now."

She grabbed the bucket she had left out by Nizael and refilled it with warm water from the kitchen. She noticed Nizael had sat up and was watching her and the injured dragon. She set the bucket down in her small workspace beside the injured wing. She put the splint in the bucket to soak, then cut a piece of shrink-wrapp and checked to be sure it was big enough. It needed to secure the break plus two handspans along the bone to either side of the splint.

Then she stepped up to the dragon's head. "I'm going to set it now," she told him. She met his eyes. "It's going to hurt, and then it will get a little better. You must hold still till I get it wrapped. Then we can fold your wing up. Okay?"

He blinked at her and looked over his shoulder, back at his wing.

"Okay," Shala said, reassuring herself.

She moved to the wing, grasped the bone on either side of the break and eased the two pieces together, rotating the back portion a bit so that the ridges she could feel on the two sections of bone were lined up with each other.

Then using her left hand, she held the join together, grasped the moist and slimy splint with her right hand and stuck it alongside the break. She held it there until the gooey surface bonded with the wing leather, then let go and grabbed the shrink-wrapp and wrapped it from one side of the bone to the other, curving it over the lump of the bone and splint on the underside of the wing and spreading it out over the wing surface beyond.

"Hold still, now," she murmured, and reached down to scoop up a handful of the warm water. She patted it onto the shrink-wrapp, covering the surface of the clear, slick stuff with water. As soon as the water touched it, it began shrinking. She smoothed the wrapp down as it bonded.

Her movements as smooth and gentle as she could make them, she rotated the wing downward, so she could reach the other side, and did the same procedure, checking as she worked to make sure the bones were still lined up properly on that side, too.

She wrapped it and wetted it and watched to make sure the wrapp did not pull the join apart as she reached for another handful of water and applied it. When the wrapps stopped shrinking, she felt along the

101

line of the bone with both hands to be certain the join was still aligned, the splints were bonded well, and that the wrapp was holding everything snug against the wing surface.

Everything looked good.

Then she held the wing at the joint to make sure he would not fold it until all the wrapp was thoroughly dry and shrunken to a firm but still-flexible shell. Satisfied at last, she stepped away from the wing and stroked the dragon's nose.

"There you go," she told him. Then she tapped his shoulder in the "close wings" signal, and he folded it up. He wasn't going to be able to fly for a while. The wrapps would dry and fall off, the splint would decompose, and the wing would heal and be as strong as before, in four tendays or so.

She stood there stroking his nose and murmuring compliments for a few moments, then heard Kharmin's bellow from the brooding barn. During all this, Shala realized, the sun had tipped down behind the hills to the west, and it was dusk and time to feed everyone again. She also realized Nizael was still watching her, had watched her the entire time she was setting the strange dragon's wing. *Oh, maybe he's jealous*, Shala thought, but she didn't have time to do anything about it just then.

She ran to check her other patient: the rider. She lit a small solar-battery lamp in the infirmary and left it on in case he woke up. He was still unconscious, though his temperature had dropped. She gave him the next dose of antibiotic as the doctor at Toronia had prescribed.

She went out to feed the animals. As she scooped grain out of the bin, her stomach growled, and she realized she had missed lunch.

Then she realized she had missed breakfast, too, worried about the pre-flight meeting and Mistress Arapunta. That all seemed so long ago.

Well, no wonder her stomach was growling. Even the dusty grain she gave the mules smelled good.

CHAPTER 8 — Sickness

"You must take the antibiotics to Reedwater!" the voice called. At least she thought that was what it said, but her dream had been very confusing.

Shala sat up and rubbed her eyes. Where—? Oh, she had fallen asleep in the infirmary, where she had stretched out on a cot after treating the rider with a late-night dose of antibiotic.

"Reedwater," the man on the infirmary bed said.

Shala got off the cot and leaned over him, checking his temperature, and the IV line. "You are definitely better," she told him.

"People in my town are dying of this infection! They must have those antiobiotics I was carrying."

Shala stared at him. "There's no one here that can take them. Your dragon broke a wing."

His eyes widened in alarm. "What? Palli? How is he?"

"Well, I need to go check and feed everyone, but when I left him last night the cast was holding, and he was sound asleep."

"What do you mean no one can take the medicine?"

"They're gone on a training flight. They'll be back late tonight."

"*You* can take it! You must!"

"Listen, whoever you are—"

"Kole! I'm Reedwater's dragonrider! You must take the medicine there!"

"I'm the only one here! I have no dragon to ride! It's going to have to wait until Aimee and Dene get back with the rest of the pack, or Sylvan comes back."

"People are dying! Every hour you wait, another person's life is on the line. That's how bad it was when I left, and it can only have gotten worse! This thing strikes abruptly—" he looked closely at Shala. "Have you taken a preventative shot? They were in the last row of the— is that what you gave me? No, of course not, or I'd still be—"

Shala raised her hands palm out and made calming motions. "The medic at Toronia told me what to do. I've been giving you the antibiotics. I took the vaccine. And I am the only one here, and I can't leave."

"Why not?" Kole said.

Kharmin's bellow seemed answer enough to Shala, but Kole just looked at her suspiciously. "I thought you said there were no dragons to ride."

"That's Kharmin. She's brooding. She won't fly. Dene is riding Oki, our spare dragon, because Kharmin won't leave her eggs. There's a packdrone with an injured foot who can't fly—even if I could get him to let me ride, which I doubt."

"What about your dragon?"

"He's not flying yet."

Kole's throat worked. "Well, make him! Make him fly and get those antibiotics to Reedwater!"

"I've already tried making him," Shala said in her quietest voice. "He wouldn't even glide. He's just not ready." She looked at her hands, which were red and dry from all the work of the previous day. "Now, I've got to feed the animals..." The animals, which included Teek and two mules. And Bodo! Maybe Bodo would get up in the air. "Let me see if I can figure something out," she told Kole and left him staring after her.

It was a little past dawn, Shala discovered as she went outside to check Palli. She fed him and Nizael. Then she made her way through wisps of fog to take care of the goats and check the sheep, who were fine. She went into the barn and looked over the mules and Alu's horse as she fed them. Yes, she could probably ride one of them, if it came down to it.

Reedwater was not that much further south than where the pack had planned to go on their training run. If Kole had arrived just a half-day sooner, or Sylvan or the training flight had delayed a bit, *they* could have taken the medicine, and it would be in Reedwater now.

Yes, but "if-onlys" and "what-ifs" are a waste of time, Andrya had always said. "Instead of living your real life, you spend all your time imagining possibilities, possibilities that never happen, and what's the good of that?" Shala heard the words in her head as if Andrya stood there telling her in person. She nodded her appreciation of her foster-mother's wisdom and went back to take care of the now squalling Kharmin.

"Okay, okay, miss Queen," Shala said. If she had fed the brooding dragon first, the rest of her chores would have been much quieter, she thought. And there she was "if-ing" again.

She fed Bodo and the packdrones last. Bodo did seem cheerful that morning. She looked the dark dragon over and signaled him to spread his wings. But he didn't. He tried, but they wouldn't even come open. It was a foggy, cool morning, which always seemed to make him worse. Frowning, Shala went and got a salve pot and began working on the knobby arthritis-swollen joints of Bodo's wings as he ate his breakfast. They finished about the same time, and she signaled the wing-spread again.

This time, Bodo got his wings open partway. "Okay, fella," Shala told him. "Fold them up." She put a warming blanket over the old dragon. She'd feed herself and Kole and then come back to check on him. Maybe, just maybe, he'd be able to fly this afternoon.

Finished with her oatmeal, and full of hope, Shala checked the paddock and then inside the barn. Bodo was still inside, huddled beneath the warming blanket. He almost seemed worse. His joints stayed swollen and stiff and his wings would not open all the way, though she worked him until he moaned with pain.

Bodo wasn't going to be able to fly today.

She tried one last time to convince Nizael he wanted to fly, but he refused to look at her. She stamped her feet on the ground near his head.

"You are a pretty useless excuse for a dragon!" she yelled. "I may have been wrong the other night, but *you* are the problem today!" She stomped off to the infirmary.

"I'm going to have to go on horseback," she told Kole, who was conscious again, but muzzy. "The horse or the mules. I don't ride well, so that's going to be so slow, it might be faster to wait until the other dragons get back," she said.

"No. If they're late," Kole said, slurring his words, "or there's an injury to delay them— No. You must go however you can." His empty oatmeal bowl fell off the bed, and Shala scooped it up in a quick catch that saved the pottery from smashing on the infirmary floor.

"Will you be okay? There won't be anyone to help you until late tonight."

Kole nodded. "I'm actually feeling much better...I'm just...tired. I will tell them what has happened and send someone along on dragonback to find you...when they get here." He sat up, looking more clear-headed. "You must leave a bottle of the vaccine here; I will have exposed you all to this thing just by being here. I will have them all innoculate themselves. You took a shot already, didn't you?"

Shala nodded. She'd already told him this, but obviously he'd been too sick to remember. "Yes, I did.

The medic at Toronia told me what to do. I've left a bottle of the vaccine here with instructions for them." She refilled the water pitcher by his bed and set an insulated jar of soup on the small wheeled cart beside him. "I shouldn't leave you and Palli here like this, though," she said.

"We are in much better shape than my town is," Kole told her. "I cannot stress the urgency enough. You must go. You must go now!" He grimaced. "Did you say there are mules, as well as the horse?" At Shala's nod, he said, "Take them, too. You can change off mounts," he said. "They'll go much farther and faster if you can switch off between them."

"But— if they're all running, how will we go farther? How can they rest if they're running along too?"

"You won't be on top of them. That's a rest." He looked at her with ferocity in his eyes. "Even if you have to run them all into the ground, you must keep going as fast and as long as you can. Do you understand me? This thing strikes so fast, and kills so quickly, there's just no way to explain—Gods! If only I hadn't gotten it, too!"

"All right, Kole. I'll take all three mounts, and I'll go as fast as I can."

"Load a bag of grain onto one of them. Stop for rest and switch animals every two or three hours and give them grain during each stop. Keep the water light but give them a little each time you stop." He dropped back on the bed, the brief burst of energy gone.

Shala left extra food out for the other animals. She grabbed her wool jacket and a blanket. She took some trail mix and granola bars, and the last, drying loaf of bread from the kitchen. She got the grain for the mounts and stood staring at Teek so tall in his stall.

His saddle was too heavy for her to lift, and if she had to keep changing back and forth—no, she wouldn't use the saddle. She wasn't even sure how to put it on, anyway.

She tied Teek's halter reins to the stall post, found some molded felt saddlepads much like the ones she and Jhude had used and strapped one on to the now-dancing horse. She tied her blanket and bag of food onto the pad strap. She would stick with what she knew, and the animals would just have to cope. She put the halters on the mules, strapped the other pads onto their backs, and put the grain aboard one animal and the water sacks, filled and dripping, onto the other.

The tray of medicine she wrapped with insulate cloth and put into a saddlebag. She stuffed several trays of syringes in with the medicine. Should she take swabs or anything? Finally, she just shook her head and tied the saddlebag onto the strap on Teek with two sets of leather thongs. That she could not lose, or it all would be for nothing.

Then she looked up at the tall horse's back. Getting on and off was going to be a problem.

She led the three animals out to the dragon paddock and climbed up onto the dragon-mounting block, then stretched onto Teek's back and sat. He stepped impatiently, ears back, but she was aboard. She would have to stop by a rock or a log each time she changed mounts, unless she wanted to drop out of a tree onto them. She shook her head, hoping she could find some way to mount.

"Hup," she said, kicking Teek's flanks. Startled, he leaped straight into a fast lope, jerking the mule's leads and yanking them into motion, too. Feeling inadequate and ill prepared, Shala was on her way. They needed to go southeast to cross the river by way of the bridge, then head south, on a path that was not

109

really a road yet, that paralleled the Yent River all the way to Reedwater.

She was sure the dragons were going to get back to Two Rivers and turn around again to find her on the road long before she ever got to Reedwater, so she wasn't going to accomplish much. She couldn't imagine sacrificing the innocent horse and mules, just to be a little further along when Dene or Aimee caught up with her.

But then she thought about Reedwater, and Jhude's new wife. Her family was there. That meant at least one household in Reedwater was Shala's family, too. And what if it was the oasis village that was sick, and the threatened people were Andrya and Jono and the others? Weren't they innocent, too?

"Sometimes 'what-if' is the right thing to ask, Andrya," she murmured. Of course, she would ride these animals into the ground to try to get the medicine there faster. Even if it saved just one person's life, she would have to do it. She wanted to. She tightened her legs against the horse's belly, tucking her feet deeper beneath the strap. Then she leaned down over Teek's shoulders and urged him to a gallop.

It was much harder to stay on the running horse than Shala could ever have imagined. The ride was more a struggle to stay on than to go faster. She rode—or fought falling off—until mid-morning, then pulled Teek to a stop near a small rock-strewn hillock and slid off on the uphill side.

She followed Kole's instructions about grain and water. Rubbing the insides of her thighs, she rearranged the grain bags onto Teek's back and led one of the mules to the front of the string, with Teek in the middle.

None of the animals liked this arrangement. The horse balked and laid its ears back. The new lead mule kicked at Teek, who shied away, jerking the back mule aside along with him. The back mule set its feet like a donkey when Teek moved again, then it reached forward and nipped at the horse. Shala swatted it with the reins and it looked at her with a hurt expression on its face. "Stop it," she said.

Shala walked to the front of the string, tightened up the reins and looked the new lead mule in the eye. "You will cooperate," she told it.

Grateful it was not a stubborn donkey, she got the mule to stand below the hillock while she stood atop the little hump of dirt and rocks. Then she jumped and crawled up onto its back.

Long ears laid flat against its head told her what the mule thought about that. She flicked the gray-brown rump with the extra length of reins. They moved out into a bumpy trot. She swatted again, and it cantered. Sort of. Teek and the other mule followed, though the mules' ears never lifted from their heads, and Teek's snorts were explosive.

From time to time she lost the rough track they followed altogether. She continued riding south, keeping the Yent on her left. The hooves of the mule found a way through the skimpy grass and over stones, dirt and fallen leaves. They were going slower now, but she felt they were still making good time.

By the time she stopped again in the afternoon, she ached all over. There was a small copse of willow trees to give shade from the midday sun. A flock of chattering birds inhabited the trees. They sounded so cheery that she glared at them.

Shala tied the mules and the horse to different trees and gave them their water and grain rations. The mules were very polite. She realized maybe they just hadn't liked having a horse between them. They were

111

different species, and just as goats and sheep had their preferences, horses and mules must also. Sweat stained their shoulders. She rubbed them down with an empty water sack. They munched up all their grain and cropped some limp clumps of grass during their brief rest.

Finished with her granola bar, she untied and took up all their reins and lined up the two mules together, with Teek at the end. That seemed to work better— Teek just had to be odd horse out. She left his lead rein extra long, so he could keep his distance.

She had worn her oldest linen pants, which were soft against her skin when they'd started out. She rubbed her thighs gently, knowing the skin was now chafed and it was only going to get worse. The linen no longer felt soft.

This time to mount, she found a tree with one wiry branch sprawled along the ground. She lined up the mule, stepped up onto the bouncy branch, and clambered aboard. They started at a fast trot, and rather than kicking the mule up into his version of a canter, she held him at the slower pace. If they could maintain it longer, maybe that would be faster in the long run, and she could stay on better. The jarring gait made her head ache, and between that and the bright sun, she could not see well.

As they went further south, they came clear of the rocky area and she picked up the pace again. Teek's canter had been easy to ride, compared with the mules' jerky paces. She had no stirrups and no experience, and kept slipping from one side to the other, but worry made her hurry.

Now and again she raised her head to search the sky. If the pack followed the plan to return to Two Rivers along the usual flight path that night, then the dragons ought to overfly her some time in the late afternoon or early evening.

If she did see them, she could whistle them down. With just one dragon, she could save a half day getting to Reedwater. The medicine could be there that night, instead of noon the next day or later.

She recalled from Dene's plans, the pack had expected to camp in a valley near a bluff that she remembered from her own trip into Reedwater. She and Jhude had come from the west, along a small creek. Well north of Reedwater town there was an upthrust of sandstone bluffs. She had not crossed that creek yet, but she thought it was not all that far south of her present position. So perhaps she was closer to them than she'd realized.

Her chances of spotting the flight in the air were not bad. A pack of dragons in the sky could be visible for kilometers. Trees were sparse here, mostly lining the river, and the sky bore not a trace of clouds or fog. She urged her mounts further west, away from the Yent and toward the valley and the bluffs.

She kept hoping and re-estimating as the sun fell in the sky with no sign of dragons. The riders, the *people* of her pack were on foot, and would be getting tired, going slower and slower. She might not see them pass until late evening.

She checked the sky every few minutes, but there were no dragons.

Some Things You Might Want to Know About the Planet Azureign

Very briefly, Azureign is unique among human colony worlds for two related reasons:

Number 1. It has rings that were probably the result of Number Two.

Number 2. It was terraformed thousands of years ago by humans who were just beginning to explore the galaxy, and who knew very little about balancing the ecology of an entire planet from scratch. This occurred well before contact with the alien species of the Compact.

This means that not everything on Azureign works quite the way anyone would like or expect.

Appalled by the botched adjustments to the planet's ecology, the Compact aliens did what they could to help (force) the humans to turn it into a usable place to live for some brave human colonists (who came there several hundred years before our story begins).

Because the Compact sets strict limits on insults to planetary biosystems—limits on mining and manufacturing, types of power the colonists can use, and so forth—the alien consortium also assisted human developers in creating what are now called Helper Species, or helpmate animals who take the place of some technological items humans and other space-faring creatures depend upon for survival.

Hence the dragons, who serve as a light delivery and communications system for the colonists of Azureign. Shortly after their apparent success on Azureign, dragon colonies were also instituted on several other colony worlds.

Other Helper Species at trial on Azureign include, for example:

Dolphin Folk, who are highly intelligent and have a language of their own and should perhaps not be a "helper" species at all, but be considered equal to humans.

Raka, who were meant to be problem solvers and laboratory assistants, but who diverged so rapidly from their original specifications no one knows what they're for any longer.

Gimbal Balls, a species of plant that produces a huge glassine sphere useful as mobile living quarters for humans and other creatures.

And many customized species of food plants especially adapted to the range of conditions on Azureign, and requiring little in the way of pest control or fertilization, such as bandova fruit.

Many humans believe the alien supervisors of the Compact utilize Azureign as a sort of testing ground for Helper Species and other ideas, because the planet was already imperfect due to the humans' botched terraforming. Some believe that the human colonists themselves may have diverged from the original species, though with minimal contact with Earth to compare, it is difficult to tell.

CHAPTER 9 — Reedwater

It was the sound that woke her, rather than the vision of dragons. Shala had fallen asleep, riding half-unconscious as Teek plodded into the darkening south. She heard the dragon wings. She heard them in her dream, then she woke up and heard them awake. She tilted her head back and whistled the shrill call-down, grateful she had been able to learn it.

She watched, expecting to see Dene or Aimee escorting the young dragons, but it turned out *no one was riding*. It was just dragons, flying. Two of them landed near Shala while the rest circled overhead, wings whirring in the dusky evening sky.

Neither the mules nor Teek had enough energy left to do more than lower their heads to the ground and not look at the dragons. Instead of running off, they tucked themselves further beneath the shelter of the trees alongside the riverbank.

She turned to her belly and slipped from the horse's back, falling a few centimeters to the ground. She achieved a wobbling trot out to the open field and the grounded dragons.

As she got closer, she could see one was Arzid; she wouldn't expect him to have a rider. But the other was Oki, and she thought Dene would be aboard, and he was not. Shala looked up at the rest of the circling dragons. Puka was up there, she could just make out her distinctive aqua-splotched tail. But there wasn't anyone aboard Puka, either.

Shala went to Oki first. The dragon's riding harness was on, but Dene clearly wasn't. She thought of Kole's bad landing at Two Rivers. Had Dene gotten sick and fallen off? She patted Oki's nose, wishing the dragon could explain. Arzid bumped her from behind. She turned to the big black and gray dragon and scratched his nostrils and eyebrows. He butted her again.

For some strange reason, Arzid was wearing a riding harness. No one should have been riding him yet, but that was a riding harness around his chest and neck. Shala stepped back toward the base of the big dragon's neck. She set one foot into the wing pocket as if she was climbing aboard and examined the riding harness. It was older and used; it must be Dene or Aimee's. But that was weird. Aimee's should be on Puka, who was flying overhead without a rider, and Oki had no Dene. She lowered herself back to the ground.

"Where's the people, guys?" she asked. The dragons didn't answer, of course, though if there was ever a time she wished they could talk, it was now. What was going on?

Then she dismissed speculation. She had a dragon to ride! "Stay!" she said to Oki, hoping he or Arzid would understand and stay put.

She ran to Teek, untied the medicines and her saddlebag. She stripped the halters and saddlepads from the mounts and threw them to the ground. She dumped out the bags of grain, so they could eat. After that, the horse and mules would just have to fend for themselves. She ran back to Oki, who scuttled backwards away from her.

"But Arzid isn't ready for a person to ride him," Shala said, as though explaining to the older dragon was going make him agree to let her ride. Shala tried again, easing toward Oki and crooning gentle words, but Dene's borrowed dragon rolled his eyes like a horse, backed two more steps and pumped his wings for takeoff.

"You would think of all the dragons who could carry a strange rider, Oki would be the most used to it," Shala muttered. But it was clear he did not want her aboard. He did look tired; perhaps that was why.

She turned and ran to Arzid. He bent his leg and lowered his left wing, inviting her to mount. "Okay, I get it. I'm supposed to ride *you*, but I don't understand why." She straddled the base of Arzid's neck, placing one foot in each of the pockets formed by the wing-shoulder joint. Arzid pumped his wings. Could he even do a ground takeoff? With a rider? She was still tying her packs to the riding harness when he lifted off the ground. She grabbed the straps with one hand and her packs with the other. In a moment they were airborne.

The rest of the pack flew up even with Arzid, for all the world as if they were escorting him. Or Shala. One dragon—Puka—flew right next to them, keeping up with Arzid even though she had to pump her smaller wings faster than Arzid did.

Shala looked down between the front wing-edge and Arzid's neck on the wing's upstroke. Teek still stood in the clearing, head down, but the mules had had enough of circling dragons, and were running north, side by side. Perhaps they would run all the way back to Two Rivers.

Then Arzid got up to flight speed, and Shala couldn't see anything.

The wind burned in her eyes, and her hair whipped her face, and the feathery hairs of Arzid's mane stung her cheeks and neck. Her eyes teared up and her vision blurred. From the little she could see, they were heading south along the river, toward Reedwater, which was where she wanted to go, so she stopped trying to see.

She couldn't breathe. She opened her mouth to gasp for breath, and a bug or something blew in. She choked then spat it out, still trying to get air.

The motion set up by Arzid's wingstrokes made her nauseous, and she felt as if the wind and the wingstrokes would throw her off the dragon's back at any moment. It was a very long way down. She tightened her grip on the harness until her fingers were numb. She decided she didn't care where they were going and stopped trying to guide him. She hunched down behind the base of the dragon's neck, which made the wind problem a little better, but her nausea worse. Arzid flew on, oblivious to her problems.

She clung to the harness, dazed. *This was terrible!* What unenlightened, idiotic dream had ever made her think she wanted to be a dragon rider?

Through a haze of nausea and weariness, Shala became aware that Arzid was slowing, and losing height. She risked a look down. The dragon circled, dropping down toward a small valley cupped in the hills below them. Shala hunched back down behind the dragon's charcoal gray neck. It was too dark to see much on the ground below. She thought she had seen lumps on the ground, too small to be dragons. More like a flock of sheep or goats, but she would find out for sure in a few moments.

The dragon landed with a thud, and then stumbled a few paces as he came to a stop. Shala worked her fingers loose from the harness and patted his neck. "Good for you, Arzid." It wasn't the dragon's fault she hated flying. He was very young to have carried a rider and he had managed a ground takeoff with a novice rider. She was impressed with Arzid's feat.

Shala dragged her bags behind her by the strap, too worn to bend over and pick them up. Then she bent anyway, and vomited, heaving up what little she had in her stomach. Shaky, she stumbled away, jerking herself and her bags aside from the reeking mess and toward the camp.

The first shadowy lump she came to was a limp human body. It was lying in the dirt, uncovered, so she thought it through and figured it wasn't someone who had fallen asleep. She knelt and rolled the person over. It was Granger, Arzid's rider. He was feverish, unconscious, and his breath was foul, like Kole's had been.

Did he have the same sickness? But how could the pack riders have been exposed? They had left before Kole arrived.

Had they gone to Reedwater?

Shala couldn't see well enough in the dark to check Granger's eyes. But if the pack had spent the previous night here, they must have had lanterns somewhere, or at least a fire. She moved away from Granger toward what must be the center of their camp, where more body-lumps lay in the dirt.

She moved through an odd silence—there was not a single sound from the people. It was as if she stood in the midst of a herd of dead sheep. She shuddered but kept walking. Then she realized she couldn't hear the sound of her saddlebag dragging in the dirt behind her, either. It was her ears that didn't work.

After a time, she could hear muffled footsteps, then other sounds. Her hearing came back a little by little— the dragons thumping as they walked on the ground, the scrape of a wing as it was opened and refolded, and then the hoarse and tortured breathing of the sick people around her.

She found the camp's fire pit, and a stock of branches. There were a few coals glowing under the ashes. She added kindling, built it up, as she had so many times at home in Andrya's stove and the firepits out in the yard where they boiled the dye water. She could build a good fire. At least she could do that.

She discovered she was not strong enough to move Granger closer to the fire without dragging him, which didn't seem like it would be good for either of them, so she took the fire closer to him. She picked a branch that was burning well on one end and used it as a torch, holding it by the unlighted end. She still couldn't see very well, but it was well enough to see the white-tipped pustules inside Granger's mouth, and a discoloration of his eyes that must be the same bloodshot and yellow that Kole's had been. She got out the tray of medicine. It didn't feel very cold to her stiff, numb fingers, but she couldn't do anything about that. She gave Granger a shot of the antibiotic.

The vaccine wouldn't do any good once people showed symptoms. She found the pack's water bags and dragged one over, managed to dribble some into Granger's slack mouth. He was unresponsive, but she remembered Kole had been at first too. Perhaps he would recover as Kole had.

But she had no IV drip. That was going to be a problem, wasn't it?

She moved on to the next person, who was little Alu. The young woman's eyes were rolled up in her head; her other symptoms matched those of this illness. Shala didn't even know what it was called, but she was more grateful than ever that the medic at the Toronia headquarters had known what to do, and that Kole had gone to the Oracle to obtain the medicines. She moved on, tending the dragonriders, one by one.

Until she got to Dene, whose body was cold and lifeless. His breath was not bad, because he wasn't breathing. She could not find a pulse. It took her long moments to realize this must mean that Dene was dead. The medicine had come too late for him.

She had come too late to save him, and he was gone.

Shala's throat ached. She put the medicine bottle back in the tray and stumbled on to Wyant, hoping she wouldn't find him cold and still as well.

Tears seeped from the corners of her eyes as she thought of Dene's quick grin, and how proud he was of his Queen, Kharmin, and her new clutch of eggs. He had been looking forward to the hatching, with wonderment and awe that his pretty Queen dragon was going to deliver a pack of her own.

Dene wasn't going to see the dragonets hatch, and somehow at that moment, that was the worst thing of all to Shala.

She made herself keep moving. Wyant was very feverish but came half awake as she injected him. She got him to drink before he slumped back down to the ground. Kiny didn't move when she checked and gave him the injection. The water dribbled from his mouth.

Shala sniffled, wiped her face, and moved on to the back side of the camp, where what must be Aimee, Erisse, and Tarva lay.

In a part of her mind, Dene wasn't dead. A part of her expected him to get up and smile and say he had just been pretending. A part of her expected him to speak with her about riding Arzid who wasn't even her dragon, and who wasn't ready for a rider. He was going to say that, she knew. Even though she also knew he was dead.

It was hard to keep moving. It was hard, too, knowing she now had the means to get to Reedwater and help the people there—but she could not leave the riders of her pack here to die. She thought about that as she worked. Not that she was eager to get on a dragon and fly again, but how long would it take to fly to Reedwater? And which dragon could she ride?

Maybe Arzid would not be able to fly again tonight, but she had a whole pack to choose from. Perhaps Puka, or Wyant's Denez could take her. She could try

122

Oki again. She could go, deliver the medicine, and return to nurse her pack riders. They did not need another shot until almost morning. Couldn't she go and return by then? But what about water for her patients?

She had a scare when she rolled Tarva over. The girl's arm was cool. But she found a bota of water beneath Tarva and realized the girl must have been trying to help Erisse and Aimee when she had collapsed on top of them, water and all. Tarva's sleeve was damp and cool, but her skin was fever-hot. Shala gave her a shot, got some water down her, and rolled her away from the other girls.

Erisse was delirious. The pretty dark-haired girl muttered and tossed her head, looking wild and terribly ill. Shala knew if everyone else had it, Erisse must too, but she did not want to waste the antibiotics if someone didn't need it. She tried to check Erisse's eyes and mouth, but the girl kept thrashing.

Of course, if Erisse hadn't been sick, she'd have been tending Tarva, not the other way around, Shala thought. In the end, she just sat on Erisse's arm and gave her a shot of the antibiotic.

She realized she was too tired to think. She was exhausted and stupid.

She dragged herself back to the fire, threw her now-stubby torch into the blaze, and slumped near the warm flames. Just a little nap. Then she'd go to Reedwater.

Shala shivered herself awake. She stared at the fire for long moments before she remembered everything. Arzid. The camp. Dene. Reedwater.

The fire had burned down some but was not out. She had slept, sitting up, for no more than a couple of hours.

She threw more branches on the fire, made another torch to light her way, and circled the camp, giving everyone water. Wyant and Tarva and Granger each took almost half a liter. All the others drank something. Everyone except Dene. She pulled a blanket over him, as if she could make his body go away and not have to think about it if she just covered it up. As if he must be cold and needed a blanket.

No, she would not think about Dene. She had to get to Reedwater, where things were certain to be ugly after so much delay. If it was this bad, here, after one day, the town must be in terrible shape—as Kole had said.

Shala went out to the small meadow area where the dragons had bedded down. She tripped over a food bag and saw that the dragons had helped themselves to the remaining chow. The bag was empty and in tatters. They were no doubt hungry and would want to hunt today. Hopefully a wild herd would be their target, and not some farmer's.

But then she found a wild deer carcass and realized they had already hunted. One of them had, at least. There was nothing left of the deer but bones and antlers and a few bits of gristle. She blinked, unable to think, and made her way over to Oki. He sniffed her hand and allowed her to scratch his nose and eye ridges. That was much better than the way he had scuttled away from her earlier that night. He got to his feet, seeming ready for her to ride. She checked the harness, and was glad she had, for one strap was quite loose. That fixed, she went back into the camp, found her saddlebags, took out the bag of trail mix and tossed some into her mouth. She chewed as she gathered up the medicine.

She left one bottle, judging it would be enough for the final two rounds of shots for the pack riders. She put a packet of syringes beside it. She had nothing to write with to leave a note but did not expect any of them to awaken before she returned. She grimaced at the thought of flying again.

She checked her pack, but she had not brought any headscarves. She stood chewing a moment in thought, then went over to where Tarva, Aimee and Erisse lay.

There had been a scarf on the ground, she thought. She had seen one, hadn't she? Yes. She picked it up, refolded it and wrapped it around her hair. That should help with the wind, a little. She took the remaining antibiotics, her water, and went back to Oki. He bent his knee, lowered his wing and let her climb aboard. Not that she wanted to.

She dropped the torch into a rocky area free of grass where it could burn out safely. Dreading what was to come, she tucked her feet into Oki's wing pockets, and grasped the harness while the sage green dragon pumped his wings. Shala stared at the mane, or ruff hairs, in front of her. There must be some way to braid them or something, so they wouldn't whip into her face. For now, she settled for gathering up a handful of the long feathery hairs and held onto it along with the harness. She did the same with the other hand. Oki started running while flapping his wings. He was going to do a running launch, unlike Arzid who had pretty much gone straight up from the ground. She shook her head, remembering. How had the young dragon managed such a takeoff?

She remembered the instructions for steering and figured out the direction they needed to go about the same time Oki got them airborne. Nausea struck. Eyes streaming, Shala thumped Oki's neck with her left knee, directing him to turn. As they rose into the dark sky, she thought she could see the shimmer of water in the Swampen Sea almost due east from their position. The ring glow brightened the night sky and lit the water with faint highlights. Wishing she could see it better, Shala gave up and ducked down behind Oki's green-gray neck. Oki's stroke and glide pattern seemed a little smoother than Arzid's had, but her stomach rebelled throughout the flight.

They turned south when they came to the Yent River. The flight to Reedwater town took less than an hour. She was at Reedwater sooner than she would have been if she had stayed on Teek and the mules—though not as fast as she might have been, if she had had a dragon to ride from Two Rivers at the beginning.

She wiped her eyes, peered down, and directed Oki to land on the packed sand of Reedwater's town square. He circled and lost height.

As they went down, the reek of decaying bodies hit her like a fist. There were a lot of dead in Reedwater. Was there going to be anyone left alive in the town at all, or were they landing in an open graveyard?

Shala crawled from Oki's back, stumbled a few steps away, and vomited. She stood shaking a few moments, then swigged her water bottle, rinsed her mouth and spat. This was going to have to stop, or she would be too weak and malnourished to help anyone.

She went to the fountain in the center of the plaza. She splashed water on her face and head and let herself drip dry as she turned in a circle looking for signs of life along the dark streets that fanned out from the central square.

Nothing moved.

Dread mounted as Shala stared, trying to figure out what to do, where to go, how to find the people that might still benefit from the medicines she had brought. There would be someone. Wouldn't there?

Would they be able to see her in the dark? She made her way to the nearest house, and feeling like a burglar, knocked on the door. No one came to open it. She tried the handle, and the door pushed open. She peeked into the dimness. Should she try to find wood and build a fire in the plaza? She went back outside and walked down the narrow alley beside the house. There ought to be a woodshed in back.

Her footsteps echoed in the alley, in the silent town.

She thought about something Logyn had said once. Her middle foster brother, who wanted to leave the village and become a monk at the Mahayana monastery, on the western coast of Shiraz: "When we cry for the dead," Logyn had said, "we are weeping for ourselves, the ones left behind."

His father, Shala's stepfather, had been killed in a sandstorm a few months before. Logyn had never mourned, not that she could see. "He has gone on to renewal," Logyn said. "He is in a better place: why would I weep?"

Stumbling over her own feet, Shala found a pile of wood. She picked up several logs and some narrower kindling, and headed back to the plaza.

She shook her head. It had been so hard to understand Logyn's attitude. She'd yelled at him. "But it's sad! He's gone, and I miss him! Don't you?"

"Of course, I miss my father," Logyn said.

She remembered him sitting there in the shade of Embry's garden wall. He crossed his legs, put his feet up onto his knees and closed his eyes, ready to meditate.

"I miss him, but I do not think it's sad," he murmured, and then he was gone in trance, leaving Shala to stare at him.

She remembered that now, that she was weeping for herself, her sadness and her own helplessness.

It did not make her weep any less.

She pulled her sparker from her pack and went to work on the shavings she'd cut from the kindling.

"Well, I am not a proper Buddhist," Shala told Oki. He had come over to see what she was doing. The fire caught, and Oki moved away from it. He went to drink from the fountain pool. He snorted, getting some water into his nostrils, and sneezed, then drank again, sucking water through his rolled tongue like he was using a straw drinking tube.

Shala fed the fire until shadows danced on the buildings that surrounded the fountain square. She gave Oki a good rubdown, trying not to think about anything except the small tasks in front of her.

The sky lightened with the weird pre-dawn tint. She sat and heard for the first time the rushing sound of dawn as it came toward her: the sun came up, by phases brightening the rings above, and lighting Azureign's sky.

Shala heard a distant shout. She turned and saw a small boy running down the street toward her.

"Kole!" he yelled. Then he was close enough to see it wasn't Kole, and it wasn't Palli, Kole's dragon, either. He kept running toward her, though.

"Did you bring help?" the boy called. "My family are all sick!"

"I have medicine," Shala said and grasped her pack as the boy waved at her to follow, turned and ran back the direction he had come. She felt a weary, paradoxical relief. She had someone she could help in Reedwater, at last. She just wished she had more energy to do it.

CHAPTER 10 — Rescue

She gave Oki the "stay" signal and followed the boy up the empty street. Their footsteps echoed on the stones of the plaza and then the street itself. They walked faster on the smooth, clean plasscrete of the street. Reedwater was a prosperous town, to afford to pave their streets.

Had been prosperous.

"My name is Shala," she told the boy. "Kole is ill, but he brought the medicine to me, and I brought it here."

He nodded, dark eyes serious in his pinched face. What must it have been like for him here? She could not imagine. She followed him, trying not to breathe the air that was so tainted with death.

"We live on Tawny Island," he said. "No one was sick there, at first. But now they are. I'm Danyon," he said. "My da is the miller for all Reedtown, but he got sick this morning, so ma made rice instead of bread for breakfast." He looked at her. "Are you hungry? You look hungry."

She probably did, Shala thought. She had thrown up everything she had eaten the previous day. "Yes, I am."

"Ma will make you breakfast." He turned a corner, and they were on another silent, plass-paved street. This one smelled worse. She couldn't think of people, human beings, at the same time she thought of what the rotting flesh smell meant. She could not think of eating breakfast.

She wrapped the borrowed headscarf around her mouth. It helped a little.

"I need to give shots, first," she said. "And the people who are sick will need to drink a lot of fresh, clean water."

Danyon nodded. "We have a big cistern on the roof of the storage house next to the mill; it's full from the rain."

Shala glanced around as they turned back to their original direction on another street. The storefronts looked familiar. For a long moment, Shala couldn't imagine why she should recognize them. Then she knew she had been here before, with Jhude. She looked around in shock. It was almost impossible to recognize this street as the same place. The colorful booths were missing, and all the people were gone.

This was a silent dead place, not a thriving town market. This was a ghost town. She shivered, walking faster. Her eyes swept down the row of buildings. It felt as if they were being watched. *The ghosts of the dead, the prayers of the living,* Shala thought. That's what she felt.

She recognized the silversmith's shop, and this— this was the fabric-seller where she had brought Andrya's work to sell. She had walked a few blocks from the inn near Netke's home, and brought Andrya's linen cloth here, and here it was, behind the sheet plass window. She recognized the pretty pale blue linen. It didn't seem right that it should hang there, looking so pretty and homey, in the midst of bitter desolation.

It was a relief when Danyan turned onto another street, this one narrow and winding along down the hill toward the river. A breeze wafted up from the water; it smelled much better than what they had been breathing.

Shala was starting to wish she had ridden Oki by the time they got to the footbridge that went out to the island in the middle of the river. The Yent flowed around it, rushing and tumbling over the rocks at the upstream end. She glanced over her shoulder, back at the rest of the town. She saw not a single living soul.

130

She worked the rest of the morning giving shots to the twenty people who lived on the island, most of whom had fallen ill the night before. She debated whether to give Danyan the vaccine, since he seemed to be naturally immune, but in the end decided it would be better than if he fell ill after she left. She gave several bottles of antibiotics and one of the vaccine to Danyan's mother Malla, who paid careful attention to her instructions about how to give the shots.

"Everyone should have plenty of water, three or four times a day at least. And you should know, it may be that you received the vaccine too late, and will also come down with it," Shala said, "so you should explain what to do to whoever gets back on their feet first." Malla nodded. "And Danyan can help; he seems to be doing fine."

"Yes," Malla said. "We thank you."

"I'm sorry I wasn't able to get here faster," Shala said. "But now I must get back to my own people who are ill."

Malla pressed a packet of biscuits and dried fruit into her hand. "For later, when you are hungry," she said.

"Danyan, can you show me the way back to the plaza where I left Oki? I'm not sure I know the way among so many streets."

Danyan lifted his chin and took her hand.

"Come straight home, Dany," Malla said. "I will need your help."

"Yes, mama."

When they got as far as the street Shala recognized, she thanked Danyan and sent him home. "I can find my way from here," she told him.

She could not leave without seeing if anyone from Netke's family might need help. Though she expected to find nothing but bodies, she made her way to the inn she and Jhude had stayed in and from there remembered the way to Netke's home. The front door was locked, but Netke had shown them a way in from the back, in case Jhude wanted to come in after her family had gone to sleep. For a tryst, Shala presumed. It was such a long way from lover's trysts to the situation in Reedwater now, Shala could hardly think about it. Was Netke okay? Was Jhude?

Shala used the back entrance, springing the back gate open with the pull bar. She walked with quiet steps across the pretty stone-floored patio Netke had taken such delight in showing them. She turned the lever on the patio door that led into what Netke called a sun porch, and from there let herself into the house. Expecting the worst, she was surprised to notice no bad smells inside the house.

Upstairs, maybe.

She checked all the rooms downstairs, then climbed up to the second story where the bedrooms were lined up along a hallway. Feeling once again as if she could get lost in the big house—it was more than twice the size of Andrya's—she was careful to pay attention and enter and exit each room by the same door. She did not get lost, but she did not find anyone, either. The house was empty. No living people, no dead ones.

Was that good? Or had they died among the first, and already been buried by others of the town? She returned to the office where Netke's father kept his desk and papers. She found a sheet of flecked tan paper and a pencil, and wrote a brief note, explaining what she had been doing in their house, and expressing her hope that everyone was safe and well. She placed it on the glossy wood of the dining hall table, setting a crystal dish atop one corner, so it would stay put.

She left the way she had come, passing the inn again, and returning to the street with the fabric-seller's shop on it. She still hadn't decided what to do about Andrya's cloth. The shopkeeper had accepted it on consignment. That meant she hadn't paid for it. The plan had been if she sold it, she would send Andrya half the money she got for it, and they would both earn something.

But she wasn't going to be able to sell it now. Even if she was still alive, most of her customers were not. No one would be buying anything in Reedwater for quite some time.

Shala stood outside the shop a long moment, looking at the blue linen. Andrya had worked so hard on that batch, spinning and weaving the fine stuff, then dying it such a pretty shade.

She thought of Logyn's teachings, and what she had read in the meditation book. This was one of those situations where two conflicting actions could be taken, and she was not enlightened enough to know what to do. What would Logyn do?

He wouldn't be in this situation—that was the truest thought she could come up with. But if he was....

She decided that if the shop were open, she would take the cloth with her and give it back to Andrya when she could. If she could not get inside the shop, then she would leave the linen here. She could not be sure if that was a Logyn kind of answer or not, but it seemed a good one for Shala.

Exhaustion made her legs shake as she walked around the camp, giving the pack riders their next shot, and as much water as she could get into them. She'd filled her own empty bota at the Reedwater fountain, but it was again empty, as were all those she could find in the camp.

She should go down to the creek and refill some of them. But when she told her legs to walk that direction, they would not go. She held the water bags, just standing there a moment, then crumpled to the ground.

Some time later—in the early afternoon according to the sun—she woke up. The sun was hot on her skin, except where the fallen water bottles had covered her. She sat up, bemused. "Guess I never filled them up." She got to her feet and did that, and went around, checking her patients again, and making them drink. Granger was still unconscious. He could be helped by more fluids, if she could just get him to an infirmary.

She looked out to where the dragons were nesting. They watched her move among their riders. She looked at Puka and Arzid again and again. Could she get some of the pack riders back to Two Rivers? Maybe Sylvan was back and could help. At the very least she could do an IV drip for Granger.

She thought about all her patients. They didn't need another shot until late that evening. Most of them had taken enough water that she thought they'd be okay—except Granger, whom she was going to take in the first trip, if she could take anyone.

It was going to take several back and forth trips to get everyone home, even if some of the young dragons could take riders. She walked out to the dragons' area, and one by one had them each spread their wings while she climbed aboard. Oki looked as if he could go again. Puka and Arzid were fine. She judged that Denez and Lizard each could handle a rider, and maybe Sparkellz. She didn't think Ozala, Sharz or Zinno were ready, though.

There were also the problems of having but two riding harnesses, with unconscious riders. Could she find enough straps to tie a rider on? Maybe she could rig something out of the abandoned horse and mule gear.

She led Oki back into the camp with her. She'd put Granger on him, and Aimee, who was also quite weak, onto Puka. She'd ride Arzid again, hopefully staying aboard with her makeshift harness. She'd keep a close eye on the two sick riders. Once they got back to the school, she could find more riding harnesses, and get everyone else home. She ate and rested. She must rebuild her strength enough to get the job done.

When the last dragon touched down in the Two Rivers yard, Shala shuddered with relief. She had met her goal of getting everyone back that night. It was pitch black, and the dragons were all as exhausted as she was, but their riders were safe.

Hardest to load had been Dene. She had put his body onto the packdrone she had dragged back with her from Two Rivers, strapping the body down as if he were a bag of supplies. He was very heavy, and awkward for her to move. She had to stop several times, and almost gave up. But she thought of Aimee, and how the girls' advisor would feel if Dene was left lying alone in a field.

Everyone was in Two Rivers now, never mind how. Now she needed to care for everyone, including the dragons.

Oki was worst off; his wings drooped even after he folded them. He had flown more than any of the others. Puka had flown two trips as well but had not gone to Reedwater on top of it. And the amazing Arzid had done more than his share, carrying her back on the first trip, then going back with Shala to bring home Tarva.

135

She ended up using Zinno after all, strapping Kiny aboard his own dragon, rather than leave him there for a last very late trip. The red dragon seemed tired, but otherwise no worse for having been "ridden," if you could call it that.

All the dragons deserved extra attention, Shala knew, but first—the people.

She helped Tarva down off of Arzid and was stripping the harness off the young dragon when she saw Alu dismount, then fall flat on her face. Shala ran over, helped the girl to her feet, and lent her shoulder as a prop, walking her to the dorm rooms.

The infirmary was full. Though Kole was now well enough to get up and empty a bed, she'd filled it with Granger, who was still the weakest among them. Aimee and Ben were in the other two beds. The rest went into the dorms.

"Dene rode Oki into town to buy something," Alu murmured to Shala as she crawled off the ladder onto her bunk. "He got sick first."

That explained how the riders had caught this thing. And why she had arrived too late to help Dene. And why Oki had been so tired that first day, Shala thought.

Kiny told her the riders had been preparing Arzid to get Dene home, when they had all fallen ill.

The dragons had known something was wrong. They left a couple of the pack at the camp, and the others flew back toward the school. Shala intercepted them, and by the luckiest of chances had the very thing the riders needed.

Now she could turn some of the responsibility over. Kole was well enough to assume nursing duties. She had hoped, coming in, that she would see Simba in the paddock, but Sylvan still was not there; he had not yet returned from his mission to save the dragons of Avordan Town.

That meant she still had to care for the animals; there was no one else healthy enough to manage the job.

She fed the dragons first, and then threw some hay at the goats and the lonesome little pony. She discovered the sheep had broken out of their pen and were eating the grass in back of the barn. She left them to it, and fell into bed and a heavy, twelve-hour sleep.

The trumpeting of dragons woke her the next evening.

Kole could feed the people but not the animals, and those were all hungry again.

Shala made the rounds with the wagonload of dragon chow, giving an extra scoop to the dragons who had flown so much. She praised Arzid, who seemed none the worse for his premature turns as a full-fledged dragon with a rider. She complimented Oki and Puka and Zinno who had worked so hard. Then she went back to handle Dene's queen.

Kharmin demonstrated her grumpiness by hissing and growling. She had been on short rations while Shala was gone.

While the queen was busy inhaling a dozen kilos of chow, Shala peeked into the brooding-barn at the eggs. The shells, which had been leathery when she had first seen them, were today hard and warm and brittle-seeming.

"I guess that means they'll hatch soon." She scuttled from the side door of the barn as Kharmin waddled back in, still munching a mouthful of chow. But Kharmin was focused on her eggs, not human intruders; she didn't see Shala slip out the side door.

How could anyone explain to Kharmin that her rider would not be coming back?

Well, maybe she was giving the dragon too much credit. Maybe Kharmin wouldn't even notice that Dene was missing. She would get a new rider, and her life as a Queen would go on. Shala chewed her bottom lip. Maybe that was how it would be, but she didn't think so.

Shala went to the bathhouse and started a tub of water filling. The hot springs had been part of the reason the school had been built on this spot, but she didn't take them for granted. Pre-heated water was still a wonderful treat. The deep stone tub filled with steaming mineral water while Shala found her soap and the herbal hair cleanser that Embry had given her as a going-away present.

Shala soaked until her fingertips looked like raisins, then finished, rinsing her hair and wringing out the headscarf she had borrowed and now made clean again.

She was clean and dry and sweet-smelling when she entered the kitchens to discover Kole had prepared a huge vat of lentil and vegetable stew. It was about half gone. She thought maybe she could eat all of the second half herself, if she just had enough time to sit down and slurp it up before she fell asleep. She wasn't going to be riding a dragon anywhere soon, so she ought to be able to make up for some of those lost— literally lost—meals.

She was on her third bowl of stew when Erisse, Tarva and Kiny came into the dining hall.

"Umm," Kiny said, sniffing the air. "Kole said there was food!"

"Stew," Shala called to them. "It's good!"

"I suppose we have to serve ourselves," Erisse said, looking around for the missing serving cart.

Shala remembered using it to get Kole to the infirmary. It was probably still there or sitting in the way somewhere.

"Let's just each get a bowl," Tarva said to Erisse. She turned to Shala. "Is it too much to hope that there's bread, too?"

"Er. I didn't see any," Shala said. "I don't know if Kole is that much of a cook."

"I would have thought you could make something," Erisse said. Her tone was cold. "But I guess I'm glad you didn't."

Mystified as to the source of Erisse's irritation, Shala raised her eyebrows. Maybe Erisse was trying to tease her. "Sorry, I've been a bit busy. Anyhow, I'm hopeless at baking." She looked back at her dish. "Besides, I've been asleep."

Erisse sniffed as she and Tarva followed Kiny into the kitchen.

Shala finished her stew, thinking of home. Early on, Andrya had hoped for help from Shala—until her tenth or twelfth spoiled cooking effort. In the face of her husband's roar of outrage at yet another ruined meal, Andrya had given up.

"You can serve," she'd said to Shala. "And you can take turns cleaning up. But you are no longer permitted to cook." They'd laughed then. Logyn had turned out to be pretty good at baking all sorts of things. Wishing she had some of his crusty cheese bread now, Shala sighed again.

She stood up, feeling satisfied, and took her empty bowl and spoon into the kitchen. She put them into the soaking tray and poured water over them. Then she waved 'bye to the other three students. She walked down the hall to the girls' dorm, almost running into Kole. He turned sideways with his tray of empty bowls to give her room to pass.

"I think everyone has been fed that needs help, and everyone else is up and able to feed themselves."

"That's good," Shala said. "The stew was wonderful. I think I'm going to sleep another twelve hours now."

Kole laughed. "I shouldn't wonder!"

But when she arrived at her bed, Shala saw the borrowed headscarf hanging from the foot rail of her bunk. She felt the delicate silk. It was dry; she should return it. Folding and smoothing the scarf in her hands, she carried it back to the dining area. She thought it belonged to Erisse or maybe Tarva.

Those two and Kiny were eating at the same table. Wyant and Tomaso were just sitting down with them. Shala smiled at Wyant, whose face was wreathed in steam rising from his bowl.

"Shala," he said, standing back up. "I wanted to take this opportunity to thank you for saving my life," he said, then sat down.

"Oh—" she started but was interrupted by thanks from Tomaso and Tarva and Kiny.

"Not that 'thanks' seems like quite enough," Kiny said with a wry grin.

"Indeed," Wyant saluted her, and then picked up his spoon.

"Of course, any of you would have done the same," she said.

What made such a compliment so hard to accept? Well, part of it was because she couldn't have imagined doing anything else. How could she *not* have helped them? So, to her, doing the right thing didn't merit a "thank you."

She glanced at the scarf she held, and then handed the pale blue silk to Erisse.

"Erisse, this is yours, I think. I picked it up at the camp to use when I needed to fly Oki in to Reedwater."

"That's not mine," Erisse said, voice cold.

Tarva blurted, "Oh, Erisse, it is too yours!" then she flinched from Erisse's scowl.

Erisse turned her head sideways to glare up at Shala from the corner of her eye. She did not reach for the scarf. Shala stood there, holding it out, beginning to feel very stupid.

"I— I'm sorry I couldn't ask to borrow it," Shala said. "My hair blew so I couldn't see when I first rode Arzid, and I knew I needed something to keep it out of my face when I went on to Reedwater, and, um...I washed it." Aware she was babbling, Shala closed her mouth.

"Keep it, rag girl. I don't need to wear it after you've had it on."

Shala felt her face go numb with shock.

She saw Tarva's mouth drop open, and Wyant and Tomaso both stopped eating and just looked at Erisse, disbelief clear in their expressions.

Then Shala saw all their eyes turn to her. Erisse's were angry; everyone else seemed stunned. Ten eyes on her humiliation were just too many.

She gulped, spun away and ran back to the dorm without saying another word, hoping they could not hear her cry.

Rag girl? *What?*

She gave her cheeks a fierce rub to erase the tears before anyone else saw them, then realized she had used Erisse's scarf to wipe her face. She threw it away from her as though it was boiling hot. It shimmered as it fell to a soft pile on the floor. Shala kicked at it, then climbed into her bunk and buried her face in her pillow.

How could she have been so mistaken about Erisse's friendship? She could see now that Erisse must have never liked her. How stupid she was! She had risked destroying her dragon's ability to fly, just for the sake of this girl's approval, when the girl cared nothing about her.

141

Had Erisse even wanted to help her and Nizael with her "plan" to make him fly?

No. Shala did not think so. Maybe Erisse had even wanted to hurt Nizael. That was a horrible thought. But certainly the other girl had not cared if he'd been injured or unable to fly permanently.

That betrayal—the complete reversal of what she had seen as friendship—was worse than anything else that had happened. The deaths at Reedwater, even the loss of Dene—those had been terrible events, but they were not like this.

This was a personal hurt, one that Erisse had *meant* to inflict. They all knew Erisse had been treated like a princess at home and was used to getting her own way. But that she would be mean and vindictive to others?

Shala could see no reason for it, and that hurt worst of all. She had betrayed her dragon for the sake of this girl's opinion, and now the girl had insulted her in the worst way. Shala bit her lip, fighting tears.

Sweet Nizael had not betrayed her. How could she have put human friendship before that of her own dragon?

One thing was certain: she would never do so again. Nizael was her friend, even if he never flew.

CHAPTER 11 — Memorial

The sunlight filtered down through the ferny branches of redwood trees. The pack riders stood in a circle around Dene's grave.

Aimee insisted he be buried under the trees. "He loved them so," she said. "He would rather be here than in New Venice, or back home."

Shala thought it was a beautiful spot. Though she knew Dene could not see it, she could understand why Aimee wanted him here. In this deepest part of the grove, just redwoods trees grew, nothing grew on the ground beneath them. There was no bracken, no bugs or seeds to eat, so no birds or squirrels to eat them: it was peaceful in an earthy, spiritual way. The long-lived trees would stand sentinel over Dene. It was a good memory for Aimee to take with her.

Shala was brought back to reality when the person beside her stepped forward. It was Alu's turn to speak. Shala frowned. She had missed what Erisse and Kiny had said. "He went to get us dessert," Alu said. "We asked if we could have dessert, out in the middle of nowhere!" She swiped at her eyes. "You were so sweet to go to Reedwater to get it for us, Dene. I am so sorry your kindness was repaid this way." She stepped back, and it was Shala's turn.

"I am sorry you will miss Kharmin's hatching," her voice quavered. "I know you were proud of your dragon and wanted to see what the little ones looked like." She stepped back, and Tomaso went forward.

"You were kind to me, when I wanted to leave. You convinced me to stay, and I am glad." Tomaso stepped back, and Granger went.

At last it was Aimee's turn. "There are no words to say goodbye to a lover and friend. You have taken a very large piece of my heart away with you," she said.

"I was always proud to stand at your side." She stepped back, then took the basket Alu handed her and sprinkled a handful of flower petals over the grave.

One by one they walked past, taking a handful of petals and sprinkling them, until Aimee stood alone beneath the redwoods, the near-empty basket of flower petals held tight in the crook of her arm.

As she walked back up the hill toward the school, Shala's hands were taken by Wyant on her left, and Tomaso on her right. They walked hand in hand out from under the trees, back into the sunlight. Dust motes floated in the sunbeams, then the warmth of the sunlight flooded over them.

In the paddock, a dragon trumpeted, shockingly loud on the still air. Kharmin's wailing answer lifted from the brooding barn.

"Poor Kharmin," Wyant said. "She's been sitting nose down all morning. She misses Dene."

"We all do," Tomaso said.

Shala squeezed their hands, grateful for their company.

Dene's death, and this simple ceremony, affected her much more than when Andrya's husband had died.

Deep in her heart, she wondered if it was because she had been a little bit glad the grouchy old man had passed on. Unlike Dene, the boys' father never had a kind word to say. She had been sad at his death, but she did not miss him.

Of course, Logyn had meditated, and Jono had been even younger than she had, and seemed to not understand his father wasn't coming back. Jhude and Andrya had mourned as Aimee did now. But Shala knew she had not. Not compared with this. And yet, this man she had known for a scant six months, while Andrya's husband had been part of her life for years.

It was odd.

She stepped over an outcropping of loose stones, setting her feet in the dying grass alongside Tomaso and Wyant's.

Perhaps it was because Dene's death represented all the deaths to her: She mourned not just the boys' advisor, but all those at Reedwater she had been too late to help.

"That's a unique way to deal with a sulking dragon," Sylvan's voice said. "Let me know how it works."

Shala jumped, then turned to the stable master as he walked up to where she stood. She made a face and went back to rubbing Arzid's feet. She ignored her own dragon. Nizael watched as Arzid got extra attention, and he got none.

"Well, I don't care if it works. I'm mad at him," she said from her bent-over position. "He can sulk all he likes."

"Hmm," Sylvan said. He moved past her and reached up to scratch Nizael's brow ridges, and Niz lowered his head and stretched out his neck to better receive the attention. The sun was bright on the paddock, and the greens of the grass and trees were brilliant in the light.

Shala finished with Arzid and stepped back, looking up at the big black and gray dragon. She glanced at Nizael and verified once again he was the bigger of the two. But what did that matter if he wouldn't fly when he was needed? "Arzid is my hero," Shala said.

"It is a wonderful thing the way he helped you through the Reedwater disaster." Sylvan shook his head, amazement in his expression. "What a horrendous set of circumstances." He smiled at Shala. "I'd say you and Arzid, Puka and Oki are pretty much the heroes of the year around here." He kept scratching Nizael's brow. "But that makes it all the more puzzling you should be mad at this big guy. He didn't cause any of it; why would you be mad at him?"

"Oh, yes he did!" Shala felt a deep cold anger seize her from somewhere inside herself where she must have stuffed it these last days. "If he hadn't been sulking—if he had flown when he could have—like Arzid did—he—they—" The rage boiled out of her mouth, tangling her words and her logic, and Shala burst into tears. "By all the paths of enlightenment, Sylvan, all those people—all dead without thought or warning or help—and he just *sat* there under his pile of hay!"

Sylvan said nothing at all, but gathered her into a hug and held her while she sobbed against his chest. She wept out all the agony of watching so many deaths, and her sense of helplessness, her feeling of standing alone, a solo reed against the wind.

"P-p-poor Kole," she gasped. "He had to go back to that mess all alone."

"He has help now," Sylvan said, patting her shoulders. "But Kole is not Nizael's fault." He grasped her shoulders and pressed her away to his arms' length, so he could look into her face. "Your dragon is sad, and he doesn't understand any of this."

"He should! It's his fault so many are dead! If it hadn't been for him, I could have gotten the medicines to Reedwater a day earlier! A hundred good people died who didn't have to for no reason other than a fat dragon who won't fly!"

"Now that's just not true, Shala of Nizael clan." Sylvan let go of her and folded his arms across his chest over the damp spot on his shirt from Shala's tears.

He scowled at her. "What on all the planets are you thinking? If Nizael *was* able to fly, you would have

146

gone with the others in your pack. There would have been *no one here at all* to help Kole and Palli, and take the medicines to Reedwater." His gaze was so fierce, Shala thought she could feel it burning straight through her head. "Kole would be dead. Granger and Alu and Aimee and your whole pack would be dead. *You*—would be dead, Shala."

Shala could feel the tears dribbling down her cheeks again. She gasped and struggled to breathe.

"So, you see, Nizael *saved* many lives. If you are going to blame him for not being grown up enough to fly, you must credit him also for the lives saved, not lost, by his youth." His glare softened. "And you must forgive yourself as well as your dragon, Shala. You are not to blame for any of this."

"I—" She stopped, gulped, and stared at the ground. Whose fault was it, then? "How could a thousand people just die for no reason?" she asked. When she looked up, she was startled to see a lopsided smile on Sylvan's face and rue in his golden brown eyes.

"Oh, Shala. You ask what humans have asked the universe since the beginnings of time. A most profound question. How could a thousand people just die? Or a million?" He lifted his palms flat out and raised his empty hands to the sky. "Better to ask, how could we live? What makes us be born, and breathe, and strive?" He shrugged his shoulders, let his hands drop. "I do not know. But I do know it is not my fault. I did not cause these lives to exist, any more than I caused them to end. Nor did you, Shala. That power is not yours, nor your dragon's nor any of ours."

She sniffed and looked at Nizael. He stretched his neck and touched his big green nose to her runny red one.

"All we have is this day and these lives," Sylvan said. "And this very fine dragon who is eager to learn to fly as bravely as Arzid has."

She stepped closer to Nizael and hugged his neck and patted his nose. She turned to face Sylvan, leaning against her dragon's powerful neck. "I— I hadn't thought about it that way," she said. "As you say, we would have been with the rest of the pack, if he could fly."

They'd *all be dead*, not just Dene and the citizens of Reedwater.

It wasn't Nizael's fault, but she had known that, in her deepest heart. It was just so much easier to blame someone than to believe it had to be...as it was. Reasonless.

The dragon raised his head. She reached up and stroked his long neck. From above her head he snuffled, stirring her hair, which tickled her face.

Blaming Nizael was not her only problem, though. She had wanted to talk to Aimee about it, but Aimee's grief was too deep for Shala to penetrate. She'd had no one she could tell this to, but now Sylvan seemed so understanding....

She blurted it out before she could talk herself out of it. "I'm not sure I want to be a dragonrider at all," she said feeling better already. Yes, she must get this out into the open now, before there were more expectations on her that she could not fulfill.

"This has been a terrible, unusual time, Shala. Most of the time, a rider's life is more pleasant."

"That's not what I mean." She met the stable master's eyes. "I mean I don't want to *ride* a dragon." Sylvan's eyebrows danced quizzically, and she hiccoughed out a very small laugh of mixed terror and relief.

148

"You won't need to ride into disaster again any time soon," he said, not understanding her problem. Well, she hadn't made it clear, yet.

"It makes me sick!" Shala said. "I threw up every time I flew. On both Oki and Arzid, so it wasn't Arzid's fault or anything! I just get so sick to my stomach, I can't keep anything down."

The humor fled Sylvan's face as he considered this. His forehead rumpled in thought, then cleared. "Have you ridden again since you returned here?"

"No. The very thought makes me ill."

"Come along," Sylvan said, moving toward Simba. "You are going to fly right now, and it will be better, I am quite sure." When he realized she wasn't walking along with him, he stopped and turned back to look at her.

"The *medicine*, Shala. When I took the vaccine, it made me ill, too, and I wasn't flying, I was sitting down. You had just taken this shot when you got on a dragon's back for the first time." He smiled and nodded encouragement. "I'm pretty sure if you fly now you'll be just fine. Isn't it worth it to try?"

Well, of course it was. Shala nodded. She was willing to try. Memory of how much faster she had been able to serve her pack and Reedwater once she had a dragon to fly bubbled through her head. Was she so eager to give that up? Of course not.

And thinking about it, she knew she had been nauseous the entire time she had been working to save her pack riders, in the air *and* on the ground. She had ignored it then. It had been so much worse while flying that she hadn't been able to ignore it.

"You know, you could be right." She cleared her throat. "Is there some trick to deal with the wind, though? That was a problem too: I couldn't breathe. I couldn't see, all I could do was barf."

"Headscarf," Sylvan said, mouth quivering as he tried not to smile.

What was funny? Shala wondered.

"Wrap it around your face and breathe through your mouth while you're in the air," Sylvan said, clearing his throat. "A pair of goggles for your eyes, or some riders just use sunglasses." He nodded again.

Then his control broke and he burst into laughter. "I'm sorry!" he gasped. "I have this picture of you leaning over, vomiting into the sky." He mimed an amazed look up at the sky. "Where did this come from?" He whooped. "It would be one of those weird mysteries, like a rain of frogs."

She had to grin, caught up by his laughter.

After a moment, he coughed, blinked, and composed himself. "Sorry." He lifted Simba's harness from the fence and waved it at his dragon. She could hear tiny snickers erupting now and then as he tried to control himself.

Shala gave up looking at him, as each time she met his eyes, it seemed to set him off again.

Instead she watched Simba amble over, using his big top wing joints as third and fourth legs. It seemed an awkward way to move when Shala thought about it, but it didn't look awkward when Simba did it. The green and tan dragon was one of the few who used that way of walking on the ground, and Shala found herself wondering if the others could not do it, or simply chose not to for some reason.

Then Simba was in front of her. She sighed a deep hiccupy breath and helped Sylvan buckle the harness on. She removed her headscarf, rewrapping it so it held her hair down firmly, framing her face. The tail end covered her mouth, and she knotted it with the beginning end, under her ear.

She clambered aboard Simba's tan shoulders.

"Bend forward over his neck, and he'll do a running start," Sylvan called. "It's a little easier than a straight lift-up."

Shala did what Sylvan suggested. Simba pumped his wings and galloped out the paddock gateway, down the path toward the lofting ridge. He seemed to glide up into the air, his takeoff so smooth Shala didn't realize they had left the ground at first. Then she saw the trees, paddock, Nizael, Sylvan, the school buildings all shrinking below her. Simba rose into the sky, and Shala felt she could just reach up and grasp the glorious rings around Azureign.

Her stomach was fine.

Even the wind didn't bother her. This was wonderful!

She leaned over Simba's shoulder and studied the lay of the land below. The lake gleamed below the launching cliff. The trees were an artist's dream of color: a thousand shades of green and brown, sepia and gold. Andrya could strive for years to dye a fabric the blend of colors that lay below.

Shala leaned against Simba's neck and wept, at last, for joy.

That night, in the dark, angry faces loomed, surrounding Shala. The faces looked human, but the fists they aimed at her were mottled green and tan, gray and black, brown and red—the colors of dragons. They yelled insults at her from mouths filled with white-tipped pustules: she was slow, stupid, clumsy and always too late.

"Where were you? Why did you not come to help us? Useless lazy girl!"

One of the faces was Andrya's husband, who had often yelled such words at her. But he had been dead for years.

That's when Shala realized she was deep in a nightmare. She sat up in her bunk, bumped her forehead on the bottom of the bunk above with a thunk loud enough to wake all the other girls, she thought. But no one else woke.

She lay back down in the deep dark of night and rubbed her forehead. She'd rather not sleep again if that was what she was going to see.

It was strange. Erisse's face had been among those shouting at her, though she had not come too late for Erisse or the others in her pack. Why would *they* yell at her? If anyone, it should be Dene.

She had run out of ideas for dealing with so many deaths, and the slinking feeling of responsibility for them. No matter what her head knew about cause and effect, her soul felt she had been given this trust, and had failed in it.

Didn't the Eightfold Path tell her so? If she was not accountable for this duty that had been placed before her, who was?

As close to silent as she could get, Shala climbed down from her bunk, careful not to bump Alu's mattress or frame. The small blonde was curled into her usual ball of blankets-with-a-pillow-on-top. She was a light sleeper. Shala had woken her before, creeping out of bed in the middle of the night.

She placed her bare feet on the cool wood floor. She lifted her jacket and pants from the trunk at her bedside and tiptoed out to the hall. She dressed in the dark, then padded barefoot down the hall to the kitchens, her nightshirt draped over her arm.

She could make some tea and perhaps attempt to bake some biscuits again. Even if they weren't very good, something warm and ready when the others got up was always welcome.

Sylvan and Shala scared each other in the kitchen. He hadn't bothered to light a lantern, but was sitting beside the stove in the dark, and she did not see him until she crashed into him. They both jumped back. Then, like a spectre from her dream he reached a hand and grasped her shoulder.

She heard herself gasp, then knew she was awake, and Sylvan chuckled.

"Couple of cave-dwellers scaring the life out of one another, here," he whispered. "Teapot's full of fresh hot & spicy."

"Oh, thank you," Shala said, taking a deep breath. Yes, she could smell the cloves, cardamom and cinnamon. Perhaps the pungent drink would help clear her head. She went to the cupboard and got herself a cup.

"What are you doing prowling the halls so early?"

Shala poured tea, then leaned against the stove. "I could ask you the same, sir," she said, with a tone of humor in her words so she wouldn't sound sassy. It wasn't going to help anyone to tell him about her nightmares, so he could giver her another pep talk.

The tenday between her flight on Simba and her relief at sharing her feelings with Sylvan had helped. But guilty feelings didn't go away just because someone told you you hadn't done anything wrong, she'd discovered. She wasn't sure what *would* make them go away, but it was not likely to be another speech from Sylvan.

"Kharmin's eggs are cracking," Sylvan said. "I heard the first one go and came to get myself awake before I go out there to keep an eye on things.

"Do they need help?" Shala wondered. Never having seen an infant dragon, she had no idea how strong or capable they were at birth. *Or on hatching,* she corrected herself, since they weren't birthed live like a goat.

"No." Sylvan said with a cheerful tone in his voice. "But sometimes it helps to keep the Queen distracted a bit; she could step on a baby without noticing it, if she gets riled up." He blew on his tea, took a sip. "I could use your help."

"My help? What am I helping with?"

"Can you please go wake Aimee up and get her out to the barn? I think if she could see some new life come into the world it would help take her mind off Dene." He cleared his throat, "Not that anything like dragonets is going to make up for losing him, but— Kharmin has no one else she knows from her own pack, so it would help her, and, I think, Aimee at the same time."

Shala took another little sip of too-hot tea and set her cup on the stove. "Of course, I'll go get her."

She padded back down the hall and in to the alcove in the dorm that held Aimee's bunk. She shook the girls' advisor awake, hoping Aimee wouldn't yell or be upset. Some people didn't take well to being awakened. Shala still remembered the time Jhude had nearly taken her arm off with a swipe from his hatchet. They never had figured out why he had been sleeping with the thing, or what threat he had imagined when he swung at Shala, but after that he made sure to leave the hatchet out in the tool shed at night.

But Aimee was a different sort of sleeper. She rolled over when Shala shook her, and her eyes popped open. She whispered, "What?"

Shala bent down and whispered back, "Hatching. Sylvan's in the kitchen."

Aimee nodded and got out of bed.

Shala grabbed her own shoes from the pile by the door, dropped her nightshirt onto her bunk, and left Aimee behind getting dressed.

Shala hopped on one foot and then the other, slipping on her shoes, on her way back to the kitchen and her tea. "She's coming," she told Sylvan.

She finished her tea while Aimee joined them, then all three trooped out to the brooding barn.

Most of the shells cracked with a loud noise once the first tiny break had appeared in the melon-sized ovals. Shala kept her eyes on a pair of eggs that lay side by side. One throbbed and began to rock. The other was quiet.

"They butt the shell with the top of their heads," Sylvan said. "Once it cracks, they stand up straight inside the egg and push the shell away with their head and shoulders." He pointed to one quieter egg. "Some stand up inside and just push, and others seem to bounce up and down a few times till the shell gives way, though how they have room for that no one can figure."

The quiet egg now had a single long crack in it. She could see the crack get longer and wider, and then sudden crazing over the shell turned into sideways cracks. Those branched out around the curve of the egg, and a piece of the shell popped up with a little dragon head under it. The dragonet shook its head, so the shell flew off, then it poked its snout beneath the arc of one side of the enclosing eggshell and pushed that piece of shell until it broke off. Then the dragonet stepped out. The pale green baby dragon took one dainty step onto the sweet-smelling crumbled alfalfa hay then looked all around for its mother.

Kharmin rumbled in her throat, sounding like a giant kitty purring, and the dragonet found her, its gaze locking onto mama who was curled at the side of the alfalfa-covered circle. It emitted a squeak and shuffled toward her. Kharmin bent her neck down to nose a couple of nearer eggs that showed no signs of activity yet, then looked back up to watch the dragonet's progress.

The feet seemed huge compared with the rest of it, and Shala was not surprised when the baby tripped over some hay. It did not fall, but it did stop and set the end of its snout on the floor, looking like a little green tripod until it had its balance figured out and stood up and began to walk again.

Compared with his three-and-a-half-meter tall mother, the baby looked puny. Then Shala compared it with the length of her arm and realized it wasn't all that small. Its feet were almost as long as her forearm. Of course, he would grow into his feet, just as the goats did their legs that were ridiculously long at birth.

Shala was surprised the little one was so determined to get to its mother. With goats, it was understandable because not only was mother safety, she meant food. The dragons, of course, had no such enticement. Here, the bonding ritual was only that: bonding.

Perhaps it's more important when you're born from an egg, Shala thought. There was a greater need to touch, to overcome the distance.

She stood up and looked over the hatching area. The throbbing egg had developed a network of cracks, but no dragonet, as yet. Nearby, two eggs cracked at once, one zapping open with enough force that the shell flew out of the alfalfa area and into the dirt of the barn. This dragonet was obsidian black, with a line of fiery red along its leading wing edge and down the center of its back all the way to the end of the tail. Its fierceness seemed to be proclaimed by both its colors and its exploding eggshell. It, too, began the trek across the hayfield to its mother. It did not trip.

But the one in the shell beside it, that had cracked at the same time, was not doing so well. Yellow and orange swirls covered this dragonet's head, a startling and brilliant color combination. But it looked around bleary-eyed, not attempting to get out of its shell.

Shala glanced over at Sylvan, wondering if he had seen that one too, and if there was something they should do. He noticed her glance and shook his head. Shala kept an eye on the yellow-orange dragonet in between seeing other dragons hatch and start themselves on the to-mother path.

The yellow and orange one pecked at its enclosing shell a few times without result. Then it angled itself inside the shell so that it faced the shortest "wall" of its prison. It walked along the inside of the shell, rolling it, so that the short side came down to the floor. Then it stepped out of the egg through the open "doorway;" the shell rocked a little behind it, still mostly intact. It found mother and walked with little gliding steps in her direction.

"Well, that demonstrates brains over brawn if I ever saw it," Aimee said with a laugh. She'd been studying the yellow-orange dragonet, too.

"Is that a Queen?" Shala wondered. "Are they smarter than the others?"

"They often are," Aimee said. "But not always. Strength is important, too, and leadership."

Shala stared at the lines of little dragons crossing the floor. Twelve of them. The first two had already arrived next to mom, who bent down and sniffed and nuzzled them each as they arrived beside her.

"This is the bonding moment," Sylvan said. "If she refuses any of them— well, that's how we get packdrones."

Shala looked at him. "Oh! I thought they were a different breed!"

Sylvan shook his head, while Aimee answered, "No one is sure what the Queen looks for, or senses, when she touches them, but there are always a couple that she doesn't like, or that aren't right, somehow."

"Why are packdrones smaller, then?" Shala asked. "If they're regular dragons—and we made sure they ate as much—wouldn't they would grow as big?"

Both Aimee and Sylvan shook their heads this time. "Doesn't happen," Sylvan said.

Aimee pointed to where Kharmin was greeting the clever yellow-orange dragonet. "If she doesn't acknowledge them as part of the pack, they are outcast. Somehow they either know that, and it stunts their growth, or she just knows by the smell that they aren't going to be big enough to fly with the pack in the first place."

"And they don't reproduce," Sylvan said, "even if we have a female and male: it's why packdrones are sometimes called mules."

Shala nodded. She knew they didn't reproduce, but thought it was because they had Queens somewhere else who made more baby packdrones—not that they came from a hatching of regular dragons.

Sylvan looked at Aimee with his eyebrows raised. "You know, I never did give the dragon reproductive cycle talk, with all the excitement we've had. We should do that soon, before the next training flight. In fact, how about this morning?"

Aimee nodded, but was too busy watching dragonets to see Sylvan's triumphant smile. He had managed to distract her from thinking about Dene. Or rather, the dragons had.

Shala saw, and gave him an approving smile.

CHAPTER 12 — Flight

"Twelve hatchlings," Shala told Wyant, "and only one of those a packdrone."

He nodded. "So Sylvan said in our surprise lecture this morning," he smiled his wry smile. "He wouldn't want to send us on our way without knowing where dragons come from! Hey, how'd you get out of it?"

"He was telling me about it in the barn when he realized he hadn't told our group, yet. So, I'd already heard it. Aimee and I got to feed and play with the dragonets, at least until Kharmin chased us away so they could all rest."

Tomaso crowded up against her and Wyant in the hallway, so Erisse and Granger could pass in the other direction. They all nodded at each other, and Shala was about to describe the yellow dragonet's shell-rolling trick for them, when she heard Erisse say her name as she passed.

"I'll bet she's no orphan," Erisse was saying. "I'll bet Shala's parents left her behind when they ran. Why would we want her in our pack?"

Granger shrugged, face red. He was obviously aware Erisse was saying this in front of the whole group, as if Shala wasn't even there. "Well, whatever, Erisse," Granger said. "The Queens will choose, so what we decide doesn't matter..." his voice faded as they walked away down the hall.

Wyant broke the uncomfortable silence that followed. "Dene would have been proud of Kharmin," he said. He acted as if they hadn't heard Erisse's remark, so Shala decided to pretend that also.

Tomaso spoke one of his rare sentences: "They have a new rider for Kharmin," he said.

"Yeah," Wyant said.

Shala hadn't heard about that. "Who is it?"

"A man whose dragon died in the epidemic at Avordan Town. He's supposed to be on his way here now." Wyant laughed aloud. "And, guess what? We're getting a cook!"

"Yeah!" Tomaso put in.

"Mistress Arapunta sent a letter," Wyant went on. "Sylvan read some of it to us. She had some things to say to the Guild about supporting the schools and the smaller packs better, after Kole's experience at Reedwater." They had stopped outside the girls' dorm room, and Wyant braced himself in the doorway, blocking Shala's entrance. "So now, all riders have to contribute a small part of their earnings to help, like a tax."

"To help retired riders, too," Tomaso said.

"Like this guy who's coming to cook and help out here at the school," Wyant nodded. "Anyway, Sylvan should be serving a town, not stuck here all the time with students. We don't have enough dragons and riders to cover our territory as it is, so he's kind of wasted here. They're getting a new stable master to post here, one who is too old to be out riding all the time. It's a way better distribution of resources."

Shala met Wyant's stare. Why was he looking at her so intently? "Sylvan said they're going to maybe hook up the solos into a loose pack arrangement," he said. "And he'll be a part of that."

"Yeah," Tomaso agreed.

Wyant slouched against the doorframe, jamming his hands into his pockets. "Umm. Alu has asked Tomaso and me to join her pack, as soon as the big pack splits into two. I don't think anyone knows what to do with Nizael."

Shala had been thinking about this a lot: how the packs would divide up. "Well, assuming he flies someday, I was thinking we might go solo." She leaned against the other half of the doorway, glancing at

Tomaso. The quiet young man was looking at her with his steady brown eyes, an unreadable expression on his face. "The Queens are already looking for their Mates, and it's getting too late to be part of any pack, now," she finished.

"You don't want to be in Erisse's group," Wyant said. "She's just plain mean."

"Oh, I think she's just nervous," Shala blurted. "Because her dragon is an obvious Queen, and everyone's watching her and Sparkellz and matching dragons and Mates."

"Well, it's kind of you to find excuses for her bitchiness," Wyant began, "but—"

"But she needn't be so mean," came Alu's voice from inside the dorm room. The blonde girl joined them at the door, her curls tousled from taking off her sweater.

She tossed her sweater behind her up onto her bed and turned to meet Shala's gaze. "Shala—" she bit her lip. "Well, maybe I'm butting in where I'm not wanted, but I think there is something you should know about Erisse. A long time ago, her family was attacked by caravanners."

Shala felt her eyebrows pinch together. Caravanners did not attack people, so this was misinformation, at best.

"Erisse's grandparents were killed, and their wagons and an entire herd of their prize horses were stolen. Her family has hated caravanners ever since, and she knows you are from a caravan family."

"We don't attack people. It's against everything travellers believe. It may have been pirates pretending to be us travellers, but it *wasn't* us."

Alu bit her lip again. "Well, I don't know about any of that, but that is why she hates you. And, well, she knows she's not as strong a leader as her Queen is. Erisse is not very good with the other dragons like you are," Alu said, "*or* with people, like Wyant is." She looked up at Wyant. "She thinks she has to bully people to get them to join with her. And if bullying them doesn't work, she treats them like an enemy. I think she's afraid of our group, because we won't be bullied."

Wyant cleared his throat. "Also, that group is going to have trouble. She can't do navigational math, and neither can Granger."

"*I* can't do navigational math," Tomaso muttered.

"But you don't go around picking on people because of it," Alu said, smiling at him. "You just take yourself off and study harder."

Wyant and Shala nodded their agreement at this, and Tomaso blushed bright red. But he was smiling while he blushed.

Alu's noticed him, Shala thought.

"Anyway, you got Tanzi to fly that maze Sylvan set up before anyone else did, navigational math or not," Alu said.

Yes, Shala thought; *Alu has been watching Tomaso.* "I never would have known you have a problem with navigation, Tomaso," she said.

Alu nodded agreement and went on, "I'm not sure, but I think Erisse is both too full of herself and her dragon to be considerate, at the same time she's insecure and frightened, because—whatever." Alu shook her head, curls bouncing. "I can't guess what she thinks. But everyone can see how she behaves. She's got Granger under her thumb, and Tarva and Kiny, and maybe Ben."

"I was thinking Ben was more sensible that that," Shala put in. "I think he's been watching everyone and will make the right choice."

"Well, if his dragon chooses Sparkellz, there's not much he can do," said Alu. "She's a strong, pretty dragon, and Lizard will have his own opinion—that Ben will have to go along with."

"We all wish Nizael would fly, Shala," Tomaso said. "So the packs can be sorted out."

"Oh!" Wyant said. "Sylvan says you're to come with us on Oki for the tenday training flight, with or without Niz."

"Yes," Shala said. Kole would be coming back for Palli soon and would drop off Oki in exchange. "Even if Niz flies by then, he won't be ready for a rider." She made a face. "Oki's a nice dragon, but he's not Nizael."

"Niz will be Queen's Mate yet," Alu said, surprising Shala with a hug. While Alu's arms were around her, Shala glanced at Tomaso. She knew he was hoping his Tanzi would get the Queen's Mate job; his eyes were downcast. She tightened her lips, not knowing what to say. She patted Alu's shoulders and they separated.

Well, however right or wrong Erisse's beliefs and behavior were, it was at least nice to have *some* explanation for the young woman's inconsistencies. The rest of the matter was up to the dragons, in Shala's opinion.

Alu's eyes sparkled. "Come on. I want to see the babies!"

Shala gave Niz an eyebrow rub, then led him out to the launching ridge. Nizael's big feet trampled the last of the spring grasses along the pathway. Yellow and white primroses gleamed among the more distant clumps of grass. The sun's rays seemed to shoot down in focused beams, intent on making all the colors bright.

When they got to the edge of the precipice, she saw the lake sparkling below. It was one of those perfect days that made her wish it was summer all the time.

She unclipped the lead rope from Niz's riding harness and stepped back. She signaled him to spread his wings and fan them. His wings came out, all four meters per side. He glanced over his shoulder at her. She imagined he was checking to see if the tractor was there. Or perhaps not; his dark eyes were calm and trusting.

"You can go when you want to, Niz," she told him, and spread her arms in the flight signal. He sat, wings spread, still looking at her. "Or not, if you don't want to." She shrugged and folded her arms across her belly.

He turned away from her, pointing his long nose down at the lake. Shala walked the few steps closer to the edge so that she stood beside her dragon just past the tip of his wing, looking down. The lake gleamed incandescent blue at the surface but swirled with molten greens in its depths. A few clouds were reflected in it, pristine white compared with the crystalline blue of the sky above and the lake beneath. Overhead, the rings glowed, seeming to emit their own light, a striking arc of white fire across the blueness of the sky. Shala and Nizael sighed at the same time.

They looked at each other, and she giggled. It was as though they shared some obscure joke.

Still smiling, she told him, "It's a beautiful day to fly, Niz, but it's completely up to you."

He turned his head away from her to look back at the lake.

Then he pumped his wings and left the ledge with so little sound it was as if he had never stood there beside her.

Nizael did not bother gliding down to the lake. He pumped his wings, circling higher and higher above her. He circled all the way around the school grounds twice. Then he flew a tightening spiral, losing height and centering in on the dragon paddock.

Shala walked back that direction, her eyes on her dragon as he left the sky. Nizael dropped neatly down to land beside Wyant's pretty Denez. He folded his wings and touched noses with Denez. It looked as though he had been sitting there beside her all along. Shala heard applause as she approached the paddock fence. Wyant, Tomaso, and Ben were all clapping, and shouting compliments to Nizael. She waved to them, a wide grin on her face.

She had never imagined how relieved she would feel when her dragon flew at last. She would have been happy with a simple glide down to the lake today, but Nizael had apparently been saving it up for this spectacular demonstration of his flight skills. Shala's cheeks ached from grinning. She walked through the gateway into the paddock and straight up to her dragon. She murmured compliments into his ear as she scratched his brow ridges and patted his nose.

"Aren't you the most beautiful dragon ever to fly!" she told him.

She heard one of the other pack riders walking up behind her. She turned with sparkling eyes to see Erisse standing there, fists clenched and a hateful expression on her face.

"I suppose now you are just going to be impossible to live with, you little glory sucker!" Erisse said.

Shala felt as if Erisse had punched her in the stomach. All the breath left her lungs, and her eyes teared up. She turned her face into the curve of Nizael's neck. He whuffed in her ear. Not even Erisse's terrible attitude could take away his wonderful flight.

But what was Erisse's problem?

"One should exchange one's own happiness with the suffering of others," she chanted into Nizael's neck scales. "Such is the *bodhisattvas'* practice." Shala finished the mantra and took deep, calming breaths.

Then she had one moment of perfect awareness: Erisse was unhappy because she felt threatened. She thought Shala and Nizael were going to take Granger and Arzid's place. Shala knew what she must say, now.

She turned, surprised to find the black-haired girl still standing there, still glaring at her. But that just saved Shala the trouble of finding her.

"Erisse, I understand now how proud you are of Sparkellz." Shala made herself meet the other girl's gaze. "She is a beautiful flier, and she is going to be a very strong Queen." Shala found those words easy to say, because they were true. "And now that Granger's Arzid is such a hero, how could anyone else be Queens' Mate? You and Granger, and Sparkellz and Arzid are perfect together. Beautiful and strong."

Erisse looked at her as though she was speaking a foreign language.

Nizael butted Shala's right shoulder with his big head, knocking her sideways, away from Erisse. She glanced over her shoulder at him and shook her head. Not now. Now she needed to return praise in return for Erisse's insults. Erisse needed reassurance. Nizael already knew he was wonderful, and she would tell him so again in a moment.

She felt warmth spread from the center of herself as she thought about what she had said, and what she needed to say to complete it. She felt her face relax, as she became certain of the rightness of her words. "Don't you know Nizael and I have already decided we want to be a solo pair?"

Erisse said nothing for a long moment. The breeze made more noise than girls or dragons did, ruffling through the hay in the dragon yard, and tousling Erisse's long black waves. Erisse brushed her hair back over her shoulder, blue eyes puzzled, but still haughty. "Well, good for you," she said. "I think it's better if you go off by yourselves, away from everyone else," she said, then turned and stalked away.

The other girl had meant that as a sort of insult, Shala suspected, but she smiled anyway. She did not want to take Granger's place.

Through several difficult situations now, she had managed to walk the right path and do the right things. And she had done them without other pack riders. She had done them alone. Well, alone but for the dragons.

Yes, solo was a good plan for them. Shala and Nizael could rely on one another now. Nizael never said anything mean to her, and she would not to him.

Nizael chose that moment to emit a long, long fart. It must have carried on the wind all the way to Erisse over by the barn, because the dark-haired girl waved her arms, trying to flap away the earthy-spice smell.

"They do that," Shala murmured.

Then she laughed and turned back to Nizael, composing rhyming, mantra-like praises of her wonderful dragon who had flown that day.

On the twenty-second day of summer, on an already-hot morning, five dragons arrived in the sky above Two Rivers. Five? Shala knew Kole was returning Oki and picking up his own Palli. And she recognized Mistress Arapunta's dragon, Palandra.

But who were the other three? She squinted against the brightness of sunlight through clouds, to better see the dragons. One was medium-sized, a rather ordinary green, tan and brown ombré. The other was a weird brownish black with dark orange streaks. No, she had not seen that one before. The third was in the sun, she couldn't see it at all.

She moved the bucket aside she had been using to wash dragon feet—they'd all waddled through the mud at the back of the paddock where the cistern had leaked and were plastered with it. When it dried, it practically glued their toes together.

Wyant raked the dried mud clumps out of the nesting area. He set the rake down and stood beside her, watching as Kole landed Oki in the yard alongside Mistress Arapunta. Then the three strangers landed. That fast the paddock area was crammed with full-grown dragons.

Nizael and the others of his pack whuffed through their nostrils and backed up, giving the five newcomers space. And respect, she thought, as she saw dipped noses and angled wings from the younger group.

Arapunta and an older woman both unwrapped their headscarves after dismounting. Kole and two other men stood beside their dragons, also unwrapping their faces.

Sylvan emerged from the office-end of the dorm building, greeted Mistress Arapunta, then turned and called Shala and Wyant over. "Get everyone from your pack out here, and Aimee, too, please."

Shala and Wyant headed for the barns. Most of the others were there no doubt, playing with the dragonets. Kharmin had become less and less protective during the last tenday, as her brood became competent on their own two feet. It was good that the little ones got used to people so they were not frightened when their own riders came to meet them. Besides, they were cute little clumsies, and would do almost anything for kibbles.

Shala found Tarva, Ben, and Aimee in the back of the main barn, clearing the last of the previous winter's hay from the loft. Wyant brought Tomaso, Alu and Tarva out to the paddock from the brooding barn.

Shala could not find either Erisse or Kiny anywhere in the barns or yards. Wasn't this Erisse's day to cook? Maybe Kiny was helping her. She went past the dorm rooms and found them in the dining hall. Erisse was on Kiny's lap, her arms around his shoulders.

Shala cleared her throat. "Mistress Arapunta is outside; we're all to come out to the paddock," Shala called to them from the doorway, and turned around and fled back down the hall before Erisse could say anything.

Wasn't *Granger* supposed to be Erisse's boyfriend now? Shala shook her head. It wasn't any of her business, but it was confusing.

Outside, the younger riders gathered around the older ones.

Mistress Arapunta held up her hands, and all the chatter stopped. "This is Kris, from Cluny in Lynly. He was posted with his pack at Avordan Town. Kris is here to meet Kharmin and see if she will accept him as her new rider." The headmistress looked at Aimee as she said this and seemed satisfied by Aimee's tight smile.

Aimee had known Kris—or someone like him— would be coming; Shala saw her looking at him in speculation. Kris had dark red hair. He wore it long, pulled back in a tail tied with thongs at his neck. Shala couldn't see his eye color from where she stood, but laugh lines crinkled the corners of his eyes and mouth.

Then Arapunta brought forward the other two strangers, an older man and woman. "This is Godfrey and Marta Davidow. They have been riders posted down south in Bouaka for many years. Bouaka just received a new pack from our Farnesse school, and the Davidows will now be in charge of Two Rivers."

In charge of? Shala wondered. I guess Sylvan is going to be sent away somewhere.

169

"Marta is a fabulous cook, in addition to being trained both as a physician and a veterinarian."

The woman stepped forward and smiled, looking everyone in the face in greeting. Her hair was dark and cut short at her ears; she was plump and quite a lot older than Shala had expected.

"And Godfrey came from a farming family before he was a rider, and will manage the crops, herds and dragonets here, as well as working with new riders as needed." Godfrey Davidow took his cap off and waved at the crowd, and his gray and black streaked hair poufed out around his head in wiry waves much the same way Shala's own hair did.

The students applauded this announcement. It would be wonderful to have someone cook their meals on a regular basis instead of trusting to the culinary skills of the student whose turn it was.

"Yay, no more of Shala's burnt biscuits and Tomaso's greasy soup!" Wyant yelled, and they all laughed. Wyant had been as terrible as any of them, which he then acknowledged. "Or my own really swell black beans and rice."

"Eww," someone said, and the others chimed in.

Mistress Arapunta smiled. "A very nice change for Two Rivers, and an easier schedule for the Davidows," she said. Then she waved Kole forward. "Kole, you know, and have had the care of his dragon Palli now for several tendays. He will ride his dragon home now.

"Oki will stay on at Two Rivers as spare dragon, along with Marta's Mamba, and Godfrey's Anemone." She stood back and waved at the dragons to introduce them. Mamba was the black and orange one. Arapunta paused for a breath, and Kole took that opportunity to step forward.

"I want to thank all of you for your help with Palli, and Shala for her rescue of Reedwater and myself and my dragon, who would surely have died if not for this young woman's good sense and dedication to duty." His smile at Shala was warm. Then he stepped back to let Mistress Arapunta speak again.

"The entire Guild appreciates your immense contribution, Shala. For one so young and new to the Guild, you have achieved much."

Shala knew her face was red, she had felt it go hot. What should she say? She had just done her best. Her fellow students applauded her also. When everyone's eyes turned away from her and back to the headmistress, she felt enormous relief.

"That is the other thing I wished to speak with all of you about," Arapunta said. "As dragonriders, our guild has had the responsibility to deliver messages and goods as fast as possible and bring help to those who need it." Her expression was serious. She met each rider's gaze, walking past and around them one at a time as she spoke. "The guild now must also stretch its responsibility to include educating the people we serve."

The sun moved out from behind a cloud, spreading sunbeams down over the group. Arapunta squinted against the glare and then held her hand up as a sunshade.

"You see, most of the other towns of Ben Yent and Lhasa have been inoculated for this disease that hit Reedwater. It is a variant of an old, old illness we brought with us from Earth. Diptheria itself has almost been eradicated, because people have vaccinated against it. This thing that struck you and Reedwater was a variant, but even the oldest form of the vaccine was effective and helped you through."

Shala could not believe the Headmistress's words. The disease could have been prevented? But of course, the vaccine she had taken had prevented her from becoming ill. It might have protected everyone if it had been given in advance.

"Small villages need help; our own schools and students need protection as well. So one of our new jobs is to carry the vaccine to all our postings and ensure our citizens and all riders are protected by a preventative vaccination program. It is going to be combined with several other simple vaccines. The Priestesses at Ysen, the Oracle, the Rangers in the southwest, and our own Guild have joined together to ensure that all the people we can reach are educated and protected.

"We believe Reedwater's remaining citizens will be happy to speak in favor of this plan, if we encounter resistance anywhere." Her eyes met Shala's and softened. "Of Kole's town of over 1200 citizens, only seventy-two are still alive. There may have been just two or three deaths if they had received this vaccination program in advance."

Shala shut her eyes.

It wasn't her fault. It wasn't Nizael's fault, or Bodo's or Palli and Kole's. She knew that, had known it, in her head.

But now she felt she believed it.

"Our thanks to Shala and Kole, who helped us to understand what our duty is," Arapunta said. She reached forward to place a hand on Aimee's shoulder, and the girls' advisor nodded her understanding.

"Sylvan is to be reposted," the headmistress was saying. "As soon as you return from your tenday training flight." She wiped droplets of sweat from her brow, dabbing the ends of her headscarf to her forehead as she looked over the assembly. "Your last dragon has flown," she stopped while the students applauded Nizael. "So everyone will go on this training flight.

"I am told that Sparkellz and Ozala will be your Queens. Your dragons will be choosing Queen's Mates. Sylvan and Aimee, who are most familiar with the way

172

your groups work, will advise you and accompany you on the flight. I expect upon your return you will know how your packs are to be composed, and whether we are to have any solos we can place." She nodded at them. "Good luck."

Shala didn't say anything. She knew there would be at least one solo team to be placed.

Of course, the dragons might have something to say about it, too. She mustn't forget that possibility. She must remember they were a team, and Nizael could be thinking something different than she was. It was still possible he might decide he liked one of the Queens, or they him. Even Sparkellz might be a choice, if Erisse was so inconstant about whom she chose to be with.

She wondered if Erisse cared what Sparkellz wanted at all. But then, who was she to criticize? She had dumped Nizael off the cliff, knowing it was *not* what he wanted.

Some Things You Might Want to Know About Azureign's Plate Tectonics and Volcanism

Recorded history of early human settlements in space is not always accurate. There is strong evidence that when the TerraForm Company began operations to turn the rocky wasteland that was Azureign into a habitable planet for man, they attempted a number of never-before-tried and very massive changes to the planet.

The Company bombarded Azureign with cometary masses for the purpose of increasing the amount of water available on the surface. In addition, other long-term projects included the introduction of terrestrial plants and animals, and soil improvements. The whole project, to be done correctly, should have taken millennia. TerraForm believed they could rush the project, because no human corporation could last for millennia.

Most colonists on Azureign are taught that all the tampering TerraForm did has made their planet unstable. Certainly, tectonic plate movement is fast for a terrestrial type planet. Some geophysical processes now occur about ten times faster than they do on Earth. Whatever the causes, Azureign is a very tectonically active planet.

What this means for the colonists is frequent earthquakes and a high level of volcanism due to subduction, rifting, and a generally hotter, more active mantle. Basalt flood plains spread across vast areas of land, making them uninhabitable. Mountains at the northern end of the super-continent have breached the atmosphere and are still rising.

Specialists predict that the lifetime of Azureign as a planet capable of supporting terrestrial life will be brief (geophysically speaking), perhaps as short a time as a mere 250,000 years. But this prediction is based only on TerraForm's *known* activities, and the 2,000 years of observations and habitation, since. Azureign's life span could be considerably longer, as its colonists obviously hope.

Encyclopedia of the Universe
Earth, 1207, Galactic Era

CHAPTER 13 — Matchmaking

They had the benefit of Marta Davidow's cooking for breakfast the very next morning, with fresh bread, muffins, scalloped potatoes and soft scrambled eggs. Shala stuffed herself, then picked up some fresh-baked trail bars for the trip. There was also a tub of fried chicken, and stir-fried vegetables and noodles for the first night's meal of their journey. Marta must've been up all night!

Outside, Shala saw Sylvan and Kole loading up the packdrones with the assistance of Ben, Kiny and Wyant. On this longer trip, the dragons would supplement their chow by hunting and fishing at the end of each day. Still, there were a lot of supplies to be loaded and carried.

She had two dragons to prepare, for she would ride Oki, and Nizael would follow, riderless. She finished putting the riding harness on Niz and went inside the dorm to get her things. He wouldn't carry her, but he could manage her pack, and some of the food supplies for his first training flight.

The other girls were loading their packs with sleeping bags, blankets, clothing and other necessities for the journey.

Shala made sure she had two changes of clothes, some washing suds and twine for a clothesline. She packed shampoo and other toiletries into a plass bag inside her goat hide satchel. With a mental run-through of her day to be sure she had thought of everything, she closed up her bag.

Sylvan rapped on the frame of the girls' dorm. Alu stuck her head out and Shala heard Sylvan say, "This is for Shala."

"Oh, good," Alu said and backed away from the door, holding a cellu-plass bag full of some rusty brown fabric, which she tossed to Shala.

"Catch!"

Shala caught. "What is it?"

Aimee had been watching them. She smiled. "Kiny said you didn't have a sleeping bag, so now you do!"

"But— how am I to pay for it? I was going to get one later, when I had some money!"

Aimee's face softened from the hard, worried lines it had been set in. "Kole was authorized by the Reedwater survivors to give you a gift in thanks. We chose this—I hope you don't mind. We know you've been cold here."

Shala hugged the bag to her chest. It was light and fluffy. "Will it keep me warm?"

Aimee and Tarva and Alu all reassured her.

"The fluff is like goose down," Alu said. "It's very insulating."

"It will keep you warm even if it gets wet," Tarva said, and Aimee nodded.

"That sounds so nice!"

Aimee handed her one of the school's plass-foam pads. "You'll want this under it, though, to keep you off the ground."

"Thank you! I need to find Kole and thank him before he leaves." She hugged the bag to herself, grabbed her satchel and went outside. The others' grins followed her out. For a wonder, Erisse was silent, not even looking up.

Kole was loading some supplies onto his packdrone. Nearby, Palli came as close to dancing as Shala had ever seen a dragon do. Just like Teek, she thought, and felt a moment's regret that she had had to let the fine horse go. Somewhere, someone had a nice white horse. Alu had assured her that Teek would find the nearest farm with food and be well taken care of. Maybe someday Alu's brothers would find him—but if not, her family considered the horse a donation to the Reedwater—and Alu's—rescue fund.

Shala zig-zagged her way through the mass of dragons and riders in the yard until she reached Kole.

"Thank you for the sleeping bag," she said, holding it up to show him.

He smiled at her. "It was little enough to do for you, after…everything. I thank you for Palli's wing. He flies as if nothing had ever happened to it," he said.

"I'm glad I was able to do it." She rolled her eyes. "We had just learned about the splints and how to set a wing bone a tenday before!"

Kole nodded. "The miller, Danyan's father, led the group in collecting a small gift of coin for you. Dragonriders contributed the rest." He gave her a quick hug, then, "Shala, my crew and I went house to house through Reedwater. We found your note in the Judge's house."

She nodded. "Netke, the oldest daughter, was to marry my brother Jhude."

Kole's expression was odd. "Well, she did, at Year Turn. And her family was at First Oasis visiting, and did not return to Reedwater until a tenday after I got back." He tipped his head. "They were shocked, of course. I gave them their innoculations," he said, holding up a hand when he saw her worried expression, "and they are just fine. They asked me to be sure you knew—they had left two tendays before the first illness appeared in Reedwater, and they and your family and village are all fine."

"Oh," Shala said. "I am so glad for them. But I think we're going to need to bring those vaccines to all the oasis villages; caravans could spread it, if anyone ever came down sick."

Kole nodded. "We are doing all we can around Reedwater. I hope your group will produce a pack for the desert, but that's not up to me." Palli butted Kole from behind, and he staggered, then righted himself with a chuckle. "I think I'm going to be leaving soon! But I wanted to wish you and Nizael good luck. He's a sweetheart."

It was her turn to hug him, then she stepped back and waved goodbye. She turned and walked to her dragons. That was a whole bundle of good news. Shala was happy that Kole did not hold a grudge against Niz. It hadn't been her dragon's fault they couldn't get the medicine to Reedwater sooner, of course, but it was nice that everyone knew that.

She stood a moment to figure out what to pack on whom. Nizael could carry a small pack, at least. He could probably carry me, Shala thought, but Sylvan and Godfrey had thought it best to wait until Niz had flown a longer distance before he took a rider aboard. She added the sleeping bag and a sack of dragon chow alongside her pack on Niz's back. He stretched his neck as far as it would bend to sniff at the chow.

"It's not for you to eat now," she said, tying everything down. Then she fastened her own food satchel and bota onto Oki, along with a second small sack of chow.

Kris stood across the paddock by the vegetable garden, watching the commotion as everyone loaded up. He would be staying at Two Rivers, to get to know Kharmin and see if she would accept him as her new rider. It was getting to be time for her to leave the dragonets, and soon there would be a new batch of riders-in-training at the school.

By midmorning, at last, the pack was on its way, flying north up the Yent River. Their eventual goal was the town of Oaks, near the source of the Yent.

The first night they camped in a lush, narrow glen. A branch of the Yent flowed around the edge of the site on the east side and a small tributary creek curved around on the southwest. Shala had never seen so many ferns and green shrubs. A huge weeping tree spread its fronds down over a clearing, making a tentlike covering above the area they would sleep in. When they told her it was a willow, she thought they were teasing.

"It's a different variety," Sylvan said, after agreeing with Alu and Kiny. "It's called a weeping willow, and they love water."

"They're like cousins to the desert scrub willow, then?"

"Yup," Sylvan said.

"Huh. Everything smells green," Shala said. "It's like the exact opposite of desert."

Indeed, there was a depth of freshness and moisture she was quite unfamiliar with. The dragons seemed to enjoy it, rolling in the soft grasses out in the open meadow and taste-sampling bracken and various leaves. Shala was astonished to see water seep out from between rocks to form a spring that ran down the western slope of the rocky hillside to join the little nameless creek.

"Fern Creek," it should be, Alu said, and Shala agreed.

"Chicken, Shala?" Kiny offered.

"No thanks," she said, and passed it on to Ben who looked up with hungry eyes.

"Shala doesn't eat meat," Alu said.

The others seemed startled at this announcement. "Huh," Kiny said. "I never noticed!"

"I could never be a vegetarian," Ben said, helping himself to three more pieces of fried chicken.

They all looked at the pile of chicken on his plate and burst out laughing.

"Guess not, Ben," Wyant said. "Maybe you want a posting on a big ranch somewhere!"

"What do you do when it's like, beef stew for dinner?" Aimee wondered, looking at Shala.

Shala met the older woman's gaze. "For awhile I tried to eat it," she said. "I wasn't so serious about Buddhist teachings, or trying to follow the proper diet, when I first left home. But I found I just do not enjoy meat. And I don't digest it well. So now I eat nuts, and a lot of bread, with peanut butter, or cheese."

"You're a Buddhist?" Erisse said.

"That's what training I've had," Shala said. "I'm trying to apply what I've learned to my life."

"Huh. Buddhist," Tarva said around a mouthful of chicken. "Is that what the desert tribes are? Oh, but you're a caravanner."

Shala shrugged. "I left the caravans when I was eleven, so I don't know. But my middle foster brother wants to be a Mahayana monk, and he taught me a lot."

"The cheese-maker?" Tarva wondered.

"No, that's Jhude. Logyn is not good with *making* cheese, but he's very good at *using* it. He's a great baker; his cheese bread is fabulous."

"*This* bread ought to measure up to your best bakery standards," Wyant said, breaking a big chunk off the last crusty loaf.

"It's very good," Shala agreed.

"I'm surprised you consider yourself a Buddhist," Erisse said. "I mean, you've been letting creatures die, showing no reverence for life whatsoever."

Several of the others groaned. Wyant shook his head, and even Granger made a face at Erisse's comment.

Erisse looked around at them all with a smirk on her face. "Oh, you don't agree? Well, I should think Alu would, with her fine horse lost, and no doubt starved to death somewhere. The school's mules are gone. And Aimee would agree with me, with Dene lying cold in the ground—"

Aimee jumped to her feet at this, stomping across the campsite to Erisse. Before anyone could imagine what was going to happen, Aimee drew back her hand and smacked Erisse across the cheek with the flat of her palm.

"Do not presume to tell me what I would agree with, you spiteful wretch!" she shouted. "I've had enough from you!"

Without a word, Erisse tossed her plate full of food straight into Aimee's face, got up and stalked away into the dark.

By this time Sylvan and several of the other students were on their feet. Alu helped Aimee wipe food from her face and jacket enough that Aimee could take the noodle-plastered denim off. Shala took it from her and went out from beneath the tree to shake the rest of the noodles off.

The tough cotton could be washed in hot water, she judged. Only hot water was going to get the grease stains out. She returned to the campfire to get the kettle and fill it.

Alu's voice was loud enough for the whole group to hear, though she seemed to be addressing Aimee. "She was the one who sweet-talked Dene into going into Reedwater. I would think she had enough sense to shut up about him."

Oh, it's guilt, Shala thought. That's what's bothering Erisse.

She knew the feeling, having suffered from it herself.

But she also knew that someone else telling Erisse she wasn't to blame wasn't going to help.

"It's an inside job," Shala murmured, remembering one of Logyn's favorite lessons. "You have to believe things your own self, in your own way; no one else can make you."

She nodded in agreement with Logyn, and was startled by a sudden attack of homesickness. She had not realized how much she missed them: quiet, meditative Logyn; bossy, tough Jhude; and always energetic Jono. And Andrya, with her calm efficiency.

The companionship of the dragon pack was not yet a substitute for her family. Could it ever be?

But no. Shala had decided to be a solo rider. It was not even something she should be considering— how to fit into the group.

She finished with Aimee's jacket and hung it on a branch to dry. Aimee was just putting on Sylvan's soft suede coat when Shala went back to her place by the fire, and her last bites of dinner. No one felt much like eating after that.

They cleaned up the dishes and spread sleeping bags around the fire. Ben pulled out his little hand-loom, and several of them watched him weave, almost hypnotized by the smooth, regular motions of his hands passing the shuttle back and forth. He made little purses, stitching the fabric together into a pouch with an overhand blanket stitch, once he had woven a long enough piece. He'd given a couple of them as gifts at Year Turn Day, and they seemed both strong and pretty to Shala, who had vowed to buy one from him if she ever had any coins.

Alu brushed Tarva's long brown hair and braided it. Tarva's eyes were sleepy, staring into the fire as Alu worked. Shala wrote down the name of the weeping willow and sketched it in the small notebook Sylvan had given her, "For your plant identification project," he'd said, with a grin. She finished her sketch, then wrapped the piece of leather-like cellu-plass back around it and tied the string.

Erisse still hadn't come back by the time they crawled in their bags to sleep.

"I think she's out by the dragons," Shala told Sylvan. "Should we go get her?"

"No," he said. "We need to separate these Queens. That's the thing that's going to help."

A horrendous shriek rent their sleep. Shala sat bolt upright, and knew it was not a nightmare when she saw other shadowy forms sitting up in the pale pre-dawn light. Then the shriek came again.

"Dragons," Shala murmured. With very great reluctance, she got out of her warm bag into the chill air.

Sylvan was already out from under the tree, heading into the meadow where the dragons had nested for the night. By the brightening dawn glow in the sky and the pale light of the rings, they could see Ozala and Sparkellz. The Queens faced each other with wings spread and heads held high on stiff necks. The other dragons had cleared out and formed a sort of ring around the two.

Ozala shrieked and darted at Sparkellz, thrusting her snout beneath the leading edge of Sparkellz' left wing, trying to tip her. But Sparkellz pushed her wing down, pressing Ozala's snout toward the ground, and battered at the smaller dragon with her big gold head. Ozala raised a foot and struck at Sparkellz with her heel claw. She missed hitting the golden dragon in the face but scraped the claw down Sparkellz' leg.

Sylvan yelled at the dragons, waving his arms, and Erisse and Alu ran out, calling their dragons to stop—not that anything the humans said could be heard over the squealing shrieks of the dragons. The other non-combatant dragons had joined in the fight by squalling and roaring themselves. Almost as if they're shouting encouragement, Shala thought.

Ozala had managed to scrape Sparkellz' leg without cutting it; Shala could see the mark down the scales even in the dim morning light, but no blood welled up from between the overlapped scales. Sparkellz arched her neck and swung her tail around, trying to knock Ozala off her feet. The littler pearl dragon leaped up out of the way and came down on top of the long golden tail. She gripped it in her claws and squeezed. Sparkellz squalled and thrashed, trying to free her tail.

Sylvan whistled the call-down signal, but Sparkellz spread her wings with a whump, and knocked him down. She didn't even notice she had done so, she was so focused on reaching Ozala. Sylvan rolled out of her way and she hop-stepped toward Ozala, buffeting her with the big gold wings, tail curving tight behind her.

Sylvan got to his feet and waved Alu and Kiny and Erisse back. There was nothing the riders could do to stop this; they'd be injured among the huge angry animals.

But their helplessness ended when a big olive green shoulder thrust between the two Queens.

Nizael! Shala thought.

Niz broke up the fight by the simple method of stepping in between the two shrieking females. He was too big to reach around, though Ozala tried, pushing her snout toward one side of his body, and then the other. Nizael opened his wings with a loud rustle-whump! and the Queens could no longer even see each other.

Ozala sat her rump down and whuffed at Nizael. No one could see what Sparkellz was doing, but Ozala turned and at last answered Alu's calls, walking over to her rider and snuffling air through her nostrils as she bumped Alu's chest with the end of her nose. Nizael folded his wings, looking over his shoulder at Sparkellz.

Without an enemy in her face, the big gold Queen had calmed down. Erisse—rather bravely, Shala thought—made her way past Nizael and to her dragon. She stroked the long golden head, murmuring to the Queen.

"All right," Sylvan called. "We're separating *now!*" He turned in a circle as he yelled names, making sure they each heard him and acknowledged: "Wyant, Tomaso, Ben, Shala and Alu, pack up!" Some of them still only half-awake, the students stood in camp a moment or two before they began following instructions.

Sylvan went out to Sparkellz and examined her foot. He stayed, talking with the Queen's rider for some moments. Erisse nodded, and Sylvan walked back under the tree.

He moved up next to Aimee, and they conversed out of hearing range, Aimee gesturing as she spoke. Shala finished rolling her sleeping gear up and tied her bedroll, watching them out of the corner of her eye. Then Sylvan turned to the riders.

"I will fly out with Ozala's group now; we will wash up and break our fast later," Sylvan called. "Aimee's group will fly out as soon as you've eaten. You will stay just to the west side of the Oak River. My group will stay to the east of the Oak, out of sight of the other Queen."

Visualizing the map in her head, Shala put her bedroll and the sack of remaining dragon kibbles on Nizael's back. He nosed the sack as she lifted it onto him. She grabbed a handful of kibbles and gave him and Oki some to munch as they others got ready, then tied the sack shut tightly.

The group she was in, Ozala's pack, would stay in the triangular area between the confluence of the Oak and Yent Rivers, while Sparkellz' pack was across the Oak, closer to the foothills of the Queensland Mountains. Was just a river's width going to be enough distance between them? She had to believe Sylvan knew what he was doing.

Shala finished tying the bags onto Niz's back. "Good job, fella," she told him, rubbing his brow ridges as he swallowed the last of his kibble snack. "I'm glad you knew what to do to stop those two idiots." He whuffed and tilted his head so she could reach the other brow better. He spread his toes as she rubbed.

"Mount up!" Sylvan called, and they did so. Six riders and seven dragons moved away from the bowl-shaped grassy area one by one and took off. Sylvan left the ground last, leading one of the two packdrones. As Oki circled, gaining altitude, Shala looked back down to the little glen. Aimee stood looking up, watching them leave.

I'll bet she wishes Sylvan went with Erisse, Shala thought. Why had the two split the group up the way they had?

Of course the Queens must be separated. But it seemed like some of the males should be split up as well, or they were going to have more dragon fights. Shala thought maybe there should be *three* groups, not just two. Of course, they only had two adult leaders, so that option was not available just now.

They flew north and a bit east, the light of the rising sun seeping above the horizon, shining into the right sides of their eyes. Shala looked down and gasped.

The ground below had become a glorious fairyland. The sunlight gleamed on dewdrops across the tops of the wild grasses below them. It looked as if each strand of grass had been tipped with golden fire, a blade-thin candle.

The fields are burning with water. How strange, she thought, *how beautiful.*

Overhead, the sunlight tinted the atmosphere yellow; the rings seemed to glow as though lit by a million candles of their own.

It was well past sunup before Sylvan found a place he liked for breakfast and landed. Simba cleared the flatter landing area, running out into the tall grass, which was long enough to brush the tops of his wings. Alu, Tomaso, and Wyant followed to land one at a time. Shala held Oki back in case Nizael wanted to land next.

She stared down at the landing site. The clearing seemed to be growing rocks. The bare, stony ground had a few scattered clumps of stubby brown grass, a different kind than the towering green blades that Simba had disappeared into. The soil in the open area looked quite dry, which surprised her, as the field was edged by the Yent, only a few meters away.

She signalled Nizael to go ahead and land before Oki dropped down into the rocky meadow, but Niz seemed to want to circle. Her scarf had slipped from her mouth, and she breathed in dusty air. It smelled like smoke. Was something burning? She glanced back up at Nizael.

Maybe that's why he's not landing. He's hunting for fire. Or food.

Whatever he was doing, he wasn't ready to land, so she signalled Oki to go down. Oki landed with his usual aplomb, and she dismounted, patting the sage-green back. "You're a good color for around here," she told him. "You look like a blob of grass and lichen." Oki did not seem impressed by this, though he whuffed in answer to her voice. She borrowed a handful of kibbles, since her remaining supply was still in the air with Nizael, and offered them to Oki. He ate them up as she moved toward the other riders.

"Shall we make a fire?" Tomaso asked.

"Just use the stove for tea, and let's be on our way again," Sylvan instructed.

Shala and Tomaso took the teapot and a bucket down to the river for water. Wyant and Alu, thinking with their stomachs, were already chewing trail bars by the time she and Tomaso got back with the water. Still chewing, Wyant unpacked and set up the stove, then set the teapot on to boil.

Wyant and Tomaso seated themselves on the ground and Alu on a rock near Sylvan. All had taken trail bars or fruit from their packs and were eating. Shala leaned against another rock, opening her sack of nuts.

"Just so you know," Sylvan said, "Aimee asked me to let her stay with that group today. We will be switching off tomorrow morning, after I decide whether this group works or not." Sylvan glanced up at the sky, where Niz was still circling. He turned to Shala. "Did you tell him to keep watch?"

She shook her head. "I thought maybe he was hunting."

They all looked up at the big green dragon. He tipped a wing and enlarged his circle to include a pass over the Yent.

"I thought I smelled smoke," she said. "Maybe he's looking for that."

Sylvan took a deep breath, and both Wyant and Tomaso sniffed the air in the same way. They reminded Shala of fala birds in the village, the mother leading the chicks in a little line, noses up. The older man shook his head. He stood looking to the west a while, where they could see a pile of clouds stacked up over the Queensland Range. He shrugged. "I don't know about smoke, but I do think we may have a storm before the day is over," he said.

Wyant turned off the little lightweight stove. "Water's hot," he announced.

Shala decided against tea. She found a place in the deep grass and went to the bathroom. Who knew how long they'd be up in the sky before the next opportunity presented?

She then went back over to the riverbank to watch her dragon as he dropped lower and lower, still circling.

Nizael flew upstream, now very close to the river surface, skimming the wide, slow-moving water with his toes. He abruptly lost altitude, dipped his legs into the water all the way to his belly, and she gulped, thinking he was going to stall out and crash in the water. But he stroked down with his strong wings, pulling himself back up again. A wriggling fish squirmed in each big green foot as his legs emerged from the water.

He pumped his wings, rose up and circled back toward the landing area. Shala headed back toward their impromptu campsite, watching as Nizael flew over the group of dragons. He didn't land, but dropped the fish, then circled back to the river.

Simba saw the fish and took off to follow Nizael, abandoning the pile of kibbles Sylvan had given him. The packdrone, still chewing the last of his own pile, stepped over to Simba's kibbles, happy to have them all. Sylvan was watching the dragons as Shala came back up to the group. Ozala had one fish to herself. Tanzi and Denez were sharing the other, though Denez tried to steal the whole thing, and Tanzi squawked his opinion of this.

"You could go catch your own, smokey-boy," Wyant told Tomaso's dragon.

It looked like Tanzi decided this was a good idea, for the charcoal and black dragon left the remainder of the fish scraps to Denez, and ran along the ground, taking flight just as Nizael returned with another pair of fish. Lizard also was busy fishing, but when he landed, he didn't share his catch.

"Does Niz think it's his job to fish for everybody?" Wyant wondered, mumbling around a mouthful of trail bar.

"I wonder," Shala said, noticing that this time Nizael dropped one fish very near to Denez, then another in front of himself as he landed. Niz took a bite of his own fish that made half the flopping silvery thing disappear all at once. "Eww, fishbones," she said. They didn't seem to bother the dragons, but Shala remembered getting one stuck in her throat. She'd never liked fish much before that, but afterward she'd rather go hungry than eat one.

Over their heads, they heard an eagle *scree* on the wind.

"Hah. He wants their fish!" Ben said, watching the golden-feathered bird circle above the dragons.

"Probably thinks they're all *his!*" Tomaso said.

"I hope he doesn't attack the dragons; it won't go well for him," Sylvan said.

Alu was watching the fishing dragons, too. "I guess the water doesn't hurt their bellows," she said, a dubious tone in her voice.

Sylvan sipped his tea. "They can push it out, pumping their wings and forcing air—and water—out of the bellows to clear them." He lifted his teacup, indicating the dragons. "They don't seem to be getting very wet today, though."

"Just their feet," Wyant said.

Sure enough, Nizael and the other fishers had wet, muddy feet. And fish guts on themselves, no doubt. They're just going to have to stay that way, Shala decided. She wasn't going to wash them off. It was a camping trip, after all.

Nizael finished his fish and took off to go get more, just as Tanzi landed, dropping several fish before setting his feet down. The gray dragon shared one with Ozala and ate another himself. Denez eyed the third flopping fish, reached her nose in that general direction, but stopped when Tanzi emitted what sounded very much like a growl. Denez prudently retreated.

Soon Nizael returned with another flopping pair of fish, and again ate one and left one beside Denez, which she ate, smacking her narrow dragon lips.

"Hmm," Sylvan said, sipping his tea.

CHAPTER 14 — Ash

They passed over grasslands and areas with copses of oak trees that afternoon. In one spot, a swath of shiny red flowers lit the low hills with a brilliant glow. Shala wondered what kind of flowers they were, even as she enjoyed their bright beauty. Poppies, maybe?

Early in the evening, they crossed the Oak River, just west of its confluence with the Yent, and camped on a grassy flat plain between the two rivers. About a million mosquitoes camped there with them.

"Really," Wyant complained, "you wonder why the Rules of Settlement had to include mosquitoes."

"Part of the ecosystem," Sylvan said. "Fish food." Then he made a face, swatting at the swarm around his head. "Or the part designed to eat people. Put some green branches on the fire," he told Tomaso and Alu. "The smoke helps keep the bugs away."

"Oh. I guess I'd better go get some," Tomaso said. "I was looking for dry wood." He walked out to the dragon's area and got back aboard Tanzi. The charcoal dragon ran along the ground then took to the air.

The other dragons were fishing again. All of them seemed to have the hang of it now, Ozala dainty in the water and on the ground, the others splashing without restraint. The packdrone looked at them like they were insane. *Which to its point of view, I guess they are,* Shala thought. *Why work when you have nice kibbles?*

"They sure seem to like the fish," she said aloud.

Sylvan grunted agreement, then turned to Wyant, Alu and Shala. "Here's what I'm thinking," he said. "Tomorrow, we'll fly along the Oak River until we're west and just a little north of Oaks town. There's a good campsite there. Then I'm going to take Lizard and Denez with me to Sparkellz' pack, and maybe Nizael, too." He rubbed his forehead, avoiding Shala's gaze.

Each time she almost met his eyes, his veered away. "I'll send Aimee back here with Sharz, and maybe Zinno, too. We'll see how that works for a day or so, then we should be able go home in our two or maybe three new groups."

None of the three students said anything. Shala looked at Alu and Wyant, noting their carefully blank faces. Sylvan looked also but seemed to misinterpret their silence.

"The town of Oaks is about another 200 kilometers northeast, up the Yent," he said. "The little lake that's the source of the Oak, where Aimee is planning to camp, is about 100 kilometers west of where we'll set up. So, you know where you are."

Wyant swatted at a mosquito on the side of his face, then rubbed the underside of his jaw. "What if we can't stand Erisse?" he wondered aloud. "Do we still have to go try to join her group?" He took a bite of something he held in his hand, probably another trail bar. He chewed, eyes distant.

"Are you going to send your dragon without you?" Sylvan asked. "She deserves the chance to see if she likes Sparkellz better than Ozala."

"What if—" The enormity of her suggestion ran aground on her common sense, and Shala bit her lip. Maybe she'd better let Sylvan and Aimee do their jobs.

"What if *what*, Shala?" Sylvan asked.

"Um. It's just that— Could Denez be a Queen?"

He met her eyes, silent.

She swept her headscarf off and tangled her fingers in her hair, rubbing her scalp. "I mean, she's bigger than Ozala, and she's becoming pretty aggressive sometimes..." She let her voice fade when she saw Sylvan's expression. The stablemaster was scowling, now.

Wyant swallowed whatever he was chewing and cleared his throat. "I've wondered the same thing," he said. "I mean, maybe it just means Denez and I should be a solo team, but she doesn't seem all that fond of either of the Queens. Maybe because she doesn't want anyone else Queening it over her?"

"We are considering your dragon for a solo posting, Wyant. But it seemed as though the human half of your team would like company."

Shala noticed Wyant's weird sidewise glance at her, then up at Tomaso and Tanzi, who were coming in for a landing. "I like *some* company," Wyant said. "But there's no way I will set myself up to be in the same room as Erisse, much less the same pack. She's poison."

Shala looked at the ground, hoping no one could see her expression. Poison was a good word for Erisse. But she did still hope the black-haired young woman's distemper would improve once the packs were chosen. Erisse was going to have to deal with her guilt over Dene, but that wasn't going to happen while she was distracted by a fighting Queen, who wanted pack hierarchy settled *now*.

As did the people, of course. Pack composition was the whole point of the training flight, after all.

Ben raised his hand. "I don't mind Erisse. And Lizard seems to prefer Sparkellz—it's just that Lizard and Arzid aren't getting along.

Sylvan nodded. "Well, I want you to join the other pack today and see how it goes. You might all like to know," he said, "that we think there may indeed be three packs amongst you. We see either a pack with Denez as Queen, or maybe a loose affiliation of solo teams, perhaps including me and Simba." He turned and waved a hand out at the dragons. "Of course, a big part of the decision depends upon what *they* want, which we're still sorting out."

Tomaso arrived and threw a great armload of green leafy branches on the fire, which emitted roiling black smoke. They wiped their running eyes, and Sylvan set onto the fire the pot of beans they'd soaked all day in the packdrone's pannier-like sack.

Shala slapped a mosquito that had found her forearm tasty and thought about how Nizael had brought Denez a fish. He hadn't brought one to either Sparkellz or Ozala. Weren't the dragons supposed to pick the strongest females to be Queens? Shala wasn't sure Denez fit that category. She sighed with frustration. Maybe she was reading too much into it, and, anyhow, it wasn't her job.

All thoughts of dragon and rider arrangements flew from their heads with the arrival of a flock of bats. The little mammals zipped and jerked as they scooped up the mosquitoes that had gathered around the group, along with some moths that had been drawn to the firelight.

Shala had never seen bats flying before, and never a huge flock like this. Some of the dragons were startled by the darting bats. Heads up, nostrils flaring, eyes rolling—including Nizael's. Shala trotted out to join her dragon in the nesting area the dragons had set up.

"Look, Niz. A gazillion little yous." She rubbed her dragon's nose as they gazed at the swarming bats, which moved off to the east little by little as they cleared the area of flying insects. She could hear Wyant's laughter over by the fire. Accepting the bats, the dragons went back to snoozing or grooming. She gave Niz a final pat and rejoined the other riders.

"That helped a lot with the mosquitoes," Alu said, satisfaction in her voice.

"Natural bug control," Ben said, "another part of the ecosystem!"

"The good part!" Alu and Wyant said at the same time. Wyant coughed and choked with laughter, and Shala went over and thumped his back.

"Thanks! I think I inhaled the last mosquito!"

"Gosh, Wyant," Shala said, daring a joke, "I know you'll eat anything, but that's ridiculous!"

He peered at her, as though to be sure what the expression was on her face, then grinned. "The bats like them! Why not?"

The others laughed and made mock of Wyant's "good taste."

It was nice with Alu and Tomaso and Wyant, Shala thought. And Sylvan.

And no sneak-attacks from Erisse.

Out in the dragons' area, she could see Nizael was using his teeth to clean and straighten the hairs of Simba's mane. He ignored Denez.

What did that mean?

Then, once again, the dragons made up their own minds before Sylvan carried out his human plans. Shala just caught the motion with the edge of her vision as Lizard lunged at Nizael. She turned in time to see them hiss at each other. Niz opened his wings, and Lizard humped up, hopping backwards in tiny little jumps, then he opened his own wings with a whump, and *scree'd*, sounding just like the eagle.

"Hai! Nizael!" Shala called, and Ben whistled. For a wonder, Lizard listened to that signal, and turned away from Shala's dragon; Lizard didn't fold his wings, though.

"Ah, I think we're leaving now," Ben said, grabbing up his pack and heading for his dragon.

"Do you know where you're going?" Sylvan called as Ben jumped onto Lizard's back.

"I think so. I'm pretty sure Lizard, does. He was looking west all afternoon as we flew!" Lizard went into the air with no preliminaries, and Ben lurched, then grabbed a handful of ruff hair and harness straps. "Bye!"

"Wow," Alu said. "Are the packs always this edgy?"

"We don't often have so many big males," Sylvan said. "Nor three females with Queen possibilities." He tilted his head and looked thoughtful. "It will be interesting to see if Jana's next clutch of eggs produces so many leaders. It might be a powerful bloodline to try and keep strong."

"Well, drat it," Alu said. "I like Ben and was hoping this would work."

Wyant and Tomaso nodded, but Shala could see from Tomaso's expression that the quiet young man was relieved to have Ben—and big Lizard—gone and apparently out of the running for Ozala's Queen's Mate. She kept an eye on the dragon area, praying Nizael would not squabble with anyone else tonight. There had been quite enough dragon excitement for one day.

She again caught a whiff of the smoke scent she had smelled earlier. She had dismissed it as probably the other group's campfire, but this was different. More like burning rocks than burning wood. And with the edge of something chemical, a little like Jhude's tanning baths for leather.

She looked around, but no one else seemed bothered.

They shared quiet conversations sitting around the campfire and cooked their beans. Alu chopped the last of the wild onions Shala had found and stirred them into the beans.

Wyant conversed with Tomaso, then turned to the rest of them. "I asked Tomo if he would lead us in a tai chi session," he said. "So, if you would like to join us, you are welcome."

Alu leaped to her feet. "Yes!"

Shala got up, too. She would like to learn what she had seen Tomaso do. He'd said at one point that it was also a meditation technique, and she thought she would find that useful.

198

Wyant used some of the green branches from the pile as a broom, smoothing the dirt and kicking away loose rocks.

Even Sylvan got up and kicked off his boots.

They spent a pleasant hour stretching, kicking, and trying to copy Tomaso's smooth moves. He ended with a little bow, and they all bowed back to him in thanks.

Wyant looked relaxed and sleepy. He waved goodnight, ducking into the tent. The others sat down in a relaxed group by the fire again. Sylvan picked up a broken harness and was repairing a strap. Shala worked by firelight on her plant drawings, filling in some of the color information. Tomaso sat next to Alu, who was fooling with her hair. Then the blonde girl snapped her headscarf out, an irritated expression on her face as she smoothed the scarf flat across her thigh.

"Shala, would you show me again how to do those foldy things with your scarf, please?" she asked. "I can't seem to get it wrapped like you do, so it stays put."

"Um, okay," Shala said, reaching for the small yellow piece of silk Alu held out. She laid it on her lap and smoothed it out with her palms, trying to stretch it bigger.

"Is that okay? I mean, I don't want to mock your customs because I'm ignorant of what they mean, or something," the other girl said, an anxious tone in her voice. "You'd tell me if this insulted you, wouldn't you?"

"Insulted? No, no, it's just—"

"What?"

"Well, it would be better if this were made of cotton or linen. The silk tends to slip loose," she explained. "And if it was a bit bigger, I think it would be easier to tie securely," she said, remembering her problems with Erisse's blue silk scarf she had borrowed.

"Maybe that's why I'm having trouble, then," Alu said. "I think I have a piece of cotton in my bag, just a minute." Alu took back the little yellow scarf, got up and went to her pile of belongings.

Shala took a deep breath of the damp, smoky air. The beans were beginning to smell good, and she caught no scent of the weird smoke that had bothered her earlier.

Alu was on her way back with a piece of gauzy orange cotton, when she seemed to stagger.

Shala felt the earth quiver, then roll. A deep groaning rumble shook the ground beneath them. *Oh, it's an earthquake*, she thought.

She wasn't as terrified of them as she used to be, when her family's ending and burial was still fresh in her mind. She still couldn't say she felt comfortable with quakes, particularly the ones around rocks and canyons. This was flat grassland, though, the ground rolling beneath them, but no boulders crashing down.

The dragons lumbered to their feet, and one of them *whree'd* in alarm. Shala saw the pot of beans shake loose from its grate and start to slide into the fire. She got up and rescued the pot with a long branch lying among the firewood. She poked and pushed it back into a secure position on the grate, and by then the quake was over.

Sylvan was scowling as he looked off to the west. The storm clouds they had seen over the mountains had rolled out across the plains toward them. "It's going to be a wet night," Sylvan said. "Let's get our gear inside before we're drenched."

Deep red lightning shot through the clouds, and the thunder rumbled like the earthquake had moments earlier. It felt like Azureign was attacking them.

"That's really close," Tomaso said, counting the seconds between the flash and the arrival of the thunder's roar.

"Poor Ben," Alu said. "He'll be wet before he gets there."

They ran to the pile of gear beside the tent and tossed stuff inside. Wyant yelped as they dumped things on top of him, then came to the doorway to help. They did manage to get their belongings inside before the storm broke, but not by much.

They ended up eating their dinner inside, crowded together in the tent with bowls of steaming beans on the floor or in laps insulated with spare clothes. They stacked their dirty dishes outside the door and crawled into sleeping bags with the sound of rain lulling them to sleep.

The next morning, Shala was awakened by a whuffing sound near her ear. She sat up in her sleeping bag and found a big green snout just centimeters from her face.

"Ahh!" she cried, startled for a moment. "Niz, what are you doing in the tent?"

He had his entire head and most of his long neck thrust through the door opening in the cellu-plass. The flap that made the door hung from his neck looking comical. Beside and behind her, Shala could hear snorts of laughter as Alu and Wyant and Tomaso saw the dragon-in-the-tent.

Outside, they could hear Sylvan laughing, too. It must look pretty funny from out there: a big green dragon butt sitting in the campsite, wearing a tent for a hat.

Nizael yawned, spreading stinky fish breath inside the tent, which seemed to transform itself into a much smaller tent than it had been a few minutes before.

201

"Eww!"

"Oh, Nizael!"

"Oh my gosh, get him out of here, Shala!"

She tried to, pushing Niz's head toward the tent flap. Startled, he jerked back, caught his little pointed ears and then his brow ridge on the door opening, and the whole tent lifted and shook. At that, Alu and Tomaso started laughing and couldn't stop, with the sort of contagious whoops that soon had Wyant and Shala rolling on the floor as well.

As though their laughter had offended him, Nizael then withdrew his head from the tent. They could see his shadow ripple across the canvas as he lumbered away, and somehow that was funny, too.

At last the giggles died down to an occasional hiccup as the four of them got out of their sleeping bags and started packing things up. Shala could smell the spicy tea Sylvan liked, and thought she detected bubbling oatmeal, as well. Sylvan had let them sleep in and made breakfast while they snoozed.

Wyant threw back the tent flap and the sun glared in. Shala stepped out of the tent, expecting a clear sunny day, but it wasn't. The sky overhead was still dark with clouds, and the rising sun just slanted in beneath them from the east. The sunshine was sideways. It looked very strange.

Puddles lay all over the ground of their campsite where the soil was hard, and slippery mud pots lurked in between. She wished she had brought her boots, as the first step she took squished mud over the sole of her sandals and in between her toes. At least the mosquitoes were gone—but now they had mud instead.

Shala shook her head. It was summer. She hadn't expected rain.

When she mentioned that later to Sylvan, as they struggled to fold and pack the almost-dry cellu-plass tent, he just grinned at her. "You're not in the desert, now. Grasslands often have rain in summer."

"Also lightning-lit grass fires," Alu said. "We have that problem every year: rain, fire, rain, fire."

"Is Ziza in the grasslands, then?" Shala wondered. "I thought it was on the northern edge of the desert." She remembered the map; Ziza was almost due west of her aunt's oasis village. It was at the delta of the Oracle River, where the water just flowed into dry land, vanishing in the desert. "The river that goes nowhere," people called it. Some thought the saying was aimed at their alien "overlords," whose tendency to do nothing mimicked the river. It (and they) started off well, but then dwindled into nothing.

"It's all grassland and swamp down to the rim of the White Rift Valley," Alu explained. "Our ranch is to the northeast of Ziza, where an arm of the Oracle River delta turns into swamp. It's pretty, though: all green in spring and golden in summer, and brown with herds of horses, antelope and cattle."

Shala had imagined the river soaking into dry desert sands, not grass and swamp. "I'd like to see that some time," she said.

She felt a pang, realizing she missed the heat and arid wildness of the desert. She even missed the stupid palm trees that gave what seemed like a scant centimeter of shade on the stony sand.

"It looks like we're going to get more storm," Sylvan said looking up at the sky. It was darker, and they heard the rumble of distant thunder.

"Should we be flying, if there's lightning?" Wyant asked.

"I don't like to," Sylvan said, "but we can't stay here. The river is already high. If it rains any more, this whole area will flood." He looked to the west and then the north. "I think the clouds are still high enough we can risk it. Just don't let your dragons get too far from the ground. If there's a lightning surge, we can drop below the trees."

They packed up and left, flying north as fast as the packdrone could go. To the west, the clouds were very low and dark. Shala thought of Aimee's group, hoping they had found a dry place to set up camp before the skies let loose the previous night.

The storm subsided before they arrived at the site Sylvan had been aiming for late that afternoon. They were now on the north side of the Oak River, which had curved around and ran almost due west, or, Shala realized, its *origin* was in the west, so the water in fact ran straight out east from the Queensland Mountains before turning south and joining with the Yent waters.

They had suffered no more rain, surprising them, and had not seen any lightning though they heard the boom of thunder from off to the west several times.

Shala smelled the rock-smoke again, and shook her head, unable to free her nose from the scent, and unable to determine where it came from.

Their new campsite was in a pretty meadow surrounded by huge granite outcroppings, some oak trees and a handful of the weeping willow trees, and some stiffer-trunked white-barked trees whose small oval leaves fluttered in the wind. Thinking of the recent earthquake and granite boulders, Shala inspected the rock outcrops, but there were no loose boulders here, nor was the area at the bottom of a steep-sided valley. They should be safe from rockfalls.

The group got their camp organized and the tent set up early enough that Wyant and Tomaso decided to try their own hands at fishing for dinner. Alu joined them on the riverbank, though she announced she wasn't going to be participating, just watching.

The dragons were doing a great job of getting their own dinner, so Sylvan again gave the packdrone extra kibbles. It showed no interest in the dragons' fish whatsoever, happily crunching its chow while the dragons feasted on fish after fish.

Shala investigated the plants at the creek side, looking for several herbs Embry had shown her the few times they had gone collecting together. The old woman had described plants that grew better where there was more water, but Shala had never seen them. She knew there had to be something here good to eat. She just couldn't figure out what.

Sylvan saw her prowling around the shrubs and grasses and walked over to where she was examining a tall velvety-leafed plant. "Keep an eye out for nettles," he said. "They like the moist soil along creek banks."

"Nettles?"

"Ah, here's one," Sylvan said, and waved her over. "Don't touch. This fuzz on the stems is very irritating if you get it on your skin," he said. "Though the leaves make a nice addition to tea."

"I was hoping for something to put in a pot of soup," she said.

"You have no faith in our skills?" Wyant called in a teasing tone. "Maybe Niz will share some of his fish— oh."

"It's okay, Wyant. In fact, many vegetarians will eat fish. Even Logyn would sometimes, it was such a treat when someone brought some in from the Sea or down from Lhasa Lake," she said. "But I do not like them."

"You don't know what you're missing," Alu put in. "Fresh pan-fried trout. Yum!"

Shala laughed and shook her head. "Not for me!" She looked around at all the different green leaves, twigs, blades, and bark. "Everything's different from what we had at home, and yet again from what I learned about at Two Rivers. I'm sure some of these are tasty!" She muttered. "But which?"

Sylvan pulled his pocket knife out and pointed to some brown and creamy-white fungi. "These mushrooms are quite good," he said, tipping one over so she could see the creamy gills. "And," he stabbed the blade as a pointer toward an innocent little low jagged-leafed plant with plain yellow flowers, "dandelions. Flowers, roots and leaves. They're a bit bitter, so you'll want not too many at a time."

"I think I saw some more wild onions," Alu called. "Over there," she pointed upriver, where the bank flattened out into an arc-shaped beach.

Shala and Sylvan went to look as soon as they had gathered the mushrooms and dandelion leaves and a few of what Sylvan promised would be bitter roots.

She finished the last spoonful of her barley and wild greens soup. "That was wonderful," she told the group. "Thank you for your help in gathering."

"Hey, I like it, too," Wyant said around a mouthful of fish. He had eaten a couple of bowls of soup, as well as the last of their fresh-baked flatbread.

Shala grinned and shook her head. "How do you eat so much and still not get fat?" she wondered.

"Boys," Sylvan said, a knowing grin on his face. "Eat like dragons until they're about twenty. Then they eat a little less than dragons, but still about twice as much as you do." He grinned. "Good thing these ones can fish, or we'd be out of food in no time."

"Hah," Wyant countered.

Tomaso started to say something when they felt the ground shake again. They jumped to their feet, staring around themselves at the granite outcrops, which moaned and shuddered but did not break or fall. The quake died away, but Shala's heartrate didn't. Her chest pounded like a herd of horses on prairie dirt. The boulders made the same horrible grinding noise as the rockfall that buried her parents. She took deep breaths, and again smelled the metallic stony smoke.

Sylvan stared through the trees past the boulders to the west. The others looked that way also, caught by the sight. The clouds above the mountains were bottom-lit by a red sunset-like glow. But the sun had set hours before—it could not be that. Even at this distance they could see clouds roiling higher and higher.

"That's not clouds," Alu said. "That's smoke!"

Then the quake started up again, intensified. Shala kept thinking it would end soon, but it didn't. She heard the dragons bellow as she fell to her knees on the shaking ground of the meadow.

Off to the west they heard an unearthly roar. The five of them all stared toward the foothills of the Queensland Mountains. They were watching as the easternmost peak in view belched out a ghastly cloud of red and black smoke, clearly visible, even from so far away.

Then the mountain exploded.

"Oh, Gods," Alu cried.

A gray and black column of ash boiled up to the heavens, so high and thick they could not see the rings above. The ash cloud flowed down the mountainside, already heading across the plain, toward them.

"The others," Shala asked, fear in her heart. "Where are they?"

"Much too close to that," Sylvan said. He spun and snatched up his jacket and Simba's pack. "You will stay here," he instructed them, "unless it is obviously unsafe, in which case you must take everything east to Oaks." He turned and met Wyant's eyes, then Tomaso, Shala and Alu's. "You must not risk your dragons, is that clear?"

Four heads nodded, and Sylvan, face grim, bent and poured water from one of their plass jugs over his headscarf and wrapped it around his face. He capped the jug, picked it up, turned and trotted out to Simba who sat up, alert in the midst of the milling pack. Without another word, Sylvan mounted and was gone, fading into the oncoming ash cloud with heart-stilling swiftness.

"Water," Shala said, and grabbed the three remaining cellu-plass jugs from beside the tent and ran to the river. She filled them, and then Wyant was beside her to help her carry them back. They stuck them inside the tent.

"We need to get masks around our faces, too," Wyant yelled, and did so himself.

Alu cleared her throat. "Can we do anything for the dragons?"

"Hope they stay calm and on the ground," Wyant said.

"Let's get inside the tent!" Tomaso called

Wyant's gaze was drawn back to the ash cloud that was boiling its way towards them. "They could have warned us about this. They must have known!"

What did he mean? Who were *they*?

One of the dragons snorted and opened its wings with a whack against a boulder. Denez. Shala saw Nizael sidle away from her, snorting. He turned to face downwind. Ozala *whree'd* in alarm, and then all the dragons did as Niz had done, huddling down together and facing downwind, letting their rumps face the ash cloud.

Then the ash cloud was upon them and Shala could see nothing. She reached out and grabbed someone's arm.

She tugged the arm, and the person, tentward along with her. After a moment that person moved. Alu, Shala thought it was and felt like from the narrow size of the wrist. They stumbled together, moving toward the tent, and what little protection it could offer from the stinging ash. Even with the scarf around her mouth and nose, it was very hard to breathe.

The ash was thick, gritty, and warm.

Shala found the tent by crashing into it. She felt along the silky cellu-plass wall until she found the zipper pull on the flap, unzipped it the rest of the way. She and Alu fell inside. Just as she began to worry, Tomaso and a moment later, Wyant stumbled in behind them. They zipped the flap closed and panted together in the dark smokiness.

Alu coughed, then sneezed, then coughed again. "It might help if we wet the scarves," she said.

Shala could hear the smaller rider unscrew the cap on one of the jugs. She felt her way over to Alu and did the same with her own scarf. When she put it on again, she found she could breathe much easier.

"The water helps," she told the guys.

She dug through the gear and found their small lantern and switched it on, hoping the solar cell had had enough sunlight to charge up the battery. The tent filled with a blue-white glow. The air was much better inside the tent than it had been outside, but she could still see dusty ash swirl in the light each time someone moved.

"I didn't know those mountains were volcanic," Tomaso mumbled, wetting his headscarf.

"Everything on this gods-forsaken planet is volcanic!" Wyant said. "We learned that in school long ago. The entire Inner Sea is a rift zone!" He threw himself down onto his sleeping bag. "When Azureign was terraformed, they disrupted the tectonic plate pattern. Plate movement sped up." He waved a hand toward the sky. "The rings are an artifact of their work—they blew up some ice moons, and dropped cometary masses, bombarding the planet to increase the water mass."

"That doesn't sound like the Rules of Settlement," Alu said.

"It was back before we knew what we were doing, before the other races in the Compact found us. This planet was one of the reasons the Ayi and Cuy and other aliens took us in hand," Wyant's voice was angry, "and showed us the *proper* way to do things." He took a deep breath, as if realizing no one there in the tent with him was to blame. "But it was too late to fix a lot of things here."

"Doesn't the Oracle keep track of this kind of stuff, though? Can't they predict where the quakes and volcanic activity are going to be?"

"Yeah, they give you a lot of bull," Wyant said. "But they have to watch their public relations, I suppose." He clenched his fists. "For the most part, they figure we have to live with our mistakes, 'we' being humans, never mind 'we' aren't the humans who screwed this planet up."

Shala was stunned. "Well, no one ever even hinted at this kind of thing, in my school." Of course, she hadn't gone to school very long, had she? Wyant and others from bigger towns like New Venice had attended classes for years.

Wyant smiled at her, making his voice gentle. "That's what I like about you, Shala. You're so naive."

Shala had no idea what to say to that, so she said nothing at all.

"The poor dragons," Alu wheezed.

"Poor Sylvan," Tomaso murmured.

No one said, "Poor Erisse," Shala noticed.

But Aimee and Ben were also with Sparkellz' rider, as were Tarva and Kiny. And their dragons also. Dragons who knew nothing about people's mistakes and animosities.

Alu coughed again. The lamp dimmed, so Shala shut it off.

"I guess we might as well sleep," Wyant said.

They lay in the tent inside a strange deep silence, as though the rest of the world had ended, the four of them the last survivors.

CHAPTER 15 — Volcano

In the morning they could see a little better than they had the night before. The sky was a terrible pinkish-yellow color, and smoke and haze filled the plains between them and the mountains. To the east it was a little better; a hazy glowing ball of light was the sun coming up.

Shala sneezed. It was still weirdly quiet, and still difficult to breathe, with tiny particles of ash and soot falling from the sky. The clearing where the dragons stood was centimeters deep in ash that swirled around the dragon's feet as they moved.

Tanzi rose tall on his feet and fanned his wings. It looked like he was trying to clear the ashy air from his bellows. With each stroke lift of the wings, when Tanzi's wings were high and the vents of the bellows spread apart, she could see that the delicate bellows structure was red and swollen with irritation. And when his wingstroke went down, a lot of ash and dust was stirred up. She went out to Tomaso's dragon and signalled him to fold his wings.

"That's making things worse, fella," she told the dragon. Until the air and ground were cleared up, the ash fall was going to be a real problem.

She checked Nizael and found his bellows likewise red and swollen. Maybe if she could wash them, sluice a bit of water over the vents, it would help.

She made her way to the creek with the big bucket. At first, she thought the water just wasn't there at all. She could see only an ash-covered mudbank where the river had been. Then she saw the sludgy ash foam on top of the sluggish water break apart, to reveal the metallic-gray water swirling beneath. She stared at the river a moment in thought, then made her way to one of the white-barked trees. She broke off a couple of small leaf-covered branches. Using them as a sort of rough sieve, she held back the ash sludge atop the water and dipped the bucket into the river. She was going to have to strain the water through some fine fabric to clean it up, but at least she had water and not ash-mud.

Wyant stood watching her when she got back to the camp. "We can't drink that, Shala. It's too acidic, and we can't filter that out."

"Are you sure?" she asked. "I thought it might help to wash the dragons down a bit."

He shook his head. "There's chemicals from the ash dissolved in the water. Some volcanic eruptions are loaded with sulfuric acid."

Shala set the bucket down. "Then all the drinking water we have is what we put into the jugs last night."

"We've got to have more water," Tomaso said, emerging from the tent.

"Clean water." Wyant turned and looked to the east. "Maybe we should go closer to Oaks. The Yent water is probably still good."

Alu coughed and leaned from the tent opening. "What do you think? Is this 'obviously unsafe' enough?" she wheezed. "I think we should pack up and leave now, before it gets so bad the dragons can't fly at all."

"Sylvan said stay here," Tomaso said, looking unhappy about contradicting Alu.

They were still standing there in indecision when Nizael let out a braying trumpet, and they heard dragon wings.

Expecting to see Simba, Shala was confused for a moment.

No, it was Aimee, atop a very ashy-colored Puka. She landed, then, still aboard her dragon, guided Puka out of the open meadow, shooing the other dragons aside to make room for more landings.

Shala looked up at the sky, Wyant and Tomaso joining her. Only one more dragon was above them. Where were the rest? She couldn't even see who this was at first. Then the dragon came in to land.

They stood transfixed with horror as the dragon approached. Ragged holes were torn in the big green wings, and they could see blackened areas, as if his wings had been burned. It was Lizard.

Those holes would mean he couldn't fly well, Shala realized. He could not judge his landing approach; his wings weren't doing what he expected.

He tilted to one side, then the other as he slowed. The bandage-wrapped rider seemed to be of little help. Lizard's feet touched down, but he was going too fast. He brought his wings down in a scoop so steep the bottom of his wings dragged on the ground as he slowed himself. He skidded to a stop with his chest against one of the big granite outcroppings.

Wyant and Tomaso ran to help the injured rider off. It must be Ben.

Lizard leaned against the boulder, head and neck slumped, his wings still open. Nizael approached from the rear, nosing at Lizard's right wing. The exhausted dragon made a half-hearted attempt to fold his wings up. With Niz prodding from one side, and then Ozala from the other, Lizard made a bigger effort, got his wings folded, and then squatted down, resting his chest and head down in the dirt. His breath made the ash swirl around his nose.

"They've got to have water," Shala said, as Aimee got off Puka and walked into their camp.

"Where's Sylvan?" Aimee said, voice hoarse, and Shala felt her breath catch.

"He didn't get there to you?"

Aimee shook her head. "You mean he left you here alone?"

"He flew out last night," Shala said. "Into the ash cloud, to find you."

Aimee's face went white beneath its coating of smeared ash. She shook her head again. "We weren't camped where he suggested we go," she said. "He must still be looking for us." She looked away.

That's Aimee's hope, Shala thought: Sylvan was either still looking for Aimee's group, or he was dead. Still looking was by far the better alternative.

Aimee coughed and cleared her throat. "Then some of you are going to have to come help us. Our camp is too close to the mountain; we've got to move the others out here where it's safer."

Alu tried to say something, but collapsed, coughing.

"You should go back in the tent, Alu," Shala said. She'd noticed the other girl coughing most of the night.

Still coughing, Alu nodded. She got her feet under herself and arrived back at the tent in time to hold the flap open for Wyant and Tomaso, who carried Ben inside. They could hear Alu still coughing inside.

"Close the tent!" Aimee called. "And wet your mask again, Alu!"

"What's wrong with Ben? And how did Lizard get holes in his wings?"

Aimee sat on the low shelf of rock nearest the campfire area. "Ash," she said. "The ash was so hot, and cinders bombed us all night." She swallowed and looked at the ground as Wyant emerged from the tent and joined them. "Ben's neck and shoulders are burned. Granger is dead," Aimee said, her voice flat and unemotional.

"My gods," Wyant said.

"Arzid's wings may be too torn up for him to fly, but I couldn't tell, because he won't leave Granger's side." Aimee went on. She coughed, echoing Alu inside

215

the tent. "Erisse's coughing worse than that," Aimee nodded toward the tent, "and she's got a lot of burns." She pulled back the sleeve of her light jacket and showed them a nasty dark burn on her left forearm. "The little chunks of hot rock flew in all directions when the mountain went, and a lot of them landed on us.

Aimee shook her head. "We were lucky, in a way. We were so close, we were under a shoulder of the mountain, and the main blast went northeast, away from us. Most of the ash blew that way, too. If we had been out there by the lake where we'd first planned to camp, I think we would *all* be dead. We got plenty as it was." Aimee took her face mask off and wiped her face with it.

"Kiny, and Tarva?" Wyant asked.

"Tarva's not too bad, but her dragon is a mess." Her mouth tightened into a grimace. "I don't think Sharz is going to make it." She rubbed her eyes, which were red and swollen.

Shala reached and took Aimee's scarf. She went into the tent and grabbed a jug of water. She used a bit to rinse the gritty fabric, then poured some fresh water into a cup and took that and the scarf back to Aimee.

"I think we can get Sparkellz into the air with a little help," the girls' advisor was saying. "And maybe Nizael or one of the other bigger dragons can bully Arzid into moving," Aimee said. Shala handed her the cup and she sipped the water in between words. "I think Sharz is just going to die." She spread the fingers of her hand and set it down on her knee with a deliberate motion. "There's still a lot of hot rock and ash landing in our camp area, so the others need to be moved away to a safer place."

Aimee seemed unaware she was repeating herself.

"Zinno?" Shala asked.

216

"Zin's got some big holes in his wings, but I think if Lizard could fly well enough to get here, maybe he can, too. I thought we could bandage the holes with some plass and glue, to help. The problem seems to be they just aren't strong enough to fly without their whole wing surface. They push, and the holes mean there's not enough resistance, so they're pushing against nothing. I think." Aimee's eyes were tearing, making pink runnels down the gray ash coating her cheeks. "Lizard had to stop three times on the way here, and he's just exhausted."

The sky above them had darkened, and Shala looked up. Blood-red lightning zipped between the clouds overhead, and then thunder rumbled through the camp. She turned to Wyant.

"Sylvan said not to risk the dragons, but if we lose all four of those that are left, that would be bad, too, wouldn't it?"

"Are you asking me permission to go?" Wyant wondered. "I'm *going*. Denez will fly. I don't think Alu should go, she can barely breathe as it is." Shala nodded agreement with his words. "That leaves either you or Tomaso to stay here and help the wounded."

Aimee had an opinion on that. "Tomaso should stay; Tanzi should be with his Queen so we can save at least one pair at the end of this." She cleared her throat and then wrapped her fresh wet scarf around her mouth and nose. Her voice was muffled, "If Shala can ride Oki and bring Nizael, I think we may be able to get everyone back here that's going to live."

"And we need to try and find Sylvan and Simba," Wyant said.

They all nodded, and Shala glanced over to the dragons' area, where Ozala and Tanzi stood side by side, staring at Lizard. The big green dragon's nose was still on the ground.

"Oh, no, he's breathing all that ash," Shala said. She ran to the tent, grabbed her old shirt and used it to filter the water she had dipped from the river. She tasted the water but could detect nothing wrong with it beyond a little unfiltered grit.

Wyant and Aimee watched her but didn't say anything. She wrung and shook her shirt out, then poured the filtered water over it again, went out to Lizard and wrapped her shirt around his nose. He groaned when she tried to get him to lift his big head off the ground. She managed to work the fabric beneath his chin, and then tied the sleeves of the shirt across his nose to hold the mask on over his nostrils. As Shala worked, Nizael walked up and watched her. Lizard seemed to breathe better after the first few breaths.

Niz whuffed, blowing ash away from Lizard's head as she finished. She stroked her dragon's nose and rubbed his long cheek. "I don't want to take you out there," she told him, "but I think we have to help the others." Lightning made the clouds glare red overhead, followed almost at once by a roll of thunder. Niz butted her with his nose. She hugged his head, then walked back to Aimee.

"We will look for Sylvan on the way," she said with iron in her voice. "We can't afford to just let Simba and Sylvan die out there, any more than we can abandon the others."

Aimee nodded weakly.

"We're just going to have to hope the lightning is busy elsewhere," Wyant added.

It began to rain then, heavy dark drops that wet the ash on the ground and turned it to mud. The rain was a blessing, because they could all breathe more easily.

Shala stuck her head in the tent. "Tomaso, you want to come help put the tarp and buckets out? The rain should clean up the air, and we need water badly enough it's worth a try."

The dark-haired boy nodded. He was covered with ashy gray soot and looked like an old, old man. He set down the cup he had been using to give the half-unconscious Ben a drink.

"I'll take care of Ben," Alu said. Her voice was wheezy, and Shala worried about the effects of ash in all their lungs.

There wasn't much they could do about it but fly away from there, which they could not do yet. She gritted her teeth as she and Tomaso worked to get a water-collection system in place. She and Nizael and Oki were going to be flying in the wrong direction. Into the volcano's cloud, not away from it.

They flew due west, crossing and recrossing the twining line of the Oak River several times as they headed toward the lake where Aimee's group had been scheduled to camp. Shala spent all her time leaning over Oki's shoulders peering down to the left and right of the dragon's neck, searching the ground for a man and a dragon.

It was a wasteland below them worse than any desert she had ever seen. Everything was gray or black, as though all the color had been leached from their world. They kept low, below the clouds where lightning lit the air above them with constant red flashes. It seemed especially unfair that they had to worry about lightning on top of the volcano's other disastrous effects.

Though the rain is a help, Shala thought, in spite of the fact that she was dripping with soggy ash. *It is easier to breathe.*

They could not tell the lake from the land when they got there, and so passed right over it the first time. It was a little flatter than the rest of the gray surface below them, but that was all. Trees, mud, and ash choked what once had been clear blue water. They spent an extra hour circling all the way around the lake, hoping they would see Sylvan and Simba, but they found no sign of them. Aimee led them away from the area. Puka had already made the trip across the plains once, and the smaller aqua dragon was faltering, her wingstrokes erratic from weariness.

Shala looked ahead, but then wished she hadn't. Smoke rose in a wide plume from the top of the volcano, and the clouds were lit a dull red above the northern flank of the mountain. Steam and smoke shot out from several places along the mountainside. The geysers were either small and frequent, or they were large and far away. It was impossible to judge distances with everything covered in ash. Perspective was washed out. Chunks of rock joined the ash and rain that fell from the sky. The clouds glowed red from fire and lightning.

It was like flying into hell.

The three riders and four dragons flew over the side of the mountain where the worst ash and mud had flowed. All the trees had blown down and lay thrown like toothpicks on the volcano's base slopes— the trunks were naked of branches and covered with ash and soot. They all pointed the same direction, away from the blast, as if they were saying that was the right way to go. Away.

At last Puka dropped low in a landing circle, and they could see the other group's ashy and torn tent standing in an ash-coated clearing. A few trees stood broken around the clearing, like gray ghost trees mourning their thousands of dead.

Aimee landed Puka in a splash of deep ash, skidding to a stop.

Denez took Wyant in for a smoother set down behind the tired pair, though Shala and Oki were circling away, and she did not see them land. She convinced Oki he needed to drop down further, too, though he wanted to stay up in the sky.

She checked behind her to be sure Nizael had followed them down, and discovered he was already below them, stooping to land. He was lined up well, but she saw him slip and skid, wing down, into the clearing. He crashed into Denez, who fell to her belly. Both dragons lumbered to their feet, looking shaken. What had happened?

She and Oki came in last, then, dropping down onto the mud-ashy ground. Like the others, Oki skidded, and she could feel how slippery the ground surface was as he scrabbled for footing. The ash and rain had made a slick layer atop the soil. Oki's feet went from under him, and he slid a ways on his belly, as Niz had. The smaller dragon came to a stop before he hit anyone, though.

Shala jumped off Oki's back, thinking to check him and Niz for injury. She fell beside Oki's sage-green feet. Then she staggered up, to look Oki over. Then again, she lost her footing in the slick mud and fell.

Wyant rose from where he leaned over Denez, and grinned a half-scared, half-triumphant grin down at her. "They're okay! It's slippery, so watch your step!" Shala went the rest of the way over to Nizael on her hands and knees and checked him anyway. Niz was rubbing noses with another dragon.

When she was close enough to see that dragon's colors through the ash, she realized it was Simba. "Oh, thank goodness," she whispered, clambering to her feet. She gave the surprised Simba an abrupt hug around his neck. Nizael whuffed breath against her neck and nosed Simba proudly, as though it had been he who had made the green and tan dragon appear.

Shala then slid-slipped her way into camp, where she was in turn seized and hugged by Sylvan. "I'm so glad you listened to Aimee," he said. "I would have come and gotten you, except she had already left to do that." He let her go and took a deep breath. "I think we can get them out of here, and maybe even move on to Oaks, where we can resupply," he said. "Water and food are running low."

"Can they all fly?" Shala asked, then flinched as piece of rock fell out of the sky and hit her cheek. It stung, and when she rubbed it, her fingers came away bloody.

Sylvan met her gaze, a complicated expression passing across his face. "Sharz died a couple of hours ago," he said, "which was a mercy, because she was in such pain." He licked his lips. "The others, I think, are in fair shape and can fly well enough. Though we're going to have to take it in short hops, with plenty of rest in between flights. You are going to have to ride Nizael, and carry some supplies, so Oki can carry Tarva."

He turned to where Aimee was unpacking the rest of the medical supplies they had brought from their camp. "Come help me patch wings." He grabbed the splint kit and some shrink-wrapp from Aimee's shaking hands. "Do you have some clean water?"

"A little," Shala said pulling her bota from behind her shoulder as they shuffled with careful steps through the camp.

Sparkellz crouched on her haunches, too unsteady to stand, in a small clearing behind the tent. The three and a half meters of her left wing were spread out and held at the tip by an expressionless Tarva. Erisse, oblivious to the tears that streaked her cheeks, smeared the underside edges of one of the bigger holes in the dragon's wing with water, and was laying a piece of plass against the hole. Sylvan thrust the supplies he carried to Shala, so he could hold the plass piece in place against the dragon's wing, assisting Erisse. The black-haired girl looked like an old gray-haired crone as she took a short section of filthy shrink-wrapp from atop a pack on the ground and pressed it onto the wet spot, overlapping bare wet wing and the edge of the plass patch with the bandaging material. She sniffed, then moved to the next hole in her dragon's wing.

"These aren't going to hold up for long," Sylvan said, "but I think they'll help enough to get away from here." He glanced at Shala, who stared at the pale gold dragon in shock. "Can you cut some shrink-wrapp?"

Shala shook herself. "Of course," she said, and did so, trying not to look at the horrible holes and burns that covered the once-gorgeous dragon.

It was hell, indeed, where innocent creatures had to suffer like this. She couldn't even imagine how bad Sharz had been, if Sparkellz was in "fair shape." Even though she hadn't seen any of the little pale green dragon's suffering, she realized it must have been terrible.

They worked for hours before they ran out of water and so had to stop bandaging wings. Then Sylvan brought out the first rider from the half-ruined tent. It was Kiny. Zinno seemed to know they wanted to put his rider atop him, but he sidled away.

"We should put him on an uninjured dragon anyway," Wyant said. "He can ride Denez."

But when they turned to find her, Denez was missing. Shala counted dragons, noticing that Nizael was gone, too, and Ozala. Zinno was still sidestepping away from them and kept doing so until he moved behind a boulder and disappeared. There wasn't a dragon in the yard.

In complete silence, Shala and Wyant glanced at each other, then followed Zinno around the boulder,

223

into a small open space made smaller by the forms of eight full-grown dragons and one tarp-covered lump.

The dragons raised their snouts to the sky and moaned an eery howl.

Goosebumps raised up and down Shala's arms.

"Sharz," Aimee said, coming up behind Shala and Wyant. "They're mourning Sharz."

Tarva burst into tears, her wails rising with the dragons'.

The dragons reminded Shala of pictures she had seen of a circle of wolves, heads tilted back, mouths open. But the sound was nothing a wolf could make, nor any other living thing she had ever heard.

Her estimation of the dragons' intelligence notched up and up. They obviously recognized the death of one of their own, and sorrowed for it. Sharz was gone.

They howled in unison, three, four, five times more. Then silence fell, but for the hissing steam and rumble of the volcano and Tarva's quiet sobs. The scene haunted Shala's dreams for tendays afterwards.

None of the dragons deserved this.

No one did.

CHAPTER 16 — Oaks

They did not get the dragons to Oaks that day. They moved everyone as far as Alu & Tomaso's camp on the Oak River, but sheer exhaustion felled dragon after dragon. They slumped in the yard area, covered with ash, like long-dead boulders.

Nizael helped so much he stared like a zombie at Shala when she came to him to ask him to fly one more time that night.

"I know, sweetie," Shala said stroking his brow ridge. She hugged his long snout. "But we have to have water. And food. Do you think you can manage?"

The Oak was still filthy with sludge, as was the sky with ash. They hadn't been able to collect any clean water from the rain because the volcano pumped out as much ash as the rain cleared from the sky, so the rain water never came down clean.

Shala and Wyant volunteered to try to get to the Yent, which ran fast at this northern end, and, coming from the east, should have water at least a little better than the Oak, and maybe a lot better.

"At least it starts farther away from the volcano," Wyant said. "The Oak is carrying us stuff from the west as well as what's falling from the sky. The Yent is just getting fallout; it ought to be cleaner."

We can hope, Shala thought, brushing some of the ash off Niz's feet before she lifted his wing and checked his bellows. Aside from being weary, thirsty, and sick of breathing ash, the big green dragon was in pretty good shape.

Better than most of the others.

She glanced at Wyant, who was working with Denez. "How's her foot?"

"Well, it would be better if the burn didn't have so much ash in it. I think it's infected." He glanced at her as he patted Denez' snout. "That's one reason why I want to go: I think if I could just get it clean and get some plass on it, it would be okay."

Nizael grunted as Shala stepped aboard, but he turned and slowly walked out to a more open area to launch. She could hear Denez following.

"Be careful," Sylvan called, voice so hoarse he sounded like Jhude. Shala waved.

Nizael ran a few meters, pumping his wings, then launched, rising into the dim ash-rainy sky.

The farther they flew to the east, the less ash they saw on the ground, but that wasn't saying much. It was less, but it wasn't gone. This journey might be all for nothing.

The sun had set long since, and the ash cloud over everything meant an early and deep darkness fell on their world. It was easy to see the lights of Oaks as they approached, for everything else was pitch black.

"I guess we pulled a little bit south," Wyant yelled as they came up to the town. They'd missed the Yent River, but the town would do.

Shala searched the ground for a place to land.

Oaks was a small town, but they must have cisterns and wells, as well as the river, she thought. They would just get their help here tonight, instead of on the Yent.

They discovered that most of the town was already asleep. They flew across the whole place before they turned back and found a landing area. There were six or seven roads in each direction along the river. Even as they landed, lights were going out in homes along the streets as people turned in for the night.

They landed in an open but fountainless square. Leaving the dragons, they made their way toward an inn that showed lots of lights. The rowdy music they could hear seemed so at odds with their recent experiences that Shala didn't even realize what it was when she first heard it. She grunted. Normal life went on; the world had not ended for Oaks.

They went to the doorway of the inn and Wyant pulled back the doorflap. Inside, instead of the drunk workmen she'd expected, Shala saw a young man and woman with flowers in their hair, who were dancing at the head of a line of fancy-dressed townspeople.

They'd blundered into someone's wedding celebration.

The music stopped as the crowd took in the two battered young people at the doorway.

"Aye, the volcano," a gruff voice said. "We thought there was no one out there to the west, for the farm folk have been coming into town for a tenday, now." The man who spoke wore a sparkling white apron, and Shala assumed he was the inn's keeper.

"We didn't know about the volcano until it blew up," Wyant said. "We've got injured dragons and riders out along the Oak River."

"You'll be wanting help," the innkeeper said, and a few people from the crowd worked their way to the front and stepped forward.

"I have a wagon," an old man said. He wore a frayed black shirt, and red and black suspenders held up his neat but old gray pants.

"Water," Shala said.

"We can bring water," the old man said.

The innkeeper raised his voice over other murmurs offering help. "We have plenty of food here," he waved a meaty arm at the laden table to the right of the cleared space the crowd was dancing in.

"Bandages," Wyant said.

"Aye, and doctors, too," the innkeeper said. He looked over the crowd. "Don't the Doctors Therayne have a dragonrider in the family?"

"Yes!" a middle-aged man called. He stepped forward, holding the hand of a woman whose black

227

and gray hair framed a face that looked so much like Tarva, Shala blinked.

"Are you Tarva's parents?" she blurted. How could it be them?

How could it not be?

The man nodded, looking worried. "Is she hurt?"

Shala and Wyant were quick to reassure them. Aside from burns and smoke and ash inhalation, Tarva was well enough.

"Her dragon was killed," Shala said, thinking they would want to know that.

"Oh, no," Tarva's mother said. "Oh, she loved Sharz so much! She wrote, telling us about what Sharz did, and how smart she was. Oh—"

"But Tarva is all right?" her father asked again.

"She's very sad," Shala said. "That's the worst thing. But we have other injured, including dragons."

"I'm not sure we can do much for a dragon," the Doctor Therayne who was Tarva's father said.

"Ben has a concussion, and most of us have burns and cuts," Wyant told them.

"We can help the dragons most with shrink-wrapp and some plass bandages," Shala said, "and most of all, some clean water."

The old man pushed past them out the door. "I'll bring up my wagon. We can load barrels of water and supplies on board," he said. He turned to look over his shoulder at them. "You're camped in the dragonriders' usual spot, there on the north point of the Oak?"

"The usual spot," Shala agreed, unsure what the man meant by "north point." But it *was* the place the dragonriders often used, she did know that.

"Sorry to break up your celebration," Wyant said to the bride and groom.

"Hey, we were getting ready to 'go upstairs' soon anyway," the groom said with a big grin. He lifted his bride's hand, bowed to the others, and led her out the back of the room.

Shala and Wyant left the inn followed by six or seven people, including both Doctors Therayne.

She heaved a sigh of relief. Now they just needed to get enough clean water to carry on dragonback and bring it back to the camp to tide everyone over until morning. Even the slow mule-cart the old man drove up in could make it out to the campsite by then.

And so it was.

"Erisse was both our savior and the cause of the deaths that did happen," Aimee said. Her brown hair was pulled back in a severe ponytail. She slumped in her chair at the table on the raised platform in the dining hall, back at Two Rivers.

Shala pushed her chair back a little bit, so she could rest her head back against the wall. The inquiry into the deaths of a young dragon and a student rider was a surprise. She had thought all the students would give their version of events in order to arrive at a full understanding. Instead the Guild questioned Sylvan and Aimee as though it had been their fault.

Aimee's face was set in stern lines; her eyes were swollen and sad. "If we had gone to the lakeside camp that we had planned to, we would have been in the direct path of the explosion. Given the state of the lake and the trees when we flew over looking for Sylvan, I have no doubt we all would be dead. Nothing survived there." She took a sip from the glass of water Marta had set in front of her, then glanced to her left where the Guild representative was sitting. Chova, his name was.

Two days after the pack had dragged themselves back to Two Rivers, the Dragonriders Guild at Toronia headquarters had sent Chova to ask questions, to make a report. Chova was cool toward them. At breakfast that morning he sat by himself and turned away the one question Wyant was bold enough to ask him with a gruff, "We will speak later." Shala thought he looked stiff and heartless. His silver hair had been cropped so it lay flat like a metal cap on his head. Like armor in a story about knights.

He waved a hand for Aimee to continue.

"We were not there at the lake, because Erisse insisted on racing the dragons as far west as we could go. Since the others followed their Queen, there was little I could do to stop them."

Even from her table five meters away, Shala could see how the water in the glass shook as Aimee sipped again, then set it back down.

Chova frowned. "How, then, did Granger and—" the Guild rep consulted the sheet of paper in front of him, "Sharz die, but not others?" He glanced out at the quiet students sitting in the dining area, then back at Aimee beside him.

Aimee opened her mouth to answer, but amidst the rest of the students, Erisse scraped her chair back on the wood floor and stood up. Her pretty black hair was shorn to a couple centimeters in length, and a part of her scalp would always be bare where scar tissue lay in a band above her left ear. "I'll answer that," she said. Shala could see how Erisse's hands clenched the back of her chair; her knuckles were white, and her shoulders hunched.

Erisse cleared her throat, then looked Chova in the eye. "They were in the air when it happened. They were competing to be Queen's Mate."

Chova frowned and consulted his sheet of paper again. "But Sharz was female," he said. "Why would she fly?"

Erisse raised her chin. "Sharz' rider was busy. I sent Tarva into the tent with a question for Aimee, so

Aimee couldn't stop us. Once Arzid and Lizard and Zinno were in the air—following me and Sparkellz—Sharz took off, too, without her rider." Erisse bit her lip. "I did not expect that to happen, and I had no way to make Sharz go back."

"Then the volcano blew up," Chova said.

Erisse nodded. "Then the volcano blew up."

Aimee turned her water glass, staring at it as if it held the secrets of the universe and perhaps she could learn them, if she focused enough. "The dragons still on the ground," she said, "my Puka and the packdrone, were below the ridgeline, and had their wings closed, so they only suffered from the heat and the smoke and ash."

Erisse spoke again. "But the dragons in the air, with their wings spread, they just—" she gulped, "*collected* every lava bomb and cinder that fell their way. Those were so hot, they burned straight through the wing leather and kept falling." Her gaze dropped to the table in front of her. "We each landed as fast as we could. I did not see Granger fall, or how bad Sharz was hurt, until much later. I was trying to save Sparkellz' wings."

She sniffed and swiped at the tears that slid down her face. "She didn't want to close her wings because it hurt so much, but that was the only way to keep her from getting hurt worse from all the lava bits that were falling." She sniffed again and sat down with a thump.

A silence fell, which Wyant then broke, addressing Chova: "My tutor in New Venice said that the Oracle station could predict things like earthquakes and volcanic activity." He didn't stand up, but in that moment, he seemed taller than Chova who sat up on the stage. "And the people at *Oaks* knew in advance. They cleared the area. So why didn't *we* know? Why wasn't the school informed?" Wyant's voice was iron hard, and cold and big.

Kiny spoke then, his voice hoarse and shaky. "Shouldn't you at Toronia have been told, at least? And you know where the usual tenday training flight goes; you would have known we were headed right into it and could have warned us off."

Chova considered this, pausing a moment in thought before he spoke. "The citizens of Oaks have more experience because of where they live. When the quakes started, they knew what it might mean, and moved everyone east. But the geological sciences are not as advanced as you seem to think," he said. "It is difficult to predict a volcanic eruption of this type."

"For *our* geological sciences, maybe," Wyant said. "But what about our alien bosses? What about the *advanced* science of the Casakin, and the Cuy, and Simbara? What about the people who made all these Rules for us to follow, because they think they know so much?" Wyant's hostile tone seemed to take Chova aback. "Why didn't *they* know? Why didn't they *warn us?*"

The Guild representative met Wyant's gaze for a moment, then looked down at his hands and heaved a sigh so deep, it was almost a groan. "Mistress Arapunta would tell you it is not our job to question these things," he said. Then after a long pause, "But she is not here."

The headmistress had gone on a tour of towns and villages and the schools in Lynly and Farnesse.

Maybe that's a good thing, Shala speculated. The Guild leader seemed very careful to follow the Rules of Settlement.

The woman could be gone all of fall season and most of winter by the time she flew all the way around the Inner Sea and home across the plains of Kendai. By then, everything that had happened at the volcano would just be a file on her desk.

232

"Since I am the one who is here," Chova said, "I will tell you I have no answer to this."

Shala's mouth blurted the words, before she thought them through. "Can we not go to the Oracle and ask?"

"The Oracle is designed to answer factual questions," Chova said, rubbing his temples with both hands. "They are not going to address a 'why' question like this. In particular because it seems accusatory of the Compact supervisors."

"It *should* be accusatory!" Wyant shouted.

Tomaso sprang to his feet like a cat. "How is it an insult," he asked in his soft voice, "to want to understand our planet?"

Shala leaned forward to see Tomaso better. She admired how he had gotten everyone's attention. *You can't hear him if you're not quiet, too.*

On the stage, Chova was nodding almost in sync with Aimee.

"If students ask the questions," Tomaso went on, "it should not seem accusatory. It should seem to be what it is: our distress at not understanding how Azureign works, and our desire to improve that understanding, so something like this won't happen again!"

Chova nodded again.

At this point, Sylvan stepped forward from where he had been standing alongside the wall to the kitchen. "Regardless of the fault of the students or leaders in this matter," he said, spreading his arms to include the entire group, "we would never have flown north if we had known there was any possibility of this event."

Chova started to say something, but Sylvan went on.

"*And* while we were in the air, travelling, we missed feeling some of the little earthquakes that might have

233

made us more suspicious of the danger." He folded his arms across his chest and stepped back to lean against the wall again. "At the very least, our Guild leaders should have been instructed on the volcanic nature of the Queensland Range. There was very little evidence we could see for ourselves. Thus, we risked ourselves and our dragons with not a glimmering of what might happen."

All the students agreed with this in a swirl of murmurs and nods.

Shala stood up. "I want to know how to fix the dragons' wings. The aliens and the Oracle know how to do that, don't they? Sparkellz, Lizard, Zinno and Arzid are never going to be able to fly like real dragons the way they are. Surely the Guild cannot afford to waste four otherwise perfect dragons? There must be a way to mend these holes in their wings, just as they can repair and grow new human tissues—when they choose."

"That's right," Wyant said as Shala sat down.

Erisse leaned across the table and took her hand. "Good for you, Shala," she said. "Thank you for thinking of the dragons."

Shala nodded and squeezed Erisse's hand. Erisse had changed in some surprising ways—the one *good* thing to come from the disaster.

Chova pressed his thin lips together. "I have no answers for you." He interlaced his fingers, clasping his hands on the table before him. "This has been a terrible year for you here," he said at last, looking around the room at them. "It seems to me that if students are concerned enough to take matters into their own hands and ask the Oracle for answers—well, the Guild will not benefit by standing in their way."

234

"Well, that was productive," Wyant said with icy sarcasm. "If you can call abandonment useful."

Alu turned off the dining room light. In the dim room, the students clustered together, lit only by beams of sunlight through the row of small southside windows. Outside they could see Sylvan escorting Chova out to his dragon. Aimee had taken herself into the dorm and her bed with a nasty headache.

It did feel as if they had been abandoned.

"But that's good," Shala said. Six other faces turned her way. "In a way, we've been given permission to do what we think is best, which is go to the Oracle and make a stink."

"He didn't give permission, Shala," Tarva said. "He just washed his hands of responsibility for us."

"Yes," Shala agreed, "which means—"

"We get the blame if the Compact council yanks the Guild's license, or something," Kiny said. "But would that be so bad?" He glanced around the circle of eyes facing him. "What's the worst they can do?"

"They could take our dragons away," Alu said.

"They'd have to catch us, first," Kiny said with a tight smile.

"If just a couple of us went," Shala put in, "the rest would not be held responsible, any more than Guild headquarters will be. I think that's what Chova was saying, without saying it."

Erisse nodded. She looked from Shala to Wyant and back but did not say anything.

Tarva stepped forward. "I'll go. I have no dragon they can take away, now." She wiped the tears that wetted her cheeks with a fierce grimace.

Sylvan's voice carried in to them from down the hallway. "You do have a dragon, Tarva." His words got louder as he walked toward them. "One who needs you very much." He came through the doorway, tension pulling his eyes tight. "Arzid is grieving, too." He stopped in front of Tarva who looked up at him with tears welling again in her eyes. "I know he is not your Sharz, but he is lonely and hurt, and does not understand why Granger has left him."

Erisse put an arm around Tarva's shoulder and gave her a hug.

"I thought it had to be a big strong guy to handle Arzid," Tarva said, her tone as dull as her eyes.

"Well, Shala has Nizael," Alu pointed out.

Sylvan nodded. "Arzid will be much better off with someone he knows," Sylvan said. "He's well trained, and you are quite strong, whether you realize it or not."

Dust motes swirled in the light beams that slanted across the wood floor. Shala was reminded of ash, swirling.

"Talk to Kris," Sylvan said. "He's been working with Kharmin and can give you some suggestions about the adoptive process, now he has a little experience." He glanced at Erisse, then back to Tarva as he finished. "Arzid's injuries are pretty serious and he still needs care that others cannot give him, because they have their own duties."

And their own griefs, Shala thought.

No one said anything, then, waiting for Sylvan to leave. When it became apparent he wasn't going to, the young riders broke up. Erisse walked with Tarva outside to see to their dragons. Wyant and Tomaso went into the kitchen to talk Marta into giving them something to eat.

Alu mumbled something about Ben, and left for the infirmary, with Kiny following her after a brief moment of indecision.

Shala glanced at Sylvan and said, "I want to see the dragonets," and walked out, too, leaving Sylvan standing alone.

Before he asks something I will not answer. She hoped he understood the pack's unspoken message: They weren't mad at him, but they *were* going to handle this themselves.

Tarva couldn't have gone, anyway, she reasoned, walking into the dusty hay-smell of the brooding barn. It had to be someone with a dragon that could fly.

She greeted the dragonets as they ran toward her in a little herd. To them, people meant food and forehead rubs. She laughed. It was nice to be with someone uncomplicated and sweet.

Some Things You May Want to Know about The Compact, or Rules of Settlement

(Author's Note: While this version is supposedly "simplified," you may find it difficult to read. Many feel that the very terms in which it is written are an enlightening window into alien thought processes.)

As agreed in the Compact between Species, colonial settlement by any species must abide by the following rules:

Colonies may be established only on worlds without indigenous intelligent life or indigenous proto-intelligent life forms, by Compact definition and examination.

Colonies must adhere to Ecological Balances as set forth in those documents by that name, including but not limited to the issues of introduction of alien and bioengineered (Helper) species; limitations on all development and growth; admixture of cultures, species and ecologies; mineral exploitation limits; biosphere exploitation limits; and technological limits.

Fair and Balanced Economies must be developed in advance of settlement.

Colony must establish and maintain at least one Oracle installation, which will oversee colonization research and data, dispense information as deemed vital to colony survival, and communicate with other Compact worlds.

Colony must establish and maintain at least one self-policing Oversight organization, religious or political or military in form, to enforce the Compact and Rules of Settlement, enforce Ecological Balances, and adjust Fair and Balanced Economies, according to its primary species' social nature and preferences within the terms of the Rules of Settlement. Such Agency(-ies) must accommodate to other species within the colony as required.

Colony must undergo Compact inspection and Oracle Report on an annual basis for 50 years, on a ten-annum basis for 200 years, and centennially thereafter, based on Cuy Native Annum timescale.

Deviations from Rules of Settlement will result in complete expulsion of population from that site, in aeternum, by Compact forces.

These Rules of Settlement shall never apply in the home system (native solar system or original ecological continuum) of any species.

The Oracle's Encyclopedia,
Terra, 25 Galactic Era

COMPACT SIGNATORY SPECIES

Ayi
Mengsee
Casakin
Simbara
Cuy
Toridani
Humanity

CHAPTER 17 — Quest

On the very last day of summer, Shala and Wyant met in the dragon paddock in the depths of night. The only sound besides their own was the lonesome call of the little birds Godfrey called nightjars, and the rustle of a big tawny owl that glided across the paddock area. It landed among the platecone and redwood trees at the edge of the paddock and hooted, as if in mournful agreement with the nightjars.

By the modest light of the rings, Shala fitted her small bag of supplies to the riding harness on Nizael's shoulders and tied it down next to her personal pack. They wanted to fly fast, so they were not taking a packdrone. Besides, if they were desperate, they could forage, or even raid the Toronia Guildhall for some additional supplies; they'd be flying right over it on the way to the Oracle's Maze.

"You might have to eat fish," Wyant whispered as he tied off his own supply bag.

She made a face. "I'll starve," she mumbled. Niz lowered his left wing and she set her foot into the shoulder pocket and swung herself aboard. "See you," she teased, and Nizael trotted out of the paddock. As soon as he had enough room, he spread his wings and took off. As her dragon rose, so did Shala's spirits. She did love to journey; nothing that had happened had changed that.

Behind them, Shala could hear the muted thud of Denez's feet as she ran, and then the sudden quiet when her feet left the ground. Denez was not as big as Nizael, but she was remarkably stubborn. She caught up with Nizael through sheer determination, and matched him, keeping even as they flew into the west. The dark line of the Lhasa River beneath them was their guide.

By the time dawn overtook them they had passed above kilometers of grasslands and reached the tree-shrouded hills of northern Lhasa. The city of Toronia lay beside the river among the foothills of the same Queensland Mountains that they had experienced the volcano in, though very far to the south and west of that place.

Their goal, the Oracle's Maze—whatever that turned out to be—lay to the north and east of the headwaters of the Lhasa, well beyond Toronia into the mountains.

Shala leaned over Nizael's neck and took pleasure in the sensations of flight. This was the first time she had been able to enjoy flying her own dragon. Nizael's wing strokes were smooth and strong. They flew over shadowy grasslands dotted with trees.

The gray desert of volcanic ashes and smoke still haunted her dreams. The volcano's ash had even followed them to Two Rivers. The Yent ran half clogged with ashy scum for a tenday after they returned to the school.

Then, as if having washed itself clean of the memory of the eruption, the water turned clear again. Shala tried to use that vision when she meditated before sleeping: the cleansing, the clarity, the renewal. The Lhasa River sparkled below them as the sun rose. Thus, they spent Summer's End Day in pleasant travel.

Shala and Wyant landed beside the rushing water for a rest and some lunch. Nizael went fishing, and she watched him stroke and dip feet into the water as she chewed her trail bar. "Guess he's not very tired."

Wyant looked at Denez, who was quite content to munch kibbles and the occasional fish that Nizael dropped to her. "Either that, or he's just so hungry, he doesn't care about resting," he grinned, his golden brown eyes laughing as much as his mouth.

241

Not unlike yourself, I suppose, Shala thought but did not say.

"Well," he said, leaning back against the slanted bole of a cottonwood tree, "how does it feel to be half of the rebel pair of our pack?"

Shala looked to the northwest where their destination lay. "I don't think there's going to be a problem with this, but if there is, we can just fly back to my home village instead of the school." She met his gaze a moment, then looked down. "The desert needs a solo, at least, and a pair would probably be welcome."

She picked trail bar crumbs from her lap, removing each tan speck from the blue linen with great deliberation. "Of course, that would mean you are going to be stuck with me, in the desert." Her eyes flicked up, back down. He was still staring at her. "I hope that works for you."

"I hoped to be in the same pack as you from the first day we met," Wyant said.

Surprised at his bluntness, she thought of and rejected six things to say, finally settling on a stumbling, "I'm glad."

She could hear him laugh as she got up and brushed dried grass blades from her pants and went to see what Nizael was up to.

At last he had caught enough fish and settled down on his haunches to munch up the pile of flopping creatures before they managed to flip themselves back into the river.

"Does that bother you?" Wyant pointed to her dragon who chomped a mouthful of trout sushi. A string of fish guts hung from his lips. The other half of the fishy carnage lay still in the grassy dirt in front of him. There was remarkably little blood.

Shala shook her head. "It's in his nature to eat fish," she explained. "I cannot deny his instincts; he is innocent of any knowledge of people's beliefs. My ideas about the sanctity of all life are just that: mine." She stared at Nizael, who ate his fish unconcerned with their opinions. "And part of honoring all life is accepting creatures as they are." She smiled and shook her head. "His table manners could use some work, though."

Wyant chuckled and waved a hand at his red and tan dragon. "She's trying." And it indeed looked as if Denez was trying to show Nizael where he could improve, for she took tidy, small bites of her fish. There was not a pile of fish wreckage in front of her, and Shala had noticed Denez did not scatter the kibbles into a crumbly mass before she finished eating them either, as Nizael always did.

Back in the air, Shala thought about what Wyant had said about wanting to be in her pack.

She had decided to be a solo, hadn't she? Did she want to be part of a pack of two? Marta and Godfrey had made it work for years, but they had been married before they became dragon riders at the ripe old age of eighteen.

Wyant's politics and opinions were harsh, she thought. He was intellectually brilliant, but rather retarded in spiritual matters. Things were either good or bad, with him, nothing in between.

She sighed. He was easy to talk to, nevertheless.

She leaned low into the base of Nizael's neck, adjusted her face scarf and freed her mind of thought, meditating as the landscape passed below her.

Trees, grass, river.

Hill, rocks, dirt.

When they neared Toronia, they took stock of their supplies. Rather than face questions from the Guildhall and risk being sent home, they decided to forage. Nizael brought down a small antelope the third

243

day of their journey, and Wyant took a portion of the meat and cooked it for himself before Niz and Denez slobbered all over it.

"Not that Denez slobbers," he said with an apologetic nod to his dragon.

"I know. Niz is the slob." Nizael was a good provider, though. Neither he nor Denez wanted any kibbles that night or the next morning.

Shala, using her own experience plus the lessons Sylvan had taught her about edible plants, gathered food each night. She had filled most of her notebook with drawings, descriptions, and cooking hints. They had fresh salad vegetables and some nuts. She rationed their rice and beans, extending the dry foods with what she gathered.

Thus, they bypassed Toronia, but they would have to stop and make a day of food collecting.

On the fourth day, they headed a bit west out of their way to the large freshwater lake that was the source of the Oracle River. They camped at the lakeside two nights, using the extra day to gather supplies. Nizael and Wyant went fishing.

Shala collected mallow root, borage leaves and pigweed. She found blackberries in a mass of vines along the north end of the lake. She followed her nose to some chocolate-colored sweet blooms she knew marked where ground nuts grew in the dirt. They had grown around the swampy areas she and Andrya gathered flax from by the Inner Sea and Shala found them along the lakeshore marsh here. She harvested several strings of the protein-rich tubers.

Denez participated in the food hunt by finding a dry sunny field where buckwheat grew wild. Shala spent most of the morning pulling plants and stripping the seeds off into a headscarf. She managed to gather quite a bit, working alongside the dragon who took dainty bites of grain heads and also ate the few late flower pannicles, including a few honeybees that seemed to love the flowers.

Then Denez rolled in the field, scaring off a flock of little rabbits when she made a nest where she and Nizael bedded down that night. Shala watched the cottontails bound off with a grin on her face, and she did not mention them to Wyant.

On the dry side of the lake, she found elderberries, a few shriveled chokecherries, and a mass of sunflowers loaded with seeds, and some of the seedless sunflowers whose tuberous roots made a tasty vegetable.

And she found many kinds of greens, both for salad and for cooked vegetables. Most of them were bitter or pungent and tart, and she added some of the berries to make their salad more tasty.

Wyant, done fishing, set a few of the fish to dry over their campfire that night. He had caught some kind of meat and cooked that, too. Done with his activities, he asked Shala what he could do to help. She gave him a flattish rock and a round, hand-sized one, and showed him how to grind up the buckwheat groats.

"It needn't be fine as flour, but the hulls have to come off, and they cook faster if the seeds are broken up."

He grunted, mashing his fingers between the rocks a few times before he got the hang of it. Then he rubbed the rocks together with the seeds in between, stripping the brownish-gray hulls off and crushing the seeds into a grainy flour she could cook with.

Shala watched him a moment, then smiled to herself and finished cleaning the berries. It was nice to have someone to help. It was also nice to have a companion who could talk. She picked the last dried leaves from her blackberries and dipped them into a bowl of water to rinse them.

She and Nizael were good at doing things together, just the two of them.

But this was nice, too.

They flew northwest again the following morning. By the end of the second day after the lake, they began their search for the only landmark they knew of that would guide them to their goal. A glass spire rose from the ground high enough in the sky to catch the light of both rising and setting sun, somewhere near the Maze that guarded the entrance to the Oracle.

At least, that's what Kole had told Shala. He spoke once of his journey to the Oracle to get the medicines for his village, and how he had found his way. With this scant guide to the Oracle's supposed location, they flew on.

And on the eighth day of their flight they found it. The spire looked like a glass arrow to Shala, an upside-down icicle in the sun to Wyant. Whatever it was made of, the translucent spear rose into the afternoon sky, caught the light of the falling sun, and scattered rainbows all across the trees and earth. It was quite pretty, but they did not have the time to admire it much because the dragons took it upon themselves to land, and no amount of encouragement would keep them airborne.

They had hoped to fly to the entrance to the caves that protected the Oracle site, but that was not to be. Instead the dragons landed at the southern edge of an open park-like area that held what looked like sculptures scattered around on packed sand. In fact a sign made of copper and set into a stone near their landing site said that very thing: "Sculpture Garden of the Oracle," the sign said. "For your Enjoyment and Elucidation."

"Elucidation of what?" Wyant said, scowling at the sign.

"Hmm," Shala said.

They tried once more to get the dragons into the air, but even when they got them to take off, both Nizael and Denez refused to fly any further into, around or over the Garden. They landed back in the spot by the sign.

"I guess we go on foot from here," she called. Wyant nodded.

In the birch woods that surrounded the open park, she saw a number of well-used fire pits, and there were flattened areas on the dirt, the size of tents. A pile of cut firewood was stacked next to the pit. They set up camp there among the trees, where others had before them. Then they found other supplicants, like themselves camped at the south end of the park.

An old white-haired man greeted them from the campsite west of them. His companion was a young woman who might have been his daughter, or perhaps granddaughter, Shala re-estimated. The young woman bowed to the dragons and greeted the riders with a tentative smile. The young woman pushed a strand of her long black hair behind her ear. "Your dragons are not going to eat our horses, are they?" Her tone was worried. "I think we have to leave them here, when we go in," she said.

Shala and Wyant walked over nearer to the others' fire.

"Our dragons will not eat your horses; they have been trained to hunt wild game," Wyant announced.

Shala winced. They were almost out of kibbles. She would not have made such a promise, and she wished Wyant had not either, because the dragons were going to have to hunt for their dinner, and the horses were awfully convenient. Was there any way to guide the dragons away from the other people's animals? She closed her lips tightly.

You hear that, Nizael? she thought in his direction. No horses or mules; only wild game.

Like that was going to do any good.

"Even when they've been pretty hungry," Wyant said, lips pouched out as he thought, "I have never seen either of them take any domesticated animal without permission."

The black-haired girl bowed to the dragons again, then extended her hand to Shala. "I am Tsu-An," she said. They clasped wrists, then she released Shala's hand and bowed toward the old man. "This is my grandfather, Ko."

Shala and Wyant both bowed and gave their names.

"I saw you could not fly your dragons past this point," Tsu-An said. "Our horses would not go, either. We could not get any closer to the entrance."

"Huh," Wyant said. "I wonder why?"

The old man said something in a language Shala had never heard before. His granddaughter listened to him, then bowed and turned back to Shala and Wyant. "He is saying that it is Oracle magic, that stops the animals. Only people may go through the Maze."

"Oh, is this the beginning of the Maze, right here, then?" Shala asked. "We have not been here before."

Tsu-An nodded. "We have not also, but cousin's uncle came to here, and told us the way."

"I think the dragons will hunt in the woods and fields back the way we came," Shala said, trying to reassure herself as much as Tsu-An.

"Do you know what it means, when it says the park is for our 'elucidation'?" Wyant asked in his usual blunt fashion.

The old man burst out with something emphatic in his language, again.

"Walk, meditate, learn," Tsu-An said, and smiled, bowing.

CHAPTER 18 — Maze

In the morning, they discovered the park somehow "knew" they were two different groups, and that Tsu-An and her grandfather had arrived first, and thus should enter first. Shala and Wyant could not take a single step onto the packed sand of the park. They could walk up to the narrow plass border, but they could not open the gate or step through it when Tsu-An opened it—but Tsu-An and Ko could and did.

Tsu-An and her grandfather waved goodbye and walked across the open sand toward the path that led between two rows of tall trees to a sculpture.

Wyant attempted to cross and was again rebuffed. "Now, what? I wonder how long we have to wait," he grumbled. He opened his day pack and took out a trail bar.

"Uhm, we just had breakfast," Shala said.

He raised his eyebrows. "I'm hungry."

"You're always hungry," she said, trying not to sound mean. "And we have no idea how long this takes or how far we have to go, so I think we should save our food."

He shrugged. "If I run out, I'll go hungry later instead of now." He finished the bar and licked his fingers with a small grin. "It's a matter of whether I carry the food outside my stomach, or in."

"I suppose." Shala remembered how much Jhude and Logyn could eat, and Sylvan's comments about "boy chow." "I hope we brought enough." She turned to look for Tsu-An and Ko, but they had disappeared.

She took a step forward, and this time the gate opened, and her leg crossed the plass dividing line without restraint. She put her foot down onto the sand on the other side, and Wyant joined her, matching step for step. They wanted to enter before the gate decided to stop them for another unstated reason.

They, too, headed for the obvious starting point, with Shala studying it, trying to figure out how she just "knew" that was the way to go.

"Those side paths dead end right there, I think," Wyant said, looking to the right of where they were heading. A small open area was visible, with a hedge around it. "I can't see a way out of the little hedgy box space."

"I have no inclination to walk there and look," Shala said. "Isn't that odd?"

"You think they have some kind of compulsion field or something?"

Shala quirked her eyebrows and made a face. "What's a 'compulsion field'?"

Wyant grinned crookedly. "I have no idea, but it would kind of explain things if there was some weird device like that."

The sun rose higher above the local hills as they approached the first sculpture and they realized something more about the garden. "Look at the shadows," Shala said.

In front of them, the metal and plass object in the center of their path had begun to move. Like an orrery, Shala thought. Their teacher had brought one to their classes at school once, to show them how Azureign's solar system worked. You could move the balls representing the planets, and the circular tracks representing their orbits, but could not change the order of the orbits or planets.

This orrery—or whatever it was—was moving by itself. Rings and globes rotated around a spindle. Each item, each piece of the sculpture, cast a dark shadow onto the packed sand, which here beneath the sculpture and their feet was very white.

Shala alternated between staring at the shifting shadows on the sand, and the gleaming globes and rings that reflected such bright light they seemed lit from within.

"Is that supposed to be Azureign's system?" Wyant said, tilting his head. There's six planets, with rings around the second, third and fourth ones."

"The second one is blue," Shala said. "But is Azureign really that small?"

"Yeah. We are not very big in the galactic scheme of things."

"Perhaps that is the lesson, here."

"What, that we're small and insignificant? Unimportant?"

Shala wrinkled her nose. "That we shouldn't bother them with trivial questions?"

Wyant snorted, and they moved on, letting themselves through a small plass gate across the walkway on the other side of the orrery.

The next sculpture was at the end of an inward curving spiral walkway between tall hedges. The basic form of the sculpture was a wall of black cubes with white bars between them. The sun shone on the whole checked board, and after staring at it a few moments, Shala realized she could see grayish-black blobs at the intersections of the white bars, between the black cubes. Or at least she could when she didn't stare straight at an intersection. The splotches appeared at the edges of her vision. When she looked directly into the junction area of the bars, they were each pure white.

"Okay," Wyant said. They walked around to the other side, and discovered the entire sculpture was translucent, and again, the sand captured shadows. A pattern of dark gray cubes and pale gray bars was clear on the white sand. They studied it awhile.

"I don't see a puzzle or a picture here," Wyant said.

"Not everything is black and white?" Shala essayed a guess. "Maybe it's not the shadows."

"Yah, 'cause what do they do when it isn't sunny?" Wyant wondered. "Ugh. It would be nice if they had the answers or an explanation written down somewhere," he said, "so we could check. But maybe it doesn't matter. Maybe it's not about the right answer—we're just supposed to think about it."

From the far side of the black cube/white bar sculpture they could see a hedge-lined exit path that led straight on to the next sculpture. They walked a few meters down that path.

"Wait," Shala came to a complete stop and looked back at the entrance path. "We came in on a continuous spiral, didn't we?"

"Felt that way," agreed Wyant. "But— It couldn't have been, because this path bisects any circle or spiral around the sculpture. We'd have seen it."

They looked back and forth a moment, then at each other. "Things are not as they seem?"

"There's a way out, no matter how it looks?"

They walked down the straight path. Shala glanced back one more time and could not see the black and white sculpture behind them. "It's not straight," she said.

Wyant glanced back, then forward again. "Okay." He gave a massive shrug, and they entered the open area around the next sculpture.

This piece looked a little like a primitive robot, with a metallic surface and a squat square-shouldered body. The leg or stand area was solid. Toward the top, it had one arm. Instead of eyes, it had four little windows in its "forehead" area. At the level where its belly would be, a sort of open bowl spread out. In the bowl were glossy, gray pebbles. A box with more pebbles lay on the ground by the robot's feet. Shala picked up one of the pebbles. "I think...it fits into this slot." She lifted it up to what would be the mouth on a person. She dropped the little stone into the slot. It made a "tick" sound, but nothing else happened.

"Huh." Wyant walked all the way around the device. When he got back to the "face" side, he reached out and grabbed the robot's arm. He pulled it down. Pictures whirled in the robot's eyes. "A slot machine!" Wyant said in triumph.

"Slot machine?"

The eyes stopped spinning one at a time. Two of the four windows showed the same picture: a tree. The third had a hawklike bird silhouette, and the fourth window showed a vivid blue sphere.

"They're a kind of gambling device," Wyant said. "My dad told me about them. But they sounded a little different from this. You spent money, trying to win more money." He put another pebble in and pulled the handle. The eye pictures flickered, stopped. A bird, a dog, a sheaf of wheat, another sheaf of wheat. Another pebble followed, then another. "You're supposed to get all the windows to match, and then you win."

"That looks hard. I wonder how many pictures there are? There could be a lot of possibilities." Shala looked at the bowl of pebbles, and the box on the ground. "Well, at least it doesn't cost anything,"

Wyant got a tree, a fish, a bird, a triangle, and started to put another pebble in when the machine went wild. Lights and holograms flashed, the machine whooped, and a bucketload of pebbles fell into and overflowed the belly bowl. Wyant stood poised with one hand on the handle, one hand at the mouth, still clutching the next pebble he'd been going to drop. "Well, that's weird," he said. "It seems to win when they're all different. Not all the same." He tilted his head, then dropped his next pebble in.

Shala composed herself to hand him fresh pebbles as he fed the mouth, pulled the arm and glanced at the windows. They "lost" a lot, and then "won" again: when the windows each showed a different picture, it gave them back lots of pebbles, but never when two or more pictures were the same.

"The richness of diversity, maybe," Shala ventured. "Each individual thing is unique and valuable."

"I think you're right," Wyant said.

They moved on, past the slot machine, through the gate and down the path.

This time the hedges alongside the path grew taller and taller until they made a real maze the two riders walked through. They found dead ends, long fruitless alleys, and little nooks and corners that went nowhere or connected back to where they'd already been. Then they passed through into an open area with benches set in a circle, and a small box on the ground in the center of the area.

Shala sat down on one of the benches. Sounds issued from the central box. Music, of some sort. Wyant knelt on the ground in front of the box, or music machine, turning his head left and right and up and down as he listened. Then he got up and moved backwards away from the box and sat down on the bench next to Shala.

Again he turned his head, presenting one ear then the other, and then looking up and down. She watched him, puzzled. Did that make the sound change? She tried it, too. While it did indeed make the sound louder in the ear that was turned toward the box, and softer in the ear away from the box as she expected, it made no other differences she could detect.

"I think it's a sound illusion," Wyant said, as the box went silent. "At first the notes were random, and then they sounded like a melody, right?"

She nodded. "One melody in each ear."

He looked at her, golden brown eyes to dark brown ones.

"No," he said, "high notes in the left ear, and low notes in the right."

"That's not what I heard."

"Huh." He looked over at the box. "I wonder how you make it go again?" They got up and walked toward the box, but nothing happened. Wyant walked all the way around it, with no obvious effect. He walked back and flopped down on the bench, taking a swig of water from his bota.

The music started again.

"The bench—" she said.

"Is a switch. Shhh."

They listened again, with the same result. She heard random notes, then gradually two melodies appeared, one in each ear. Wyant again also heard two melodies, but all the high notes of both melodies in his left ear, and all the low notes of both in his right.

He swigged some more water. "Weird. What the heck is that supposed to mean?"

"We don't hear the same thing. We all, um, have different experiences?"

Wyant sighed. "I don't see how this is getting us to the Oracle."

Shala glanced up at the sun. "Well, it's taken us two or three hours to get this far. If we want to get through the Maze today, we need to move faster."

"Right," he said, capping his bota. He rooted in his pack, then pulled out the small muslin sack she had given him the night before. He took out one of the baked ground-nut tubers and popped it into his mouth. He chewed a bit, then made a face. "These were better last night when they were hot." He swallowed, grimacing, but took another tuber and put it in his mouth.

They walked out of the music box area past the gate and down a curving path that at least led closer to the hillside where they believed the Oracle's cave was located.

The path was a very long arc. By the time Wyant finished the last tuber from his sack, they were walking *away* from the hills.

"Nice," he said. "Back the way we started from."

They found several more "sculptures" and spent time looking at them, making their way through the maze.

What turned out to be the last sculpture looked like nothing so much as a pile of junk. Pieces of metal were fastened to one another in no apparent pattern or design. Wyant walked up and pressed on one piece of metal that looked a lot like a fork. It did not move whether he pushed, pulled, or leaned against it.

"Not kinetic," he muttered.

She looked up at the sky. The sun had edged well down in the west, and was poised on the hilltops, ready to dive down into sunset. It had taken them all day to get here. She stared up at the sculpture, then down at the ground.

"Oh my gosh, Wyant, look at the shadow."

On the ground was the clear-cut shape of the orrery, a shadow version of the first sculpture they had seen. She walked toward the shadow area, sat down and looked up at the sculpture, trying to match up solid spaces and holes with areas of darkness and light in the shadow. "It's casting the shadow, even though it looks nothing like the orrery."

He joined her, looking disbelievingly from the shadow to the metal construction and back again. He shook his head. "I would say it was impossible, except I can see it."

As they sat there, she thought she could detect very slight movement. "Oh, it turns. And, look, there's lights set into the ground and on poles—for when it's not sunny."

"Eh?" Wyant looked where she pointed at the ground. A narrow seam in the sand was a metal groove. "Hah. Lights! And it's on a turntable. Okay, that explains how there's always light shining through at the right angle to make the right shadow shape. But how the devil did they make the construction so the shadow looks like this instead of a misshapen lump? It's very cool!"

"From chaos comes order?"

"Again, things are not as they seem?"

"From the end to the beginning, everything is connected," a strangely accented voice said.

Shala and Wyant jumped to their feet. Standing in the archway at the end of the exit aisle was a figure wearing a voluminous green hooded robe. The fabric of the garment swayed as from a breeze. Beneath the bottom hem, Shala could not see any feet. Instead, there was what looked like a fuzzy green mushroom stem.

"Only one of you may enter to fulfill your Quest," the alien said. "The other will wait outside or return to your camp." It pointed, through the cloak, to a straight, hedge-lined path that went down the side of the Maze area toward the distant birch trees where they had set up camp.

Wyant looked at Shala. "I think you are the better choice," he said.

"But you wanted most to come."

"I'm not very good at politesse. You're good at talking to all sorts of creatures." He met her gaze, face serious. "Unless you do not wish to."

"I—" Shala rubbed her forehead, "I can go."

"Besides," Wyant said with a wry grin. "I've eaten everything in my pack. I should go back to camp."

He gave her a quick hug, then stepped back and watched her.

"Once you leave the Maze, you cannot return," the alien said.

Wyant shrugged. "I'll wait, then. You go, Shala. Get our answers."

As Shala stepped forward next to the caped alien figure, it said, "Your friend is more sensible than I gave him credit for." Before them, the double doors set into the archway swung open with no sound. "Please enter."

With a last glance over her shoulder at the watchful Wyant, she passed through the archway into the Oracle's den.

CHAPTER 19 — Oracle

There was a familiar odor in the air. Shala looked sidelong as they entered. The alien's skin was faintly green. She thought the smell was coming from it.

Then she recognized the scent: The alien had the same cinnamon-earthy smell as dragon farts. She sucked her lips inside her mouth and pressed her teeth together to keep from laughing. Once she had composed herself, she turned and looked frankly at the person walking beside her.

Its eyes were tilted downward at the edges. The pupils glittered, as though shards of green ice made up the iris. The rest of the eyeball seemed ordinary enough: white, and ovoid, though perhaps there was a greenish cast to the white.

The nose was very flat, with just a bump at the tip where the nostrils rose away from the upper lip. The mouth was the most human part of its face, though it still looked a little off. She couldn't figure out what about it told her the lips were not human, but they weren't. The ears, if ears there were, were hidden beneath the hood of the cloak.

Was this the Oracle? She felt a sense of disappointment, if it was.

"I am part of the Oracle's staff, one of many who serve, here."

"Oh. Can you read my mind?" Shala asked, grimacing at her recent notion that the creature smelled like dragon farts.

"I cannot see your thoughts. But it is a common thing among Questers, to think perhaps whomever greets them at the entrance may be the Oracle." It paused, indicating they should turn left. Shala risked a glance down at its feet. Or where its feet should be. When it moved forward, the flesh of the mushroom stem surged, something like the body of a caterpillar or a snake. It left a wet-looking trail on the floor behind it, like a snail. "The Oracle is a machine," it said. "A vast complex computer, but still, a machine."

"You serve—"

"We collect and input data. We guide and assist questants from your planet and others nearby. We prepare reports and determine policy for the planet of Azureign. This policy and information is given to your people by way of the Priestesses at Ysen, the Guildhall at Toronia, the Rangers in Jarana and Ubaria and Ozangi, and other such centers of human thought and politics."

While she had someone willing to answer simple questions, Shala prioritized the many she had. "Was that a compulsion field, that air wall fence thing out there around the gardens?"

"No."

For a moment Shala thought that was the end of her answer. The creature led her through a tall narrow archway into a small, dimly-lit room.

"The field is a result of a sonic generator. You were held back by a wall, but it was a wall of sound—the same that prevents animals and fliers from entering the Maze."

It indicated a chair, and she sat down in it.

"Sound that we could not hear?"

"That you could not hear. Very specific sound waves, pitched at a range you cannot hear, but some of the staff here can. Thus, we are alerted someone has entered the Maze and what progress they are making."

"What is the purpose of the Maze?"

"There are multiple purposes. Some are to our favor, some to the questant's. For example, we have had time to view our cameras and identify you and your companion and gain some notion of the reason for your visit. You have had time to organize your thinking and determine the precise question you wish to ask the Oracle."

"Question?" Shala's heart sank. "We only get one?"

"We? You are alone, here."

"I represent my people, and our dragons, and we have several questions."

"You are an elected representative?"

Shala thought about that for a moment. She and Wyant had been elected by the rest of the pack. And then Wyant had voted for Shala to go in, at the entrance. "Yes," she said. In a way she was. She hoped the creature had been telling the truth about the mind-reading.

"Then you may be permitted to seek more than one answer. Please write down your primary inquiry on this piece of paper." It indicated a single unlined white sheet that lay on a wood table next to a pair of sharpened pencils. "I will endeavor to determine the number of inquiries you will be permitted, Shala of Two Rivers."

She opened her mouth to say she was not from Two Rivers, but stopped, since that was true, in a way, too. By the time she figured out how to explain, the creature was gone, leaving a wet trail behind it.

She slid the chair across the cool plass floor. The table was made from a glorious rosy red wood with a burled grain, finished with a dull sheen. She admired the surface, running her fingers lightly over the wood, which was so rare among the desert peoples. Then she sighed, and picked up a pencil.

The most important inquiry would be how to mend the dragon's wings. Or was it how to predict volcanoes? No, it must be the wings. Perhaps she could say it in a way that would ask both questions.

"Our dragons were injured in a volcanic explosion," she wrote. Then she erased "volcanic explosion" and added the word "unexpected" to the line. "The leather of their wings was burned through by lava and hot ash. One dragon died. Four remaining dragons of our pack cannot fly. I wish to ask: How may the wings be mended, and how can this be prevented in the future?

That was really two questions, she knew, but maybe the Oracle was not that fussy. She wished Wyant had come instead of herself. A computer was a machine, not a creature; how could she talk to it? He would be better at this, with his logical thinking.

The moment she set her pencil down, the door opened, and the creature that had guided her here, or one exactly like it, entered the room.

It was followed by a perfectly ordinary human person, a boy about ten, whose arms were full of boxes, book cubes, and clear plass sacks of liquid. The boy grinned at her. There were plass wires across his teeth, and Shala wondered if it was some kind of muzzle to keep him from biting.

The boy handed her a small insulated plass pack. "Rider Kole has inoculated your own oasis village. This is for the other villages in the White Rift Valley who have not been inoculated against the diptheria-plague that hit Reedwater. You must ensure they all are given a dose." He stepped back, and the green-robed alien stepped forward. With the fabric of the robe covering its "hands" it set down a box on the table, and lifted the lid.

Inside the box, packed in little plass-segmented sections, were rolls of what looked like plass strips, some clear tubes of a smoky gray fluid, and white opaque tubes. "To mend the dragon wings," the alien said.

"Attend well: This webbing is impregnated with tiny biological machines called makers, or menders, by some of your people." It pointed to the rolls of plass with its robe-covered fingerlike digit. "You cut it a little larger than the hole, then lay it over the hole in the wing. Then you take this," the smoky gray liquid in tubes, "and paint it over the entire piece of webbing. It activates the menders."

It looked at her and she nodded her understanding.

Next it pointed to the white tubes. "This is a cream that you will rub into the entire web-covered area and a few centimeters into the normal wing leather around each hole, once every day, until the skin has regrown on the wing; it reduces scar tissue and will keep the wing leather flexible." It smiled at her with its almost-human lips. "Of course, the dragons must not fly during the two or three tendays it will take their wings to heal." It folded its fabric-shrouded arms into a lump at its belly beneath the cloak, and stepped back, looking something like a small, green Buddha.

It was the boy's turn, again. He grinned at her once more and she almost asked him about the wires on his teeth, but then was distracted by what he said. He held up a book cube. "The most up-to-date book about Azureign's plate tectonic processes, volcanic regions, likelihood of quakes, volcanoes and other danger areas—in common language for the layman. And, updated maps with similar information," he held up the second cube.

"Of course geologic processes are slow and cannot be predicted exactly, but these maps will show which areas are most likely to experience earthquakes or volcanic eruptions, or tsunamis, and so forth, and which should be avoided for safety."

Then he lifted the third book cube, a mischievous twinkle in his eyes. "This is my own addition, a cube with the sources and explanation of the sculptures you saw today, including the twelve proper solutions of the holographic mandala puzzle, and how the laser alignment puzzle works, and all the others." He twisted his lips into a very crooked grin. "The sculpture puzzles change all the time, you know, so the answers won't help if you ever need to come again!"

"Oh," Shala managed.

"You were correct about the puzzles being designed to elicit thought and conversation, and for questants to perhaps gain a new perspective. For example the orrery—the moving planetary display at the beginning—is to help questants realize how their own system is laid out.

"The next one, the black and white sculpture isn't the puzzle," he said. "The spiral entrance hedge maze with the straight, or slightly curved exit, is the puzzle. It's designed to help you look at things from a different perspective."

"Of course, you cannot move on in the Maze until you find some sort of 'answer' or idea. The Oracle and its attendants were pleased at how you and your partner cooperated to consider answers and find solutions."

"Oh," Shala said again.

Then the alien stepped—or slid, Shala thought—forward again, holding the plass sacks of clear liquid.

"For your desert pack," the creature said. "To be painted on dragon wings at the beginning of each storm season, in the autumn." It gave a little bow, rather like Tsu-An's bows. "To protect the wings from sandstorm damage. The sandstorms can come up quickly and cannot be predicted with any great accuracy, so this will help your pack." It oozed, or glided or whatever it did to move backward.

"Bye," the boy said, still with his cheerful grin and wire-covered teeth. He gave a little one-handed wave and went out the door.

"Please carry your Answers to your people," the alien said, standing by the doorway.

"I'm done?" she asked. But she still had a dozen questions.

It waited by the doorway. In a mind-reading act of her own, Shala realized there weren't going to be any more answers, and she had best take her things and go. Now, before they took something back.

She snatched up the things they had brought her, barely able to carry it all, and joined the alien at the archway. The outside of her arm brushed the white wall as she went through, and she was surprised to feel warmth. She had thought it was made of stone, but this was some kind of very hard plass, or ceramic, like tiles, maybe. Like the floor.

She stopped at the doorway, where the alien still stood, rather blocking her way. It was staring at her, she realized when she looked at it.

"What is this?" the alien asked, pointing at her chest.

"What?"

"This, this jewelry you wear."

Oh. He meant her mother's pendant. She went back to the table, set down the armload of things, and fished the chain out from beneath her shirt. The pendant globe dangled at the end of the chain.

"It was my mother's."

"It is ours," the alien said.

Shala scowled. "I don't think so. It was the only thing she gave me before she was killed. She wouldn't have had something of yours. She said it was my great-grandmother's."

"Yes," it said. "It was given to that woman in answer many, many years ago. It was a trial, to see if the device would work as we hoped. She promised to wear it, and test its working."

"She said nothing about that to me. What is it supposed to do?"

"Do you understand pheromones?"

265

"Chemicals animals produce, usually to attract a mate with scent."

"Many other purposes, as well. This has makers to...soothe various animals. To help with herding."

Well. That explained away Shala's "ability" with animals. It hadn't been her at all. She frowned.

"There are much better ones now, made as a result of this testing and others. Usually these are given to veterinarians and sometimes herders."

"The dragon schools should have them," Shala said, thinking about the grouchy Queens and the fights that sometimes broke out between the Queen's Mate candidates.

"This will be considered," the alien said. "That one, I believe, no longer functions."

It didn't? Maybe she *did* have a gift with animals, then. She would never know for certain, it seemed. Shala let it drop back onto her chest. "It is all I have from my mother," she said. "If it doesn't work, you don't need it back, right?"

It tilted its blobby head to one side, then the other. "Best to destroy it," it said after a few moments of silence.

"It's mine. It is all I have left from my mother, my only token from my family."

"This is important to you, this thing of ours from your mother's ancestor?"

"Yes."

It stared at her for a moment, then turned and emptied the doorway. Shala picked up all her "answers" and followed it quickly, hoping it was going to lead her back to the entrance. She'd not been paying close attention when she'd come in.

"We are finished, here," the alien said.

"I'm not sure I understand," she said.

"It is well," the alien comforted her. "You have your answer."

"Why the Maze? Why only one person to ask and why only one question? And who, or what kind of person are you?"

It smiled its little pale green almost-human smile. It led her to the big double doors she'd come in. "Your companion waits outside. It is well," it said, "for you look as if you need help to carry your answer."

Shala passed through the doors. Wyant leaped to his feet and took three fast steps to her, eyes wide as he caught a bag of the sandstorm protector just as she lost her grip on the sack. She turned quickly to look behind her, hoping for one more answer, but the doors had already swung shut in the same eerily-silent way they had opened.

"Okay," she said. "That was without question the weirdest thing that's happened to me ever in my life," she said as Wyant relieved her of the box of wing-repair menders.

"What's all this?"

"That box is the wing repair stuff. They seemed to think this would fix them so their wing leather would regrow, back into a normal healthy wing, and they would be able to fly just fine." She didn't realize she was crying until a big tear plopped from the end of her chin onto the other bag of sandstorm fixit she hugged against her chest.

"So we got everything!"

"Well, except for some explanations of all this, and about volcano warnings," she said, "though the little boy said there were some answers on his cube."

"Little boy?"

She rolled her eyes. "Let me tell you about it."

She talked non-stop as they made their way down the long aisle, back to the birch forest and their camp.

Her entire time in the Oracle's cave had been so brief, the red light of sunset still glowed in the sky, lighting their way—yet she had not done telling Wyant about her brief time with the Oracle's people even as he set the wing-repair kit reverently on the ground next to their campfire pit.

"Muzzle?" he asked when she got to that part of the description.

"Well it wasn't to keep him from talking, because he spoke just fine, except maybe for a little lisp." She tilted her head. "Maybe it was fixing his lisp?"

Wyant sucked his own teeth in thought. "You know, I think I have heard of this thing, it is a way to make really crooked teeth be straight."

"I've never seen anyone with crooked teeth before," she said.

"Neither have I, but people on Earth and maybe other places don't always grow their teeth in straight, so they fix them by moving them slowly into alignment." He nodded to himself. "Yeah, I bet that's what it was. Maybe he wasn't from Azureign?"

She shrugged. "He looked just like us except for the teeth thing. How could I tell?"

Wyant shook his head. "The alien you described was a Simbaran. Maybe the boy came from somewhere else, too."

Shala glanced at the sky then back to where the dragons had rested the night before. They weren't there. Probably out hunting.

While they were gone, someone had replaced the firewood they had used. The pile was as full as it had been when they first arrived. She put some of the stacked logs into the pit, added kindling and got her sparker out. "I'm starved, so I'm going to make my dinner now." She glanced up at him. "I bet you're hungry too."

But he didn't rise to her teasing. A frown wrinkled his forehead. "So, I guess we should stay tonight, and start back to Two Rivers in the morning?" he said, examining one of the book cubes.

"Yeah. I'm happy to go back with all this great stuff, the Oracle's not mad at us, and the Guild should be ecstatic!"

Wyant nodded, still seeming rather distant. "I was half-hoping we'd be kicked out of the Guild, and could just go our own way."

Shala stood up and took a step toward him. He met her eyes. "You know, the Oracle itself said there was going to be a desert pack." She gestured toward the wing fixit kits. "With Sparkellz fixed up and able to go to Midford after all, Alu will get her wish to go to Oaks," she smiled, hoping to see his lopsided smile in return, "and that means Denez must be the desert Queen."

As if they'd known their riders were talking about them, Nizael and Denez appeared at that moment over the birch forest. They landed in their nesting area, and Denez reached over and picked up a fish from the pile Niz dropped in between them.

Wyant snorted. "Desert Queen!" He shook his head, the crooked smile beginning to appear. "How can they fish in the desert?"

"You never heard of sandfish?" she asked him in a teasing tone.

"Really?" His smile was full now, and she laughed to see it.

"Oh, yes," she said. "One of the desert's many mysteries!"

CHAPTER 20 — Pack

Later that night they were joined by two unknown dragonriders, who landed and set up their camp in the space Tsu-An and Ko had used.

"We never did see them again," Shala said, glancing from Wyant to the campsite's new occupants and back again.

"Tsu-An and Ko? I did. They came out while you were inside," Wyant said, also watching the dragonriders who were minding their own business, setting up camp. Their dragons rose into the air and flew off, presumably to hunt.

Shala wondered if the strange dragons would go where Nizael and Denez were off hunting again, or if they would keep to themselves.

"Ko seemed happy with his answer," Wyant said, "but Tsu-An did not. They had to begin their journey home right away, I guess."

"Should we, um, go over and say hello, or what?" Shala jerked a thumb over her shoulder at the other pair of dragonriders.

Wyant made a face, then shook his head. "I don't know. Maybe not."

They finished eating their dinner about the same time Nizael and Denez returned from wherever they had been. Niz wasn't carrying any dinner in his claws, so they must have eaten whatever they had found...wherever they found it.

The sound and sight of their dragons brought the other two riders right over into their camp.

An older man with long graying hair pulled back into a braid helped an even older grand'erly man step over the rocks. "Hello," the one with the braid called. "We didn't realize there were other Guild members here."

Wyant and Shala exchanged a quick look. They weren't supposed to be there, and they weren't official dragonriders yet, either.

"We're not quite Guild members, yet," Shala decided to say.

"Students?" the grand'er asked. "They're sending students to the Oracle, now?"

"Um." Shala reached a hand out to support the old man who looked as if he was tottering into a fall among the dead branches she'd piled up for kindling. On his other side, the gray-braid man grasped the grand'er's elbow, and met her eyes.

"I believe I know who these two are," he said. Was his tone threatening?

Shala's heart quailed. Were they going to get into trouble now, after all?

Gray-braid took in the plass-wrapped supplies they'd received from the Oracle, which rested on the ground by their gear. With a wordless cry, he left the older man's side and knelt down to look at the packs. After a brief inspection, he arose, disappointment in his eyes.

"What did you get?" he asked, still not sounding very friendly.

Wyant took the situation in hand. "A bandaging and repair system to fix holes burned in dragon wings by volcano fire," he said. He didn't mention the vaccine, or the sandstorm protectant or volcano information. Or the Maze cube. But then, the boy said the maze changed all the time. The cube probably wouldn't be any help to these men, anyway.

The grand'er managed to fold himself down onto a rock. Gray-braid squatted next to their fire, which had burned down to the glowing ember stage. "Did you ask them about arthritis cures?"

Shala shook her head. "They only let you ask one question," she told him. Then without knowing quite

271

why, she made a decision to trust him. She stepped forward, bent down and stuck out her hand. "My name's Shala. I ride Nizael."

He clasped wrists, grinning. "Yes, I've heard of you. My name is Climt. My dragon is Axel, the big blue one."

"Heard of her?" Wyant said, not giving his name.

"Rescued Reedwater, fixed Palli's broken wing, transported sick riders on baby dragons, and helped save her pack from an attack by volcano. Heard of her. You are?"

"Wyant." He reached over and clasped wrists with Climt.

"You solved the Maze?" the grand'er asked in a wheezy voice. He sounded like the pack had, after breathing volcano ash for three days.

"It's not very difficult," Wyant said. He glanced at Shala. "You want to show them?"

She fetched the proper cube from their stack of the Oracle's answers.

Climt took it from her and shook it awake.

As he stared at the first few puzzles demonstrated on the cube, Wyant told him, "It won't be much help. They said the puzzles change all the time. But that's what they're like."

Climt nodded, flipping the cube through more puzzles, then snapped it off and handed it back. "They told us we'd have to solve puzzles," he grinned. "No one knows if they ever repeat any of them or not."

Shala said, "I believe even if you don't solve them with an exact 'correct' answer, you can pass through the Maze and get to the Oracle anyway. They didn't seem very strict about it."

The other dragonrider nodded again, then glanced at the old man. "You ready to eat, Hap? I think our pot of beans and rice is done," he announced.

"You're asking for an arthritis cure?" Shala asked him, thinking about his question.

He met her eyes. "We're going to ask if there's something for dragons, as well as people."

Thinking of Bodo, Shala said, "I hope you succeed."

Climt helped Hap to his feet, and the two made their way back to their own campsite.

"Good luck," she called to them.

"Well, they were just ordinary people, too," Wyant said. "I don't think we had to have an authorized Guild representative come here to ask for help. Why did Chova imply we would be breaking somebody's rules if we did it ourselves?"

She thought back. It was hard to remember. "Did he say that?" she wondered, "Or did we just make up that part ourselves?"

He made a wry face and grinned at her. "Here we thought we were being heroic rebels or something, and we were just doing what everybody does!"

"I don't care. As long as it worked!"

As Nizael's big wings pumped, Shala looked down at the buildings of the Two Rivers School. The horse barn had been whitewashed while they were gone, and it glowed in the noon sunlight like a beacon lit to guide them home.

Below and beyond the launching cliff, the lake gleamed blue, and the mixed forest edging it seemed an especially wondrous assortment of greens and golds.

She was struck by how much she had missed the others in her pack. Even Erisse, who had been much changed by the volcano and its aftereffects.

The others came charging out of the dorm, even Ben, whose head was no longer wrapped in bandages.

Nizael dropped to the ground and ran a few steps to clear a space for Denez. Shala saw Sylvan and Aimee, Kris and Marta join the pack riders.

Her own big grin told them what they wanted most to know, but Wyant shouted, "Yes!" and leaped off Denez before she even stopped moving.

"They can fix their wings?"

"They gave us stuff to do the job," Wyant answered. Relief was plain on Erisse's face, and she smiled. It was a small smile, but an honest one.

Shala was pleased to see Ben move up next to Erisse and take her hand. They stood there with their half-bald, scarred heads together in the sunlight. She wished she had asked for a cure for their burn scars. Why hadn't she thought of that?

Of course they were only supposed to have *one* request, and the Oracle had given them three answers. Plus the boy's gift of the Maze & geology cubes.

"Come tell us everything," Alu said.

First she and Wyant took care of their dragons, while the others carried the supplies into the dorm dining hall. Shala was startled to discover a little dragonet running across the paddock. Kharmin was lounging in the sun, surrounded by a flock of them. The Queen sighed, resting her head on one of her blue-green feet.

Nizael walked in his clumsy two-legged amble up to Lizard, touched noses, then he turned to Sparkellz and nuzzled her. With her wings folded, the pale gold Queen looked almost normal. She arched her neck and greeted Nizael with a soft *whree*.

Promising Niz a foot rub later, Shala grabbed her pack with the book cubes in it, and the insulated tray of medicines for the desert people. She put the tray into the cold-box in the infirmary, which she was happy to see was now empty of all injured people, and made her way to the dining hall. She could hear Wyant already telling the story of their journey.

"So, is there going to be a desert pack?" Shala asked. She looked around at everyone. "I assume the pack assignments have been made?"

Sylvan nodded, capturing all their attention as he stepped forward. "Here is the final pack list," he grinned, glancing around at the circle of intent faces, "if you want to know it, that is."

They all groaned, and he laughed out loud. "I figure you *already* know, so this is just confirmation.

"All right. Soon-to-be-perfectly restored Queen of the pack for Midford: Sparkellz." Sylvan smiled at Erisse, who returned a small smile and a nod. "Joining as Queen's Mate will be Arzid, with Tarva as rider. Ben on Lizard is backup Queen's Mate for that pack."

He held away the piece of paper he'd been "reading" from, to meet their gazes. "By the way, the guild wants to institute a more formalized dragon breeding program. We're going to create bloodline books and use them to obtain the strongest possible offspring through each Queen." He cleared his throat. "We may have to send Arzid off on an errand out of town some day to accomplish this plan and give Lizard his chance." Ben nodded and Tarva's eyebrows raised, then relaxed.

"To Oaks, as we promised the good citizens there, we send Queen Ozala, with Queen's Mates Tanzi and Zinno, riders Alu, Tomaso and Kiny."

Shala glanced at Tomaso, who was staring at Alu, as if lost in a dream. Then Alu met his gaze, smiled at him, and Tomaso flushed bright red. Well, that hadn't changed!

Kiny ducked his head in acknowledgment. His dragon might mate with the Queen, but Alu was all

Tomaso's girl. From the admiring looks the dragons had received from Oaks' helpful citizens, Shala did not think Kiny would have any trouble finding a whole clutch of girlfriends, and perhaps a wife among them someday.

"And for that already infamous desert pack," Sylvan said, "we have Denez as Queen, Nizael as Queen's Mate, and Simba as backup Queen's Mate, if Denez will accept him. Also added to this loose pack, which will be spread over a lot of territory, will be Kole and his dragon Palli of Reedwater, whose town is rebuilding, but does not have enough population to support a full-time dragon and rider, right now."

Sylvan dipped his head. "Finally, Aimee will return with Kris to New Venice, where the rest of their pack are awaiting their Queen's return, and—" he pointed out the window to where Kharmin lay covered in dragonets, "I am pretty certain Kharmin is just as eager to get home."

They laughed, for one dragonet had just clambered from the Queen's neck up to the top of her head and stood perched on top of her brow ridge. She shook her head, and the little one tumbled off, then leaped to its feet. Wings spread, neck thrust forward at the end of its stiff little neck, the dragonet was giving its mother a squawking complaint about her treatment of it. Kharmin set her head back down on her foot and closed her eyes.

"I hope you are pleased with the final assignment." Sylvan said, "You are welcome to fly out to your new homes as soon as your pack is ready to go."

Aimee's voice carried over to them from where she stood in the hallway door. "I thank you for your help through my grief," she murmured. "And I wish our time together had been more...normal."

Alu and Erisse, as if they had practiced the move, went to Aimee and hugged her, one on each side.

"I'd say we're just about the strongest packs ever to come out of this school," Kiny said. "Gods, after what we've been through, we've got to be ready for anything!"

They laughed at that, but there was a layer of sadness beneath the laughter.

On the third day of the third tenday of Fall, Shala guided Nizael into a landing between the oasis village's well and Simba. She dismounted, and watched as Wyant on Denez came down.

Shala looked around. This was where it had all started, for her. It seemed strange that the little cluster of houses seemed so much the same, when she felt so much changed.

"I cannot believe you were here less than a year ago, looking for riders," she said to Sylvan.

Wyant dismounted from Denez, stroking her face as she leaned forward to stick her snout into the cistern. "Here, now!" Wyant pushed her head back. "Wait for a bucket, you slob!"

Shala had to laugh. Wyant calling Denez a slob?

It was Renel who ran out with a bucket, of course. The boy filled it, paying more attention to the dragons than to what he was doing. Then Syvan helped him drag it out to where Denez could reach it. Renel took care of each dragon in turn, refilling the bucket as though he'd always done that for dragons.

"Hi, Shala!" Renel said, glancing up from his work. He walked around the animals like an old dragon-wrangler might, touching a neck or a shoulder to let them know he was there, scratching brow ridges and rubbing long noses, wet from the fresh, cool well water. He seemed impressed with Shala's big green dragon.

"That's Nizael," she told Renel, just as Jono and Andrya came out of her old house. Andrya shaded her eyes from the sun, a big smile on her face. Behind her, Shala could see Netke, who waddled out, big with child.

That didn't take long, Shala thought, but then corrected herself. No, it had been half a year since Reedwater, after all, and they had been married before that, at Year Turn.

"Jhude and Logyn are out with the goats," Andrya said.

Shala introduced Wyant and Denez. "And you know Sylvan and his Simba."

"Are you here long?" Jono asked.

"Long enough for our first errand as your official pack," Wyant told him.

"Please come over here, Jono." Shala pulled a packet of syringes and a bottle of vaccine from her pack. "I'm sorry to say this," she said to her littlest foster brother. "But it's going to hurt, just a bit."

"We already got shot!" Jono said. "The dragon man who was here before, to tell us about Reedwater."

"Yes, he gave you one inoculation. This is another kind, for other diseases."

She swabbed his arm, checked that the vaccine bottle had injected the correct amount of fluid into the syringe. Then she set the blunt end of the syringe against his arm and pressed the button.

"That's it?" Jono said. "Foo, it didn't hurt at all!"

Renel had watched the whole process. "Do I get some, too?"

"Everyone does," Shala said, swabbing a clean spot on his dusty, dark brown arm. "Especially kids, and moms and dads and grand'ers." She grinned as Renel crossed his eyes, then ran off to pet the dragons again.

One by one, the villagers received the vaccine.

"Your shot will protect the baby," Shala explained to Netke. "But once it's a year or so old, it should have one, too."

"He," Netke said with a grin. "We all think it's going to be a boy."

Shaking her head, Shala smiled at her sister-in-law. "It's hard to imagine Jhude as a father!"

"Or me as a grand'er," Andrya said, widening her eyes at the thought.

Netke laughed aloud. "It's hard to imagine me as a mother, for all of that. But soon, now!"

Embry came out with a bottle in her hands. She handed it to Shala. "Some more of that herbal shampoo, if you want it."

"Oh! I love that, Embry! And I think I can sell a bit of it to my friends in Oaks, too, if you have extra." Shala swabbed the old woman's arm. "This may give you a little fever, but it will protect you—"

"I heard about Reedwater," Embry said, shaking her head. "That's not going to happen here."

"Good. You are protected against the Reedwater thing from the shots Kole gave everyone—he did get everyone, didn't he?"

Embry nodded.

"This prevents some of the other things people can get, like the fever that the Dylun's baby got, when I was little."

Embry nodded again, then made way for the Dylun clan. They brought her a pair of fala-birds in thanks, or payment, depending upon how she thought of it. Shala thanked them in return, and handed the birds off to Wyant. He'd know how to clean and prepare them. As well as eat them, of course.

Netke made her farewell, to go inside and get started cooking the family's dinner. Andrya was about to join her, when Shala cried, "Oh, wait!" From the bigger pack still on Nizael's back, she took out the packet of linen she had rescued from Reedwater. "I washed it, and you've all had your shots, so it shouldn't be germy," she explained to Andrya, "but I thought you would want this back."

Andrya held the soft fabric against her cheek. "I'll make some baby things," she said.

"I can try to find other places to sell it, if you like."

"Maybe from the next batch," her foster mother said. Then, "You are coming back here, aren't you?"

"Yes. Eventually. We haven't worked out the exact timing and how we're going to split up, but we will be spending a few days in various oasis towns and making the round from one end of the desert to the other. We'll probably use Esfa town as a sort of headquarters," Shala said. Andrya gave her a hug and went inside.

They waited by the well for each of the villagers to come for their inoculations.

Embry stayed out there with them, admiring Shala's plant notebook. They talked about herbs she might like to have next time the riders came to visit.

Jhude and Logyn came home in the late afternoon, and that started the news session all over again, while Shala gave them their shots.

Logyn went into the house and came out with a fresh loaf of cheese bread. The whole family followed him outside to say goodbye.

Shala hugged everyone one last time.

Then the three dragonriders of the desert pack climbed back on their dragons and flew southwest, into the desert sun.

People, Places and Things of AZUREIGN

People

Student Riders—Z-year pack at Two Rivers:

Alu
: Blonde, tiny, pretty, perky daughter of rich ranching parents; from near Ziza, in Lhasa. Rides Ozala.

Ben
: A nice boy, quiet; rides Lizard. His family is in shipping, from Avordan Town.

Erisse
: Black wavy hair, deep blue eyes, beautiful, popular; her boyfriend is Granger. She rides Sparkellz. Her father governs a large province in Ben Yent.

Granger
: Erisse's boyfriend. Rides Arzid. Ginger-red hair; from Midford; his father is a blacksmith.

Kiny
: One of Erisse's followers; he rides Zinno; sandy brown hair, green eyes; his family are merchants on the Queensland/Lhasa border.

Shala
: of Nizael Caravan, brown fluffy hair, dark eyes, dusky tan skin. Rides Nizael. Her foster family raises goats, makes fabric in first oasis village.

Tarva
: Rides little Sharz; follows Erisse; stocky brunette; her parents are physicians in Oaks; she's youngest of six; her family (the Doctors Therayne) help the dragonriders.

Tomaso
: Quiet, shy, hopelessly in love with Alu; rides Tanzi; dark hair & eyes; family are farmers on the Ben Yent plains; practices T'ai Chi.

Wyant
: Cute, brown hair, golden brown eyes; rides Denez; intellectual family from

New Venice. His mother is a professor, his father a biological scientist.

Other dragonriders:

Aimee Female advisor for Z year; permanently stationed at New Venice; gray eyes, brown hair.

Arapunta Headmistress from Guild headquarters/Central School at Toronia; rides Palandra.

Chova Guild rep investigating dragon & rider deaths; cropped silver hair.

Climt Dragonrider at Oracle.

Dene Male Advisor for Z year; permanently stationed at New Venice; his dragon, a Queen named Kharmin, is brooding, so he's riding Oki; Aimee's partner.

Godfrey Davidow Retired rider, spouse of Marta; a farmer & stablemaster; rides Anemone.

Hap Dragonrider at Oracle.

Kole Sick rider from Reedwater, rides Palli

Kris Kharmin's new rider; his dragon died in the Avordan Town plague; long straight dark red hair.

Marta Davidow Retired rider from Djameno(?); vet, medic & cook; rides Mamba.

Sylvan Stablemaster, veterinarian; rides Simba, light brown eyes and hair.

Other folks:

Andrya Shala's foster mother, widowed a few years previously; makes cloth.

Benar Oasis villager whose mules Shala & Jhude borrow.

Clio Andrya's husband, Shala's foster father (died when Jono was little).

Dylun   chicken & Fala-bird-raising family with walled yard in oasis village.

Embry   Old woman of oasis village; makes herbal soaps & cleansers.

Jhude   Shala's oldest foster brother in oasis village. Raspy voice, makes cheese.

Jono   Shala's youngest foster brother (younger than she by several years).

Judge family Netke's family in Reedwater

Logyn   Shala's middle foster brother, wants to be a Buddhist monk.

Netke   Jhude's wife-to-be from Reedwater, of the Judge family.

Therayne   family; Tarva's parents; physicians in Oaks.

Dragons

First-Years (Z pack):

Arzid   m. Big, black and charcoal gray. Possible QM candidate. Granger's.

Denez   f. Pretty tan and reddish brown; Wyant's.

Lizard   m. Big green. Ben's dragon.

Nizael   m. Olive green. Huge. Queen's Mate candidate. Ridden by Shala.

Ozala   f. Pearly white; sweet-tempered; possible Queen candidate. Alu's dragon.

Sharz   f. Very small, very pale lime green, ridden by Tarva.

Sparkellz   f. Pale gold, iridescent wings, Queen candidate; Erisse is her rider.

Tanzi   m. Gray & charcoal medium-sized male; Tomaso's dragon.

Zinno   m. Burgundy red and pink, smallest male; Kiny's dragon.

Adult dragons:
Anemone Godfrey Davidow's dragon.
Axle Adult dragon at Oracle.
Bodo m. Old adult (B) dragon with arthritis; dark brown.
Jana Queen. Z pack's dam (mother).
Kharmin Queen of K pack; mother of new "A" pack; ridden by Dene; blue-green.
Oki m. Oki's rider was killed in a brawl; sage green; kept at Two Rivers as a spare; packmate of Kharmin.
Mamba Marta Davidow's dragon
Palandra Arapunta's dragon
Palli Kole's dragon from Reedwater; pale brown.
Puka f. Adult (K pack) dragon ridden by Aimee; mottled aqua.
Simba m. Sylvan's dragon; green and tan; dignified.
Sufax Adult dragon at Oracle.

Species in Compact
Ayi Human-like bipeds with telepathic (?) abilities (pejiin).
Casakin Bipedal, furred, catlike; considered not as bright as humans or ayi.
Cuy Amorphous, most "advanced" life forms in the known universe.
Humanity (Includes humans, and some bioengineered colonists and itinerant traders whose genetics are dubious.)
Mengsee Insectoid; love mechanical devices.
Simbara Green, slightly humanoid; unipedal, called "slugfoots."
Toridani Nothing is known about their appearance; they communicate only

with Cuy, via electronics, never "in person."

Zenaan   Belligerent humanoids; quarantined to their home system.

Critters and Things

bandova   A melon-like fruit dragons are fond of

bodhaata   A kind of ungulate similar to an antelope/kangaroo.

comarre rice   Tall, very dark brown drought-tolerant rice from Comarre colony.

dinah-nut   High protein nuts that grow on scrubby trees/big bushes; "spicy" odor.

fala birds   Something like a game hen or small duck.

gimbal balls   A species of plant that produces a sort of glassine sphere useful as mobile living quarters for humans and other creatures; a Helper Species.

ground nuts   Tubers in strings, grow beneath the ground; marked by sweet chocolate-scented and colored flowers above ground; found in marshes; probably adapted from peanuts from Earth.

packdrones Smaller than dragons. Lesser in size and temperament; not assigned a rider or a name with a pack's letter.

platecone tree Flat ring or disk of branches separated by ~meter of bare trunk; branches don't start until about 3m up from ground; waffle-like cones hold delicious nuts; no one knows their origin, but not Earth.

sandfish   A possibly mythical "fish" that supposedly lives in sand.

splaid fungus Each shelf grows on a dead tree, delicious baked.

285

Places

Avordan Across the peninsula from New Venice in Ben Yent, where dragon plague (dysentery) was.

Bouaka Town in southern Kendai.

Cluny City in Lynly.

Esfa Village at midpoint of White Rift Valley, where Shala may have been born.

New Venice City in Vai Tilden where Dene & Aimee are from.

Oaks Town on the northern extent of the Yent River, where the tenday training flight usually ends; where Tarva is from.

oasis village Nameless tiny village where Shala grew up, in the hills on the north end of White Rift Valley; sometimes called First Oasis.

Oracle Office of off-planet species in the hills of Lhasa, where master computer for Azureign is, and where citizens can apply for scientific and medical aid

Oracle's Maze A garden, sculpture garden and maze outside the Oracle's headquarters in the Queensland Mountains.

Reedwater Town on Swampen Sea that becomes sick with a variant of diphtheria, where Kole is from, & where Shala rides with the vaccine.

Toronia Town where Dragonrider Guild Headquarters is located, near Oracle.

Two Rivers Dragonrider Guild training school, at the border between Lhasa and Ben Yent, on the Yent River inland from the Swampen Sea.

Ziza Town in the Lhasa grasslands on the delta of the Oracle River, at the edge of the desert; where Alu is from.

Acknowledgements

The tailless "dragon" displayed between sections is a pterosaur from: *Claessens LPAM, O'Connor PM, Unwin DM (2009) Respiratory Evolution Facilitated the Origin of Pterosaur Flight and Aerial Gigantism. PLoS ONE 4(2): e4497.*

https://doi.org/10.1371/journal.pone.0004497

About the Author

Joy Oestreicher has always loved dragons and cats, the unreal and the real. She has written several tales set on Azureign and in the Azureign universe, one of which ("Vet-o-Saurus,") appears as a short story in *A Starfarer's Dozen,* from Harcourt Brace, edited by Michael Stearns, 1995.

Bonus: Original cover artwork
(watercolor)
By Samantha M. Schumacher